Disney's

ART OF ANIMATION

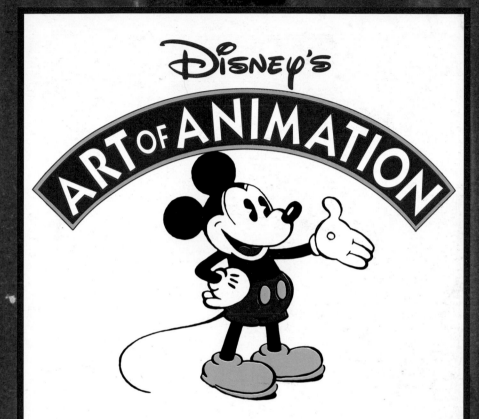

Disney's ART OF ANIMATION

FROM MICKEY MOUSE TO BEAUTY AND THE BEAST

By Bob Thomas

A WELCOME BOOK

HYPERION
NEW YORK

A FEW THANKS

To those in Disney's West Coast offices who gave us invaluable picture help: first and foremost to Karen Kreider, in the Publishing Division, who was grace under pressure; to David Pacheco for both his slide collection and his knowledge, and to Debi Dooley, Dave Smith, Robert Tieman, and Rose Motzko in the Archives; Joanne Warren and Jan Loveton in the Photo Library; Kay Salz, Doug Engalla and Larry Ishino in the Animation Research Library; Howard Green and Steve Rogers in the Publicity Department; Esther Ann Ewert, Grace Simpson, and Annie Stevens in the Disney Art Program; Michael E. Stern for his expert photography; and finally, to Don Hahn, Stacy Slossy, Tony Rocco, and Laura Perrotta in the Feature Animation Department, who took time away from their own horrific deadlines to aid us.

In the Hyperion office in New York, Bob Miller ranks as one of the great morale boosters, with endless, cheerful, and solid support from Lesley Krauss, Marcy Goot, Kris Kliemann, and Mary Ann Naples—all of whom have been important to us.

And to my staff: Mary Tiegreen and Dianna Russo who conceived the design; Markus Frey and Steven Gorney, who carried it forward; Natasha Fried, who watched over every step; Jennifer Downing, for keeping us calm and tranquil; and to Hiro Clark, for everything.

—Lena Tabori

Produced by
Welcome Enterprises, Inc.
164 East 95th Street
New York, NY 10128

ISBN: 1-56282-899-1
Text Copyright © 1991, Bob Thomas
Illustrations Copyright © 1991, The Walt Disney Company, Inc.
Pages 109, 118, 119: Illustrations from *Who Framed Roger Rabbit*
Copyright © Touchstone Pictures and Amblin Entertainment, Inc.
Page 196: *The Swing*; Jean-Honoré Fragonard;
National Gallery of Art, Washington; Samuel H. Kress Collection.
Pages 20 and 21: *Gertie the Dinosaur*; Collection of Jeanne and Mike Glad.
Page 34: *Horse in Motion*; Collection of Stanford University Libraries,
Department of Special Collections and University Archives.

FIRST EDITION
10 9 8 7 6 5 4 3 2 1
Printed and bound in Japan by Toppan Printing Co., Inc.

To My Grandson
Matthew Clayton Goff

ACKNOWLEDGMENTS

Walt Disney said to me in 1957: "All these years I've been taking the bows for the cartoons and the animated features. I did that for a purpose: to establish the Disney name as a guarantee to the public of good family entertainment. Now I want to give credit to the guys who made all those pictures."

The result was *The Art of Animation*, a history of animation at the Disney studio, together with an account of the making of *Sleeping Beauty*. Little had been written about animation at that time, and apparently the book helped inspire a young generation to seek careers in the field.

Now I'm writing about that new generation and the challenge they are making to Disney achievements of the past. Parts of *The Art of Animation* are included in a different form in Chapters 1 through 7. I have also drawn on previously unpublished interviews I did in 1957 with Walt Disney and his artists.

I am grateful to Esther Ewert of the Disney Art Program for originating the idea for the book, and to Bob Miller for including it among the first of the Hyperion books, appropriately named for the street on which Mickey Mouse, Snow White, Pinocchio, Bambi, et al., were born. Martha Kaplan provided judicious suggestions. The editorial assistance of Patricia Thomas was indeed invaluable.

My gratitude also to Don Hahn for leading me through the animation process and to the following for help in my research:

Gretchen Albrecht, Roger Allers, James Baxter, Robby Benson, Bill Berg, Baker Bloodworth, Janet Bruce, Karen Comella, Brenda Chapman, Ron Clements, Patti Conklin, Lorna Cook, Fred Craig, Marc Davis, Andreas Deja, Roy E. Disney, Michael Eisner, Randy Fullmer, Will Finn, David Friedman, Ed Ghertner, Howard Green, John Hench, Mark Henn, Jim Hillin, Ollie Johnston, Jeffrey Katzenberg, Glen Keane, Lisa Keene, Vera Lanpher, Angela Lansbury, Brian McEntee, Alan Menken, John Musker, Paige O'Hara, Jerry Orbach, David Pruiksma, Chris Sanders, Peter Schneider, Tom Schumacher, Grace Simpson, Tom Sito, Dave Smith, David Ogden Stiers, Shari Stoner, Frank Thomas, Robert Tieman, Donald Towns, Gary Trousdale, Kirk Wise, Linda Woolverton.

BOOK ONE
HISTORY OF A NEW ART

CHAPTER ONE

A MOUSE IS BORN

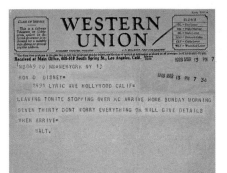

PRECEDING SPREAD: *Mickey Mouse in the
1932* Mickey's Revue (INSET) *and the 1935*
The Band Concert (SPREAD).

LEFT: *Ub Iwerks during the feverish months of
creating Mickey Mouse.*

BELOW: *Story sketches for the 1928 Oswald
cartoon* Tall Timber.

A Star with Two Fathers

Don't worry everything OK
Will give details when arrive
Walt

Walt Disney hid the bitter truth in this telegram to his brother Roy. Everything was not OK. The Disney brothers' enterprise had been shattered by the double-dealing of their New York distributor. Walt had spent February of 1928 in New York trying to renegotiate the contract for his cartoon series Oswald the Lucky Rabbit, hoping to raise the price per cartoon from $2,250 to $2,500. The distributor, Charles Mintz, offered $1,800. "But that's impossible," Walt protested. "We couldn't make a profit."

Then Mintz dropped the bombshell. He declared that he owned all rights to Oswald and warned: "Either you come with me at my price, or I'll take your organization from you. I have your key men signed up."

Walt was desolate. Not only had he lost his star performer, Oswald. He also was being deserted by almost his entire staff, most of whom he had brought to Hollywood from Kansas City. Only his key animator, Ub Iwerks, had remained loyal. Five years before, Disney's Kansas City cartoon studio had gone bankrupt. Now, at 26, he faced the same grim prospect in Hollywood.

How Mickey Mouse was born may never be known. Walt told the story, embellished over the years, that on the train ride back to California he had concocted a new character, based on a friendly mouse who had visited his drawing board back in Kansas City. Ub Iwerks told another version: Walt returned from New

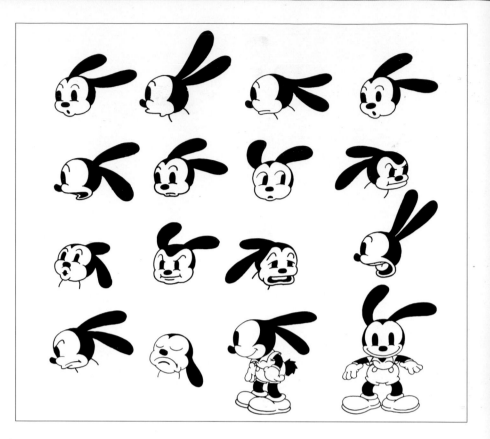

Walt told me in 1957: "Mickey had to be simple. We had to push out seven hundred feet of film every two weeks. His head was a circle with an oblong circle for a snout. The ears were also circles so they could be drawn the same, no matter how he turned his head. His body was like a pear, and he had a long tail. His legs were pipestems, and we stuck them in large shoes to give him the look of a kid wearing his father's shoes.

"We didn't want him to have mouse hands, because he was supposed to be more human. So we gave him gloves. [Mickey went gloveless in the first three cartoons.] Five fingers seemed like too much on such a little figure, so we took away one. That was just one less finger to animate.

"To provide a little detail, we gave him the two-button pants. There was no mouse hair, or any other frills that would slow down animation."

ABOVE AND OPPOSITE BOTTOM: Plane Crazy, the first Mickey Mouse cartoon, was made as a silent, then released in sound after the success of Steamboat Willie.

TOP: Model sheets of Mickey (OPPOSITE) and Oswald (RIGHT) demonstrate the difference in their ear designs.

York discouraged, and Walt, Roy, and Ub held a meeting to discuss a new character. "How about a cat?" one of them suggested. "No, can't compete with Krazy Kat," another replied. Ub riffled through some magazines, looking for animals. Finally they decided on a mouse. Except for the brick-throwing Ignatz of the Krazy Kat series, mice had been overlooked in cartoons.

Whichever version of Mickey's birth is correct, it is agreed that Walt's wife Lilly did the naming. She rejected the proposal to call the new character Mortimer. "I think he should be called Mickey Mouse," she announced.

The three survivors of the Walt Disney organization had to act fast—and secretly. Walt was obligated to produce three more Oswald cartoons, and the defecting animators would be remaining at the studio for three months. Walt worked up a story line that capitalized on the nation's passion for Charles Lindbergh. Ub began animating Plane Crazy in a locked room, surrounded by random sketches. If anyone knocked on the door, he quickly covered up his real work and substituted bogus drawings so the intruder could not see the character that lay aborning on his workbench.

Mickey Mouse was nothing very new; in fact, he bore a strong resemblance to Oswald. Except for the ears. While Oswald's were long and floppy, Mickey's were perfectly round, sitting atop his head.

The simplicity of design was created out of necessity on Ub Iwerks's drawing board. Mickey was essentially a series of circles that permitted Ub to work at superhuman speed. Bill Nolan had held the cartoon industry record for the number of drawings per day: six hundred for Krazy Kat. Ub turned out seven hundred. The entire cartoon consisted of 8,500 drawings.

To maintain the secrecy, Walt set up a little shop in the garage of his house on

MICKEY MOUSE   MODEL №1

771-49

Lyric Avenue. Lilly, Roy's wife Edna, and Walt's sister-in-law Hazel Sewell inked and painted Ub's drawings onto celluloid.

Plane Crazy previewed well though not sensationally at a Hollywood theater in May 1928, and Walt was encouraged to start another Mickey Mouse cartoon, *Gallopin' Gaucho*. He traveled to New York and engaged a film dealer to sell the new series. But no distributor was interested in cartoons about a mouse, or any other character. Short subjects were a minor part of the movie business, which was now struggling to cope with the talkie revolution.

The Cartoon Finds a Voice

Walt returned to Hollywood without a contract. He called a night meeting at his house with Roy, Ub, and the three remaining loyalists, Les Clark, Wilfred Jackson, and Johnny Cannon.

"Roy, what do you think about trying sound?" Walt began. The entire industry had been thrown into a turmoil the previous October when Warner Bros. introduced sound with Al Jolson in *The Jazz Singer*. Walt continued: "You know they've got the track right on the film now, so you can't get out of sync."

Always the cautious brother, Roy considered the proposal from all aspects. Was sound practical? What would it cost? Was it worth the gamble?

Walt admitted the financial outlook wasn't good. The loss of Oswald had robbed the studio of its income. Walt had mortgaged his home. Many weeks he and Roy didn't get paid, though their employees did.

"I think we ought to do it," Walt decided. "I think sound is here to stay. Think

Studio workers agreed on the symbiotic relationship between Walt and Mickey. First of all, the voice. Out of necessity, Walt uttered Mickey's squeaks in Steamboat Willie. When Mickey began to articulate, Walt auditioned voices. He listened and said impatiently, "No, it's more like this, more like this," and he demonstrated with a Missouri falsetto. Finally his animators said, "Well, Walt, why don't you do it?"

More than the voice, Walt contributed his own adventurousness and sense of wonder to Mickey. In the early years, Walt guided every Mickey Mouse cartoon from beginning to end, and that's when the best of them were made. Animator Frank Thomas observes: "Mickey was Walt, and Walt was Mickey. Mickey reached his height in the days when Walt did the voice in that awful falsetto of his. When he started making feature films, Mickey declined."

ABOVE: *Disney (second from left) and coworkers gag it up to plug the studio's song, "Minnie's Yoo Hoo." Left to right: Johnny Cannon, Walt Disney, Bert Gillett, Ub Iwerks, Wilfred Jackson, and Les Clark; seated, left to right: Carl Stalling, Jack King, and Ben Sharpsteen.*

TOP RIGHT: *Mickey Mouse scripts with Disney's typed continuity and Iwerks's story sketches.*

what we can do with it! Think of how we can use music! Think how much better we can tell stories and put over gags with sound!"

Disney expounded on the values of sound: the gags could be socked across with a well-timed sound effect; the characters would exude more personality if you could hear their voices; the action could be timed to the rhythmic beat of a popular song. Walt put Ub to work on the third Mickey Mouse cartoon, *Steamboat Willie*, a takeoff on the Buster Keaton comedy *Steamboat Bill*.

Wilfred Jackson, whose mother had been a piano teacher, devised a way to synchronize music to film by using a metronome. "We know how fast film will run— ninety feet a minute," said Jackson. "All we've got to do is figure how fast the beat of the music is, and we can break it down into frames."

Walt whistled "Steamboat Bill" while Jackson played his harmonica. The metronome ticked out their rhythm. The system worked. But would audiences respond to music and noises emanating from a cartoon? Walt decided to make a test. He invited the workers and their wives to the studio one night. Roy ran the projector outside the window to eliminate sprocket noise. While *Steamboat Willie* was projected onto a bed sheet, Jackson played his harmonica, Ub and Les Clark beat on boxes and pans, Johnny Cannon made animal sounds, and Walt said a few words of dialogue. The illusion was successful.

Walt next faced the challenge of recording the sound track on the film. He left for New York, stopping in Kansas City to meet Carl Stalling, a theater organist who had helped the Disneys with a much needed $275 loan. Walt persuaded Stalling to compose a score, which was timed to the beat marks Ub had made on the screen.

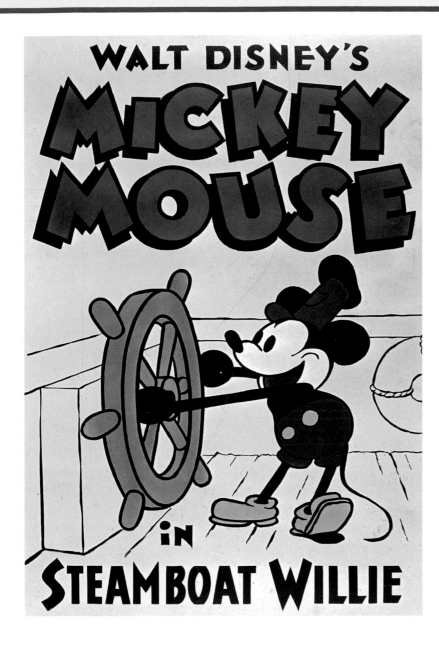

WALT DISNEY'S MICKEY MOUSE

IN STEAMBOAT WILLIE

Iwerks's drawings for Steamboat Willie *demonstrate the elasticity of* Mickey Mouse.

Walt continued to New York with the written score and the completed film. The big recording companies were either too busy or too expensive for the young cartoon maker from Hollywood. Walt found a slick operator, Pat Powers, who offered to record *Steamboat Willie* with his own bootlegged equipment.

The first session was a fiasco. The conductor refused to follow the beat marks on the film, and the musicians couldn't keep up with the frantic action on the screen. Walt had already written checks totaling $1,500, which Roy had scrambled to cover. Now Walt decided to sell his Moon roadster to raise more money for a second session. Finally *Steamboat Willie* was recorded, with Walt himself supplying the voices of Minnie and a parrot that shouted, "Man overboard! Man overboard!"

Steamboat Willie had its premiere engagement at the Colony Theater in New York on November 18, 1928. The 7 1/2-minute cartoon drew better reviews than the full-length movies released that week. Critics were delighted with the first sound cartoon. Within weeks, Mickey Mouse was a nationwide sensation. In three years, he would be a national institution.

Story sketches for Orphan's Benefit *(1934). The film was noteworthy for three events: Dippy Dawg's name was changed to the permanent and appropriate Goofy; Donald Duck in his second film made his first featured appearance, raging as his onstage performance draws jeers and brickbats; and Clara Cluck made her Disney debut.*

Goofy and Donald went on to vast fame. Clara's single talent—clucking operatic arias as a barnyard soprano (voiced by Florence • Gill)—proved limiting. She appeared in only seven cartoon shorts, including the 1941 color remake of Orphan's Benefit.

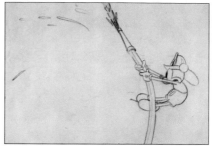

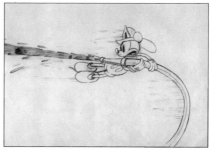

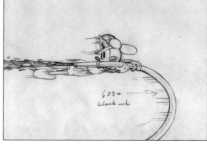

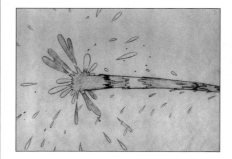

"Remember, He's Just a Mouse"

What was that special alchemy that made audiences around the world respond to Mickey Mouse? Hundreds of theories have been proffered, philosophical and Freudian, profound and crackpot. An intriguing hypothesis is presented by John Hench, who performed several functions in Disney animation beginning in 1939, and remains resident guru of Walt Disney Imagineering, which plans the theme parks.

"I have always been mystified with the power of Mickey Mouse, how he can go everywhere in the world, never to be questioned or suspected of being an American export," says Hench. "It is mostly a matter of déjà vu, apparently, because people seem to recognize something about him."

Hench compares Mickey's appeal to twelve-thousand-year-old fertility symbols that central European tribes carried with them. "They were small stone objects, but they were built on Mickey's formula of hooking together a series of circles—in Mickey's case, spheres—in a dynamic way. He expresses simple ideas: that life is dynamic, that it isn't static. He has this remarkable way of recalling these feelings in people everywhere."

At first, Walt and Ub dreamed up the plots. They sat in the inner office of the tiny studio. Ub drew sketches of the action, and Walt typed the dialogue on the bottom of the sketches, using three fingers on the keyboard. Then he handed them to the animators in the outer office.

Walt soon realized the need to include more minds in the story sessions that were held at night around the dining table in Walt's five-room bungalow. In the center of the table was a film can containing candy.

"How about letting Mickey be a fireman this time?" Walt would propose.

"Good," Ub commented. "Minnie could be caught in a burning building."

TOP LEFT: *The 1941 color remake of* Orphan's Benefit.

ABOVE: *Animation drawings of Mickey in action in* Mickey's Fire Brigade (1935).

As the studio grew, Walt continued seeking ideas from everyone. In 1932 he circulated a two-page synopsis of The Wayward Canary along with this note:

The following story strikes me as having wonderful audience appeal.
This is a wonderful chance for personality stuff with all of the characters.
Special cute action of Mickey and Minnie trying to teach the canary bird to sing.
Pluto trying to sleep with the piano annoying him.
The love making of the two birds.
The villainous looking old cat. (Note this cat is not human—it is carried as a real cat.)
The frantic efforts of Mickey, Minnie and Pluto with the wild canary, all trying to rescue Minnie's bird from the old cat.
Pluto's heroic fight and rescue of the bird.
The happy finish with the entire group bandaged up as they sing and play.
Pluto all bandaged up still trying to sleep—then finally joining in with the tune by howling in goofy manner.
Especially the fight sequence where all four characters are chasing the old cat all over the back yard trying to rescue the little helpless canary.
So let's all hop to it and have some good belly laughs ready by
TUESDAY NIGHT—JUNE 14th

"We could have the ladder slide down the pole and jump on the fire wagon," Jackson suggested. The talk continued far into the night until the script was completed.

More so than any other cartoon character that preceded him, Mickey Mouse remained the same basic, well-defined character in each film. He could adopt a variety of occupations and engage in outrageous adventures, but the steady, well-meaning, straight-shooting Mickey always shone through. Walt saw to that. Story men who engaged in flights of fancy suffered his withering comment: "Mickey wouldn't do that."

Mickey was so much a part of Walt that Walt couldn't articulate what Mickey could and could not do. That was spelled out by a story man in 1939:

Mickey is not a clown; he is neither silly nor dumb. . . . He can be funny in a variety of situations. . . . His first successes were hero roles, such as *Cactus Kid, Gorilla Mystery, Pioneer Days.* . . . Other early successes showed him as an accomplished musician, dancer, etc., in *Opry House, Shindig, Birthday Party,* etc. . . .

Later Mickey's audience value improved when he began getting into difficulties and accomplishing things under pressure, as in *Barnyard Broadcast.* . . . Mickey can still be entertaining when things are running smoothly. . . .

Mickey is seldom funny in a chase picture, as his character and expressions are usually lost. . . . He is at his best when he sets out to do a thing with deadly determination despite annoyances and menace.

For the first two years of Mickey Mouse, Walt Disney and Ub Iwerks devoted their energies and talents to building their creation into a minor masterpiece. The equity of their partnership was signaled by the title card of *Steamboat Willie:*
"A Walt Disney Comic by Ub Iwerks."
Ub drew most of the first five Mickey cartoons, with the drawings in between the major moves supplied by Clark, Cannon, and Jackson. Ub also drew the first batch of Mickey Mouse comic strips, which King Features started distributing to

Above: **Mickey's Nightmare** (1932).

Opposite: *Walt and his key coworkers stand behind a row of Mickeys in front of the Hyperion studio in 1930. Left to right: Dick Lundy, Tom Palmer, Johnny Cannon, Dave Hand, Bert Gillett, Wilfred Jackson, Bert Lewis, Walt Disney, Les Clark, Ben Sharpsteen, Norm Ferguson, Floyd Gottfredson, Jack King.*

newspapers in January 1930. With the studio expanding, the Disneys hired a group of New York animators in the spring of 1929. Only then did others besides Ub begin drawing Mickey Mouse.

When Mickey Mouse was firmly established, Walt Disney began gazing at new horizons. It was a pattern that would dominate the rest of his career: having achieved one goal, he needed another, more challenging one. He never lost his concern and affection for the star who made him famous (Walt referred to him as "Mickey Mouse," whereas Donald was dismissed as "The Duck"). Periodically Walt would bring Mickey's career back from idleness and neglect with a prestigious new vehicle. And Walt was ever vigilant to preserve Mickey's character and dignity. When story men allowed their imaginations to overreach Mickey's capabilities, he cautioned them, "Remember, he's just a mouse."

CHAPTER TWO
ANIMATION BEFORE DISNEY

Early Attempts at Animation

From an eight-legged boar in the Altamira caves to Marcel Duchamp's *Nude Descending a Staircase*, human beings have always tried to capture movement in their art. Presumably, the artist in a cave in northern Spain thirty thousand years ago was dissatisfied with his drawing of a four-legged boar and added the extra legs to trick the eye into believing the animal was running. The critical reaction to his art is unknown, but Duchamp was excoriated when his painting of overlapping figures was displayed at the New York Armory Show in 1913.

A forerunner of today's comic strip can be found in an Egyptian wall decoration circa 2000 B.C. In successive panels it depicts two wrestlers struggling in a variety of holds. Illustrating proportions of the human figure, Leonardo da Vinci showed how the limbs would appear in various positions. Giotto's angels seem to take flight in his repetition of their movements. The Japanese used scrolls to tell a continuous story.

True animation could not be achieved until people understood a fundamental principle of the human eye: the persistence of vision. This was first demonstrated in 1828 by a Frenchman, Paul Roget, who invented the thaumatrope ("wheel of magic" in Greek). It was a disc with a string or peg attached to both sides. One side of the disc showed a bird, the other an empty cage. When the disc was twirled, the bird appeared in the cage. This proved that the eye retains images when it is exposed to a series of pictures, one at a time.

The thaumatrope was simply a visual trick. The phenakistoscope ("an optical deceiver" in Greek) achieved real animation. Invented by Joseph Plateau in 1826, it was a circular card with slits around the edge. The viewer held the card up to a mirror and peered through the slits as the card whirled. Through a series of drawings on the card, the eye perceived an acrobat doing flips or a horse performing tricks. Another important principle had been discovered; the spaces between the slits operated the way the shutter of a movie projector does today.

The same technique applied to the zoetrope ("burning life" in Greek). In 1860 Pierre Desvignes inserted a strip of paper containing drawings on the inside of a drumlike cylinder. The drum twirled on a spindle, and the viewer gazed through slots on the top of the drum. The figures in the drawing magically came to life, endlessly repeating an acrobatic feat.

PRECEDING SPREAD: *Newspaper cartoonist Winsor McCay infused his Gertie the Dinosaur with personality. Here Gertie encounters the woolly mammoth Jumbo* (SPREAD). *J. R. Bray spoofed the safari trips of Theodore Roosevelt in Colonel Heeza Liar's African Hunt* (INSET).

OPPOSITE: *In drawing proportions of the human figure, Leonardo da Vinci animated the arms and legs (circa 1492).*

TOP LEFT: *An eight-legged boar portrays movement in a prehistoric wall drawing in Spain.*

TOP: *The thaumatrope had a bird on one side of a disc and a cage on the other. Twirling the disc, the viewer perceived the bird in the cage.*

BELOW: *Wall decoration about 2000 B.C. shows how Egyptians made an attempt at animation.*

Top: *By spinning the cylinder of the zoetrope, the viewer sees an acrobat leaping through a hoop.*

Above: *Walt Disney demonstrated the phenakistoscope on the "Story of the Animated Drawing" feature of his* Disneyland *television show.*

Again, the persistence of vision. Animation could be simulated as long as the eye had a brief pause between seeing the next picture in a sequence. The afterimage supplied the bridge to the next picture. The thaumatrope, phenakistoscope, and zoetrope provided entertainment in many a Victorian parlor.

In 1892, another Frenchman, Emile Reynaud, brought animation to show business. A painter of lantern slides, Reynaud was fascinated by the early attempts at animation. He improved on the zoetrope by replacing the slits with mirrors stuck side by side on the revolving center. The mirrors reflected the individual pictures on the inside of the drum, providing movement. He called his invention the praxinoscope.

He carried the idea further by drawing his pictures on black strips of paper. A separate card provided the background for the action drawings. The animation, which consisted of only twelve different poses, could be played against a variety of backgrounds.

Still Reynaud wasn't satisfied. Instead of the twelve poses on paper, he painted five hundred on hard, transparent gelatin. Small holes were punched in each picture, like the camera sprockets of today. The holes meshed into the teeth of a large wheel, rotating at the same speed as thirty-six mirrors in the center. Each picture was lighted individually, reflected on a mirror, and projected onto a screen. Reynaud's Théâtre Optique attracted a half-million Parisians between 1892 and 1900.

The kineograph was simply a flip book inside a large viewer. A series of progressive actions was drawn on successive pages. When the pages were riffled, the drawings seemed to move. The kineograph first appeared in 1868 and continues today in the form of children's toys and peepshows in penny arcades.

Animation in Motion Pictures

The development of the motion picture camera and projector by Thomas A. Edison and others provided the first really practical means of making drawings move. But the possibilities weren't explored until almost a decade after the movie industry was born. Three important figures were associated with the beginning of the animation industry: J. Stuart Blackton, Emile Cohl, and Winsor McCay.

Blackton was a young English-born adventurer who pioneered American films as one of the founders of Vitagraph in 1899. In 1906 he issued a short film *Humorous Phases of Funny Faces*. A sensation with audiences, the illusion was created by the simplest of means.

Comical faces were drawn on a blackboard, then erased. The camera was stopped after each face was photographed. The "stop-motion" provided a startling effect as the facial expressions changed before the audience's eyes. Blackton also experimented with animation in *The Haunted Hotel* (1906), *The Magic Fountain Pen* (1907), and other films.

Paris-born Emile Cohl was a political cartoonist who protested to the

Gaumont film company that it had stolen one of his cartoons for an ad. The Gaumont manager was impressed with the young man and gave him a job as gag man at the studio. In 1908 he made a two-minute film called *Phantasmagoria*, a work of rare imagination that required two thousand drawings. Movie audiences had already marveled at photographed objects moving on the screen; they were astounded to see drawings come to life. Cohl created all the drawings himself, as he did for one hundred other cartoons he made in France and the United States in the next ten years.

Working alone, Cohl produced crude art work, enlivened by his caricaturist talent. He created a little man, Fantoche, who is considered the first regular character to appear in animated films. Cohl anticipated the gags of later animators with hens that laid alarm clocks, obelisks that sighed, and a man who flew with his coat as a rudder.

Winsor McCay, dapper cartoonist for Hearst's New York *American*, was the first to apply showmanship to film animation. One day his son brought home something he had found in the rubble of a burned-out drugstore. It was a flip book to advertise a pharmaceutical firm. When McCay riffled the pages, he could see the action of the Bob Fitzsimmons-Jim Corbett heavyweight boxing match in 1897, the first championship fight on film.

McCay was fascinated. He turned the book over and on the blank pages drew pictures of his comic strip character, Little Nemo, in antic poses. Nemo moved! Using a stop-action camera, McCay produced his first cartoon film, *Little Nemo*, in 1908.

None of the three trailblazers of animation remained in the industry they helped to found. McCay, tired of multiple drawings, returned to newspaper cartooning. The innovative Blackton moved on to other kinds of filmmaking and died broke in 1941. Cohl went back to France before World War I and made no films after 1918. He died in utter poverty in 1938.

In 1909, Winsor McCay played vaudeville theaters with Gertie, the Trained Dinosaur, in a tour that awakened America to the magic of animation.

McCay appeared at the side of the stage in evening dress, carrying a whip. He introduced Gertie, an amiable dinosaur that appeared on the screen and did tricks more or less at her master's bidding. Gertie lifted her foot on cue, tossed a mammoth by the tail and danced to music.

Audiences were astonished. McCay wouldn't divulge his secrets, but his methods were simple. He carefully pinned a transparent sheet of paper on a drawing board with a 7-by-10-inch border outlined on it. Within this frame, he drew his action and background. The next piece of paper was placed over the first and the action varied slightly. The background was entirely retraced.

McCay repeated this process 960 times to achieve a minute on the screen. The painstaking McCay spent twenty-two months to make twenty-five-thousand drawings for The Sinking of the Lusitania, released in 1918.

ABOVE: Gertie the Dinosaur (1914) *was McCay's most outstanding achievement.*

TOP LEFT: *J. Stuart Blackton and one of his Funny Faces.*

The Industry Emerges in New York

"The early years of animation in New York were an exciting time," recalled Dick Huemer in 1957; he had started in 1916 and later became a Disney director. "The business attracted a strange breed—signpainters, salesmen, cartoonists—most of them failures. The rule was: if you could hold a pencil, you could animate.

"But we were a dedicated lot. We were pioneering a new industry, and having a vast amount of fun doing it. And money. As a kid I was making a hundred and fifty dollars a week. Some animators made four hundred dollars a week. Big money in those days." The New York animators buzzed with each innovation in the industry. J. R. Bray, a staff artist for the humor magazine *Judge*, produced *The Dachshund and the Sausage* in 1910, which is considered the first cartoon telling a story. The plot concerned a dog prevented by a pesky flea from eating a sausage. Bray also created *Colonel Heeza Liar*, a satire of the exploits of President Theodore Roosevelt, which became the first cartoon series.

Bray devised the practice of printing backgrounds on translucent sheets so the scenery would not need to be copied on every drawing. The characters were animated on these sheets; when a figure overlapped a background line, the line was scratched out.

Earl Hurd, who became a Disney story man in the Thirties, approached Bray in 1914 with the idea of tracing animation drawings in ink on celluloid sheets. The inked "cels" could be photographed against any background. The Bray-Hurd system became the standard practice in the industry.

Another pioneer, Bill Nolan, discovered the panorama or "pan" shot in 1913. Puzzled at how to show a figure skating against a small, framed background, he went to a drugstore and bought a roll of shelf paper. He drew a long scene on the paper. His figure remained stationary while the background scene was pulled past the camera, giving an illusion of speed.

Raoul Barré was a brilliant young artist who began animating in France, then moved his studio to New York and created Silas Bumpkin in the series *The Grouch Chasers*. Unlike other cartoon makers who worked in secrecy, Barré believed in letting

TOP: *J. R. Bray* (TOP) *and his* Colonel Heeza Liar's African Hunt, 1914 (RIGHT).

ABOVE: *Max Fleischer and his* Out of the Inkwell *star,* Koko the Clown.

OPPOSITE LEFT: *Ad for Raoul Barré's first cartoon series.*

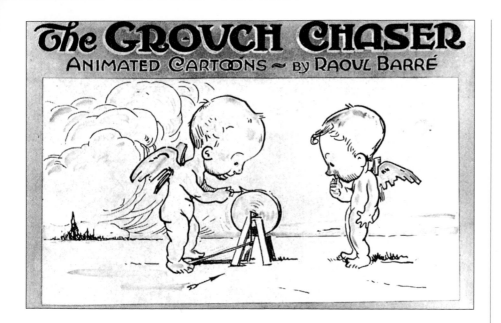

The GROUCH CHASER
ANIMATED CARTOONS ~ BY RAOUL BARRÉ

others know about his animation methods. He was the first to institute an apprentice system, a standard practice in cartoon studios today.

Barré's important contribution was the peg system. He punched holes at the top of the drawing paper. The holes were standard on the top of each sheet, fitting over pegs at the top of drawing boards and assuring an exact and rapid alignment of the drawings. Because the punched paper was heavier and not as transparent as previous paper, Barré devised the idea of drawing over a sheet of glass with a light under it.

Max Fleischer entered animation in 1917 with his ingenious *Out of the Inkwell*, in which the cartoon figure Koko the Clown interacted with Fleischer himself in live-action. Fleischer improved on the "rip and slash" technique first developed by Raoul Barré. The background of a scene would be drawn on one paper, the animated parts placed on top of the background. To reveal as much of the motionless parts as possible, pieces of the superimposed paper were cut away. The technique saved on animation costs and was widely used for a time. It was abandoned when Paul Terry introduced a complex method of laying cels on top of each other—one or more for the animated figures, one for background.

Absence of Personality

The new technologies helped the animation industry flourish during World War I and in the following years. Audiences were fascinated by the antics of the bizarre characters. The caliber of material didn't need to be high. Whenever stuck for a gag, an animator drew one character thumbing his nose at another. Like the flung custard pie in Mack Sennett comedies, it was always good for a laugh.

Most characters were devoid of personality, which is probably why none survived the advent of sound. The closest to achieving immortality was Felix the Cat by Pat Sullivan and Otto Messmer. He was a mischievous character who could survive a variety of scrapes, like Charlie Chaplin, but without being earthbound. His one great gimmick was pacing back and forth, deep in thought with hands behind his back, as he contemplated his next move.

*F*elix the Cat was the most popular star of silent cartoons. He was named Felix for "felicity"—a gesture toward improving the reputation of black cats. The Felix cartoons outshone competitors in the Twenties with their sophisticated humor and clever drawing. Like other silent stars, Felix was doomed by sound. His comedy was based on pantomime, and dialogue seemed out of place. The last regular Felix cartoon was released in August 1928, three months before the debut of Mickey Mouse. Several comebacks were attempted, including a television series, but Felix never recaptured his Twenties prominence.

TOP: *Pat Sullivan drew the Felix the Cat comic strip as well as the animated cartoons.*

ABOVE: *Felix the Cat's trademark was his pondering walk, which he could even perform on a tightrope.*

Many of the early cartoon characters were lifted intact from newspaper comics: John Foster's Katzenjammer Kids, Jack King's Happy Hooligan, Raoul Barré's Mutt and Jeff, Leon Searl's Krazy Kat and Ignatz Mouse. Readers of the funny pages could recognize their favorites on the screen; they knew that Mutt was the guileless short fellow, and Jeff was the tall one who was always getting him in trouble.

But the use of newspaper comic figures never proved successful in the long run. Many of them were not fully developed personalities in either medium. Many appeared in one-joke situations which became boring and predictable by repetition. All of them, especially the human characters, suffered in the transition to animation.

ABOVE: *The cinematic nature of comic strips such as* The Katzenjammer Kids *made them ideal for transference to movie cartoons.*

TOP RIGHT: *(From left to right) Horace Horsecollar, Clarabelle Cow, and Goofy make a merry threesome in this animation drawing.*

Paul Terry's Farmer Al Falfa was also a popular figure, but he was merely a human stooge amid a cast of animals. Most of the time he was the villain, and the story concerned the barnyard animals ganging up on him.

Animation of the human figure remained primitive. Audiences were amused by stylized animals cavorting on the screen. But there was something jarring about seeing a human in jerky, unrealistic movements. When animation became commercialized in the Twenties, little effort was made to improve drawing methods. The same tried-and-true systems prevailed: the Circle Formula and the Rubber-hose Method.

The quickest way to draw a character was to use circles, as Ub Iwerks did with Mickey Mouse. Round head, round eyes and nose, round body. The animator never had to worry about angles; no matter which way a character moved, he could be drawn with circular strokes.

Arms and legs moved like rubber hoses. No such things as elbows, knees, and wrists concerned the animator. Tubelike and rubbery limbs could be drawn fast and moved in any direction or elongated if necessary.

Speed and economy won out over reality. As long as characters were drawn with the Circle Formula, they would be as flat as those in the newspaper comic strips. There was no illusion of depth, as there was in live-action movies. The Rubber-hose Method further robbed the cartoon of realism.

The greatest handicap for conveying personality during the first two decades of the animation industry was the absence of sound. In today's cartoons, voice is the primary means of establishing character, and sound effects are a major tool for comedy. In silent films, dialogue was expressed in two ways: balloons above the characters' heads, as in comic strips; or full-screen titles. The first technique was totally unrealistic, the second interrupted the action.

Some animators tried to eliminate dialogue and tell their stories in pantomime, using crude facial expressions to indicate emotion. Not until Walt Disney and Ub Iwerks created Mickey Mouse did true personality appear in a cartoon. They were able to capitalize on sound for voices, sound effects and music. More importantly, Mickey was a dimensional character, bristling with gaiety and surprise, ever beguiling the audience. That was Disney's priceless contribution.

Storytelling in Early Cartoons

"Plots? We never bothered with plots. They were just a series of gags strung together. And not very funny, I'm afraid."

In 1957, Dick Huemer recalled his years of animating in New York cartoon studios before joining Disney.

"Usually there were three animators on a cartoon," said Huemer. "If we were working on a Mutt and Jeff cartoon, one of us might say, 'Let's make a picture about Hawaii.' Okay, fine. So each of us would work on a third of the picture. A couple of weeks later, we'd make a hookup. 'Where have you got 'em?' I'd ask. The other animator might have Mutt and Jeff on a surfboard at the end of his sequence. So I'd begin mine on a surfboard."

The gags were primitive and often based on violence, as is still true of cartoon shorts. One character would beat another mercilessly, only to have his victim instantly recover and return the favor. Perhaps the villain would swing a rapier and reduce the hero to baloney slices, which would be miraculously rejoined.

Anything could happen. An explosion would blow the features off a man's face, then he would pick them up and reassemble them. When Felix the Cat paced in a quandary, his tail detached to form a question mark over his head.

Albert Hurter and a few others strove to elevate the standards of animation. For a wartime Mutt and Jeff, Hurter drew a stunning display of an American flag flying over a captured German submarine. He made one series of forty drawings that were repeated and another of thirty drawings, also repeated. Ordinary animation would have depicted the flag in five to ten drawings, constantly repeated. Another artist, Dick Friel, created a beautiful water splash in forty or fifty frames instead of the usual eight.

But in the mid-Twenties, commercialism took over the animation industry. Big studios like International decreed to animators that a waving flag had to be accomplished with four or five drawings. A splash was depicted by four circles in the water. Animators were given quotas on the number of the drawings they had to produce each day. Cartoons had to be manufactured in quantity and cheaply, because theater owners would pay only small fees for "fillers" before the feature attraction.

The same gags were worked and reworked. Audiences became apathetic. The novelty of seeing cartoons move on the screen had long worn off.

The cartoon industry struck a depression. Studios shut down and animators were jobless. Many of the brilliant ones, discouraged by orders for speed and simplicity, departed for other fields of endeavor. The cartoonists who remained feared that the cartoon was doomed to an insignificant role on a movie bill.

"Although anything was possible in the world of the cartoonist, we had to discover what we could do bit by bit," commented Ted Sears, another cartoon pioneer who became a Disney story man. "The early artist didn't think of defying gravity. It was discovered by accident." Sears said that the man responsible was Albert Hurter, a Swiss-born artist whose drawings helped inspire Three Little Pigs, Snow White and the Seven Dwarfs, and Pinocchio. Hurter was animating an Alpine adventure of Mutt and Jeff. One scene showed Mutt leaning against a railing next to a precipice.

When the scene was photographed, the camera operator neglected to include the cel with the railing. The finished product showed Mutt leaning against thin air. Raoul Barré, a literal-minded Frenchman, was angry that a mistake had been made. But Hurter and the other artists laughed, realizing a new comedy device had been discovered.

The law of gravity was promptly repealed in every New York cartoon studio. Cartoon characters could walk on air, water, ceilings, clouds or sides of skyscrapers—and did.

TOP LEFT: *Sketches for Horace Horsecollar, Clarabelle Cow, and Clara Cluck illustrate the Circle and Rubber-hose techniques of animation.*

ABOVE: *Mutt and Jeff was another comic strip adapted to animation.*

CHAPTER THREE
DISNEY BEFORE MICKEY MOUSE

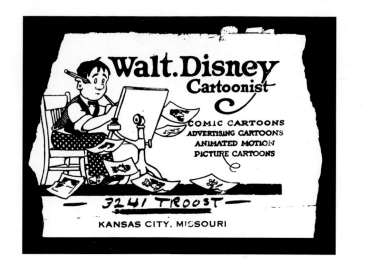

Kansas City and Laugh-o-Grams

"Everything is going fine with us and I am glad you made up your mind to come out. Boy, you will never regret it—this is the place for you—a real country to work and play in. . . . I can give you a job as artist-cartoonist and etc. with the Disney Productions, most of the work would be cartooning. Answer at once and let me know what you want to start. . . . At the present time I have one fellow helping me with animation and three girls doing the inking etc. while Roy handles the business end."

Walt Disney was writing from Los Angeles on June 1, 1924; to his good friend in Kansas City, Ub Iwerks. Walt and Roy had put up a sign Disney Brothers Studio on a small store at 4649 Kingswell Avenue and started producing Alice Comedies with the help of another animator, Rollin (Ham) Hamilton.

To fulfill his ambitious program, Walt needed help. He beseeched Ub to join him. Ub was a prodigious worker and a far better animator that Walt had ever been. Ub's arrival in California signaled the end of Walt's drawing career.

They had met in 1919 when both were seventeen and working for the Pesmen-Rubin Commercial Art Studio in Kansas City. Ub, born Ubbe Ert Iwwerks, was a Dutch immigrant's son, a high school dropout with a talent for lettering and airbrush work. Walt, born Walter Elias Disney in Chicago and reared on a Missouri farm and in Kansas City, had delivered mail, driven an ambulance in France after World War I, and turned to artwork against his father's wishes.

Laid off at Pesmen-Rubin after the Christmas season, Disney and Iwerks opened their own commercial art enterprise. Then Ub spotted an ad in the Kansas City *Star*:

Artist
Cartoon and Wash Drawings
First Class Man Wanted
Steady, Kansas City Slide Company
1015 Central

The two failed young entrepreneurs agreed that Walt should apply for the job. Walt was hired, and a month later he wangled a job for Ub. The company, which changed its name to Kansas City Film Ad, produced commercials that appeared in movie houses. Ub and Walt plunged into the world of animation.

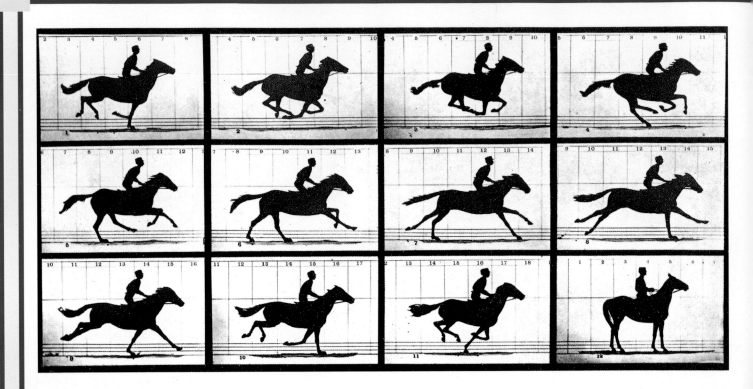

Dissatisfied with the primitive Film Ad animation, Walt wanted to know how the New York animators created their cartoons. At the public library he found a handbook by Carl Lutz and a book of Eadweard Muybridge's sequential photographs of animals and human figures in movement. He photostated the Muybridge photos, and he and Ub studied them to improve their drawing skills. Soon they were producing gag-filled cartoons for Film Ad.

TOP: *Eadweard Muybridge made sequential photographs of a horse galloping, settling a bet that all four feet are off the ground at one time.*

The methods were crude. Paper figures were cut out and pinned to sheets with background drawings. The figures were photographed on one frame of film, then moved slightly and photographed again. Walt prowled through all the departments, learning to operate the camera himself.

Walt moonlighted to produce Laugh-o-Grams, brief comic cartoons that appeared in three Kansas City theaters. They were successful enough to encourage Walt to incorporate Laugh-o-Gram Films in 1922. He convinced Ub to quit his job at Film Ad, and they hired five animators, most of them still in their teens. Laugh-o-Grams began making wry versions of *Little Red Riding Hood*, *Jack and the Beanstalk*, *Cinderella*, and other fairy tales.

President of his own company at 20 with a staff of ten, Walt Disney did some of the animation, operated the camera, and even washed the cels so they could be reused. To help keep the company solvent, he filmed news events for New York newsreel companies and took baby pictures for Kansas City parents. But such efforts were not enough, and Laugh-o-Grams was sliding into insolvency.

"We have just discovered something new and clever in animated cartoons!" Walt enthused in a letter to a New York distributor. He described his plan for a series of one-reelers in which child actors would intermingle with cartoon figures "not like *Out of the Inkwell* or Earl Hurd's, but of an entirely different nature."

The series would be called Alice Comedies.

The distributor encouraged Walt, and with his dwindling staff he embarked on his first short cartoon, *Alice's Wonderland*. Halfway through production, Walt ran completely out of funds. He described his plight to his older brother Roy, who was being treated for tuberculosis at a veterans' hospital in West Los Angeles. "Kid, I think you should get out of there," Roy counseled.

Disheartened, Walt decided to leave Kansas City. Laugh-o-Gram Films declared bankruptcy. By taking his camera door-to-door to photograph babies, he raised enough money to buy a one-way railroad ticket to California.

Young Man in Hollywood

After the Laugh-o-Grams fiasco, Walt Disney turned his back on animation. He had carted his camera and cartoon gear with him to California in 1923, but he kept the trunk locked. His ambition now was to become a motion picture director.

"No openings." Disney heard the same response at every studio. "Come back when you've had some experience."

The only experience he could acquire was riding a horse as an extra in a cavalry movie. His finances became precarious, and he had to borrow $5 from Roy to pay their Uncle Robert for board and room. Roy, who remained under treatment at the veterans' hospital, advised his brother, "I think you'd better give the cartoon business another try, Walt."

"No, I'm too late," said Walt. "I should have started six years ago. I don't see how I can top those New York boys."

Besides, there were no animators in Hollywood, and Walt realized his own shortcomings as an artist. He was confident in his skill at telling stories and devising gags, but he realized that Ub and the other animators at Laugh-o-Grams were better draftsmen. Eventually Walt had no choice except to unlock the trunk and

Advertising card for Disney's first cartoon enterprise.

construct a makeshift cartoon stand in Uncle Robert's garage. He returned to his stunt of making brief cartoons about local events and sold a series to the owner of a theater chain.

Alice's Wonderland continued to haunt Disney. He dispatched a letter to the distributor, Margaret Winkler, who had expressed interest in the series, telling her that he planned to embark on an ambitious program of Alice comedies. He convinced his Kansas City creditors to release the impounded film so she could view it. She responded favorably, offering $1,500 per negative.

"Let's go, Roy!" Walt exclaimed. "This is the break we have been waiting for."

The lifelong partnership began: Walt, the restless adventurer, ever seeking new goals of creativity; Roy, the steady hand, finding ways to realize his younger brother's dreams. Roy borrowed money to establish the Disney Brothers Studio, and production began on a new film, Alice's Day at Sea.

The bustling company of eight persons, including young new recruits from Kansas City, produced 56 Alice shorts before their modest popularity waned in 1927. The novelty of combining a real girl with cartoon figures had worn off, and new plots were hard to find. Disney's distributor, Charles Mintz, who had married Margaret Winkler and assumed control of her business, had become increasingly critical of the Alice cartoons. Carl Laemmle, the boss of Universal Pictures, told Mintz that he would like a cartoon series about a rabbit. Walt leaped to the idea and collaborated with Ub on rough pencil sketches of a proposed character.

"If these sketches are not what you want, let me know more about it, and I will try again," Walt wrote.

Ub and the staff hurriedly created the first of the Oswald the Lucky Rabbit cartoons, Poor Papa, in April 1927. Universal responded that the animation was jerky and repetitive, Oswald was dull and unfunny, and the story was merely a succession of gags. Walt stoutly defended Ub Iwerks, "whom I am willing to put alongside any man in the business today." He admitted that Oswald could be made "a younger character, peppy, alert, saucy and venturesome, keeping him also neat

In combining live action with cartoons, Walt first filmed Alice, played by young Virginia Davis, against a white backdrop. Then he and Ham Hamilton made drawings to augment the action and reexposed the negative, frame by frame. After completing six Alice comedies, Walt felt secure enough to send for Ub Iwerks.

TOP LEFT: The animals give Alice a welcoming parade in her first cartoon, Alice's Wonderland, 1923.

Top: *Disney made fifty-seven Alice comedies from 1923 to 1927. The first Alice was Virginia Davis, seen here in the sixth of the series,* Alice and the Dog Catcher.

Above: *Left to right: Friz Freleng, Walker Harman, Walt Disney, Margie Gay, Rudolf Ising, Ub Iwerks, Hugh Harman, Roy Disney.*

and trim." But an excess of plot in a one-reeler would eliminate the funny stuff, he warned.

Walt and Ub worked long hours to inject more appeal into Oswald. Slowly the rabbit evolved into a rounder, softer, more accessible character. Unlike the New York cartoon studios that employed every cost-cutting method possible, Walt refused to stint on quality. He didn't allow his animators to use cycles—repeating the same action over and over to save production time. Rough animation was photographed and reviewed in a makeshift projection room—the origin of the "sweatbox," as it is still called. If the rough animation did not meet Walt's standards, it was returned to the animator for improvement.

Such attention to quality added to production costs—and Roy's headaches—but it paid off at the box office. Oswald the Lucky Rabbit cartoons attracted warm reviews in the trade press, and even the New York animators began marveling at the ingenious cartoons from the West Coast. The Disney brothers, who had moved into a new studio on Hyperion Avenue near Mack Sennett's comedy factory, added to the staff and began producing Oswald cartoons every two weeks.

The future seemed unlimited—until Walt journeyed to New York to renegotiate the contract with Mintz. Then the bombshell: Oswald had been snatched away, along with most of Walt's animators. In his eagerness to sell Oswald, Disney had failed to notice that Universal owned the copyright. "Never again will I work for somebody else," Disney vowed to his wife Lilly. Enter Mickey Mouse.

TOP LEFT: *Alice (Margie Gay) faces the firing squad.*

ABOVE: *The beginnings of the Disney studio on Hyperion Avenue.*

Exit Ub Iwerks

The avalanche of acclaim in the world's theaters and press for Mickey Mouse produced one casualty: Ub Iwerks.

Perhaps it was inevitable, despite the mutual bond of the two young animators who had risen from the Pesmen-Rubin Studio to preeminence in the cartoon world. Both were similarly ego-driven men, though Walt was more outgoing and Ub withdrawn. Walt was a showman, a born actor and a visionary. Ub was the hard-striving artist, unmatched in his fluid style as well as his volume of output. Walt was Irish and quick-tempered. Ub was Dutch and stubborn. He watched with growing discontent as Disney won world recognition as the father of Mickey Mouse, while little attention was paid to the artist who had given Mickey form and movement.

Friction between the two partners surfaced in 1929, when Ub was animating most of the Mickey Mouse cartoons. Disney made a practice of returning to the studio at night to take care of business matters and review Ub's drawings. Walt often created his own exposure sheets (the form detailing the action, dialogue and music, frame by frame), causing Ub to complain the next day, "That's not the way I planned it." He discarded Walt's sheets and made his own. After several complaints, Walt agreed not to interfere.

Disagreement between the two creative partners continued. Ub believed that his drawing of Mickey played the key role in the series' success, and he was jealous of any encroachment on his domain. Walt's concern for Mickey was intensely proprietary; he had learned from the Oswald experience to retain complete control of his enterprise.

In January 1930, Ub Iwerks announced he had accepted an offer to create a cartoon series of his own. He was leaving the Disney studio.

"I can't believe it," said the astonished Walt. He and Ub had worked side-by-side all day and into the night for the better part of eight years. They had spent more

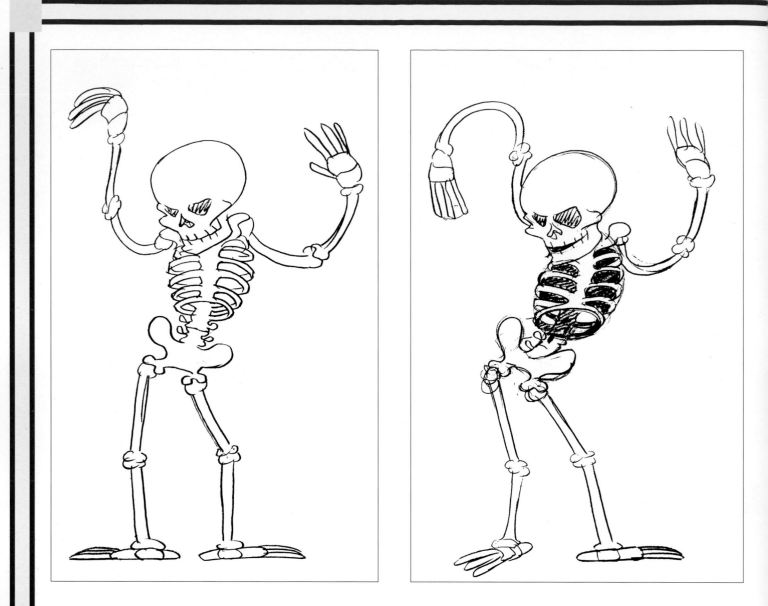

time together than they had with their wives. Walt was hurt, as well as apprehensive because the studio was losing its most gifted animator.

Ub could not be dissuaded. He relinquished his 20 percent interest in the Disney company for $2,920 and opened the Ub Iwerks studio in Hollywood. He launched a series called Flip the Frog. While technically proficient, the series lacked the personality and storytelling that Walt had injected into Alice, Oswald and Mickey Mouse. MGM released Flip the Frog, but it faded after thirty-seven episodes. Ub invented another series about a boy, Willie Whopper, but it failed to catch on.

For ten years Walt Disney and Ub Iwerks maintained an icy relationship. Then in 1940, Ben Sharpsteen convinced the two old friends to reconcile. Ub had tired of trying to maintain his enterprise in the fiercely competitive Hollywood; he wanted to pursue his real passion: developing technical processes. Walt welcomed him back to the studio. Both were undemonstrative, but their fellow workers recognized the deep bond between the two men.

Ub Iwerks became a valuable member of the Disney company. He designed the first multihead optical printer that facilitated the combining of animation and live action. He continued developing new techniques and devices for Disney and Disneyland until his death in 1971.

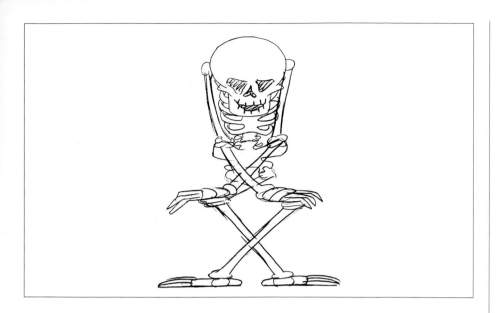

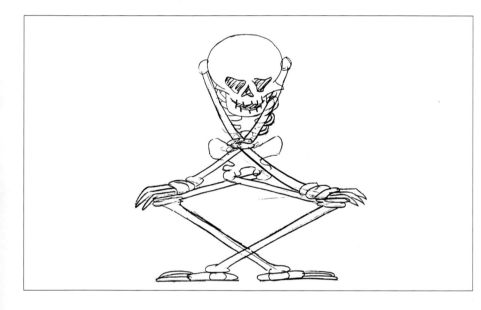

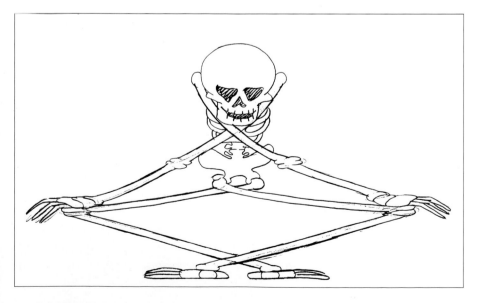

Disney was determined his studio not be overwhelmed by one character, as had happened with Alice and Oswald. He welcomed the suggestion of Carl Stalling, the studio's music director, for a series of shorts based on musical compositions. Stalling's first idea was a graveyard frolic to the music of Grieg's March of the Dwarfs.

Both Disney and Iwerks sparked to the idea. They devised a series of gags with skeletons floating out of graves and cavorting in a loose-boned chorus dance that even incorporated some of the Black Bottom and Charleston dance steps of the Twenties. There was no story, just one ghostly scene after another.

Iwerks plunged into the animation of The Skeleton Dance with the same demonic fervor he had given to Steamboat Willie. "I am glad the spook dance is progressing so nicely—give her Hell, Ubbe," Walt wrote from New York. "Make it funny, and I am sure we will be able to place it in a good way."

Disney masked his discontent with Ub's intransigence. Although Les Clark animated the opening scene, Iwerks insisted on drawing every remaining frame, allowing assistants only to fill in details. Disney disliked having his best animator tied up, but his arguments made no headway with the inflexible Ub, who felt he could achieve a flow of action only if he drew every scene himself.

Disney's distributor viewed The Skeleton Dance and complained, "They don't want this. MORE MICE." A theater manager termed it "too gruesome." But the public was charmed, and Disney was encouraged to launch a new series called Silly Symphonies.

CHAPTER FOUR
PREPARING FOR GREATNESS

Color Comes to Animation

To achieve what he envisioned for animation, Walt Disney needed color, lots of it. He had instructed his technicians to experiment with nitrates and other solutions that might provide color on film, but nothing worked. The only thing possible was the tinting that had been done since the earliest movies—blue could be used for a night scene, red for a big fire. Early attempts had been made at hand-tinting details of the actual film, but that proved laborious and impractical.

During the Twenties, Technicolor developed a two-color process that was used successfully in films like Douglas Fairbanks's *The Black Pirate* in 1926. But the process was expensive and failed to provide true color, so producers lost interest in it. Then in 1932, Technicolor devised a method of combining the primary colors on three strips of negative. The process would not be ready for live-action movies until 1935, when *Becky Sharp* was released. But the process was suitable for cartoons.

"That was what we'd been waiting for," Walt recalled later. "When I saw those three colors all on one film, I wanted to cheer."

Roy Disney was not as enthusiastic. The company had just entered into a distribution deal with United Artists, said Roy, warning that United Artists would not advance more money for color.

Walt argued that the excitement of color would bring longer playdates for Disney cartoons and hence return more money to the company. When his brother expressed concern that colors might not stick to the celluloid or would chip off, Walt replied, "Then we'll develop paints that *will* stick and *won't* chip." He added that color would help popularize the Silly Symphonies, which had never matched the bookings achieved by Mickey Mouse.

As often happened, Walt prevailed. He insisted on strict terms with Technicolor: Disney would have a two-year exclusive which would prohibit other cartoon makers from using the three-color process.

Flowers and Trees *opens with the woodland animals enjoying the delights of spring. The camera switches quickly to the bright figures of an orange centipede, yellow daisies, and tan mushrooms.*

The hero and heroine are introduced. Both are trees, she a demure sapling with a yellow trunk, a light green clump of hair, and dark green fans on her arms; he with a dark brown thatch and a light brown trunk. The villain is a nasty gray stump with a green tongue.

Spurned by the heroine, the villain rubs twigs together, Boy Scout style, and tosses flames in her direction. Bright red and yellow flames dance everywhere, threatening trees, birds, flowers, and mushrooms alike. The birds save the day by divebombing white clouds that spray out the fire. The hero and heroine are wed and clinch against a bright rainbow.

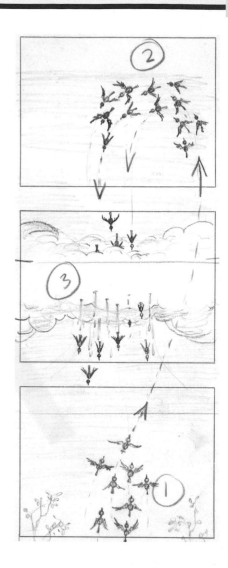

Disney called a halt to a new Silly Symphony called *Flowers and Trees*, which was halfway through animation. The backgrounds were repainted with color, and so was the action. The studio was pioneering all the way. Disney artists had applied color to cels to give more tone to the black-and-white shorts, but its extensive use had never been attempted.

"The colors were basic," commented Wilfred Jackson, one of the earliest Disney employees. "We had no choice in those days. Later we had our own standard paint mixes at the studio. But then we had to use commercial poster paint or whatever we could find. Some of it faded, some fell off the celluloid. We had to feel our way along."

Some studio artists favored muting the colors and attempting subtle shades. "We're paying a lot for color," Walt decreed. "Let's use it."

Jackson remarked, "Walt was right. In those days, there hadn't been many pictures in color. Audiences were impressed by the bright reds and greens and yellows. After color pictures became more common, we could afford to be more subtle."

By today's standards, the coloring of *Flowers and Trees* is far from subtle. But its release brought fresh praise for Walt Disney's inventiveness, as well as the extended bookings that Walt had predicted to Roy. The Academy of Motion Picture Arts and Sciences, honoring the cartoon medium for the first time, gave the Oscar to *Flowers and Trees* for best cartoon short of 1932.

Color brought a new dimension to cartoons, but also new problems. Before color, it was simple to make characters legible; they were outlined in black against a light background. Color required close coordination so animated figures would "read well" against backgrounds.

A red character against a purple background would be disturbing to the eye. A green figure standing before a green tree would disappear into the foliage. The issue was often solved by keeping the characters in lively colors and graying out the backgrounds.

"Look out the window and you will see there is gray in everything—the trees, the sky, the mountains," pointed out veteran Disney color-stylist Art Riley. "By painting our backgrounds with overtones of gray, we can make the scenes look natural and allow the animated figures to be legible." Gray need not be a somber color. Warmth can be found in gray-violets and gray-greens.

"Absorbing color is like eating a steak. The first few bites seem wonderful. But too much steak can make you tired of it. So can too much color."

OPPOSITE TOP: *The vivid hues of nature proved ideal for Disney's burst into color.*

OPPOSITE BOTTOM AND TOP LEFT: *Story sketch pages for* Flowers and Trees.

ABOVE: *The story artist captures the movement of birds in flight.*

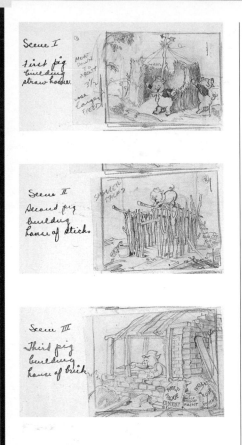

ABOVE: *Story sketches show the differing houses of the Three Little Pigs.*

TOP RIGHT: *Artist's concept of the Wolf's comeuppance.*

Triumph of Character: *Three Little Pigs*

Walt Disney, who enjoyed showing off his cartoon domain to famous visitors, was escorting Mary Pickford through the studio one day in 1932. "America's Sweetheart" adored Mickey Mouse, and she listened raptly as Walt explained the process of creating a Mickey cartoon.

The party stopped at an office where a new Silly Symphony was being planned. On the walls were drawings of three pudgy little pigs and a terrifying wolf.

Walt had started preliminary work on *Three Little Pigs* a few months before. Albert Hurter created charming sketches of the characters, and a story was being developed. Walt argued that the short needed an added value, perhaps a jingle to help tell the story. Frank Churchill, a Disney musician, picked out a tune on the piano. Ted Sears, the story man, contributed couplets that helped tell the story. The chorus fell into place: "Who's afraid of the big bad wolf?" They couldn't think of an ending to the chorus until Pinto Colvig, the voice of numerous cartoon characters, suggested a few bars on a fiddle or fife.

"Why don't you do that 'pig' thing for Mary?" Walt suggested.

With Churchill on the piano, Sears with a fiddle, and Colvig playing an ocarina, the song was performed for the famous visitor. "If you don't make this cartoon about the pigs," Miss Pickford threatened Walt, "I'll never speak to you again."

Disney had already been convinced of the possibilities of *Three Little Pigs*, especially during a time when millions of Americans were "trying to keep the wolf from the door." He assigned Dick Lundy and Fred Moore to animate the pigs, Norm

Ferguson for the wolf. Bert Gillett was the director, but Disney oversaw every phase of the production. In a memo, he exhorted his staff to contribute more comedy for the cartoon:

> . . . . The building of the houses holds chances for a lot of good gags. All this action would be set within rhythm and should work out very effectively. . . . Pull quite a few gags of the wolf trying to get into the little houses, and the pigs' attempts to get rid of him. Chances for funny ways in which the little pigs attack him, the different household props they would use. . . . The idea of the pigs having musical instruments gives us a chance to work in the singing and dancing angles for the finish of the picture. . . . Might try to stress the angle of the little pig who worked the hardest, received the reward, or some little story that would teach a moral. . . .
>
> All gags must be handed in by Friday afternoon December 30 at 4 P.M. I expect a big turnout on this story in spite of Christmas.

Production moved swiftly, and Walt delivered *Three Little Pigs* to the New York distributors. "How come you give us a cartoon with only four characters?" one of them demanded. "We got our money's worth with [the April 1933 Silly Symphony] *Father Noah's Ark*."

Disney shrugged off the comment. He knew from Los Angeles previews that he had a hit. He wrote to his brother Roy: "At last we have achieved true personality in a whole picture."

Released in May 1933 at the depth of the Depression, *Three Little Pigs* was acclaimed by the nation. The wolf was on many American doorsteps, and "Who's Afraid of the Big Bad Wolf?" became a rallying cry. Theaters billed the cartoon over the feature attraction, and many kept it week after week as the rest of the bills changed.

The plot was simplicity itself. The two frivolous pigs would rather sing and play than build suitable shelter against the evil wolf. The industrious pig constructs a wolf-resistant brick house. The wolf arrives and blows away the straw and twig

TOP: *The sketch illustrates the stealthy approach of the Wolf.*

ABOVE: *Disney listens with satisfaction to the voices of the Three Little Pigs (Pinto Colvig, Mary Moder, Dorothy Compton) singing "Who's Afraid of the Big Bad Wolf?" Composer Frank Churchill on piano.*

BELOW: *Animation drawing of the straw-building Pig.*

houses of the two silly pigs. They rush to the house of their serious-minded brother. The wolf is foiled, falls into a boiling kettle, and flees. The pigs celebrate with a song.

Some of the picture is crude. As a hangover from silent days, exclamation marks appear when the pigs are terrified and when the wolf slaps his hands, pretending to walk away.

But it is easy to see why *Three Little Pigs* proved a sensation. It is full of clever uses of sound and color. Mortar makes a juicy sound when slapped on brick. The pursuing wolf is crowned with a treeful of red apples and then a rotten brown one. His face turns blue, then purple as his huffing and puffing fails against the brick house. Character is the element that makes *Three Little Pigs* great. The first pig plays his flute to a gay song and kicks his feet nimbly. The second pig shows his flighty nature as he fiddles and jigs. They sing in boyish falsettos. The builder pig talks his songs in businesslike tones and works with sharp, deliberate motions. He is in overalls, not the sailor suits of his brothers.

The wolf is a shaggy, stealthy villain who slinks from tree to tree with an evil eye. He drools at the prospect of succulent porkers for dinner and concocts cunning schemes to snare them. The ending is perfect: the triumph of good over evil and industry over sloth.

Character, plot, and songs combined in 8 1/2 minutes of rare entertainment. The distributors clamored: "Send us more pigs." Walt, who detested repeating himself, refused, but Roy convinced him to try three more: *The Big Bad Wolf*, *Three Little Wolves*, and *The Practical Pig*. None approached the success of the first picture. Walt often commented in the years to follow: "You can't top pigs with pigs."

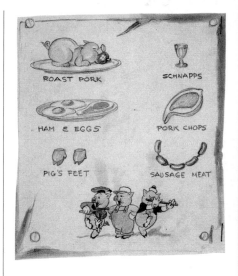

Disney reluctantly brought back his new villain to menace Little Red Riding Hood in The Big Bad Wolf *(LEFT). He also appeared in* Three Little Wolves *(OPPOSITE AND TOP). Except for a wartime government film, the Wolf's theatrical career was over.*

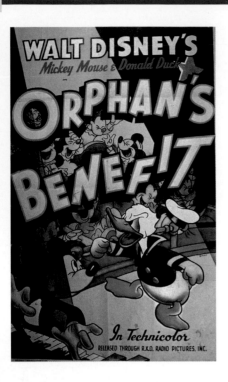

Donald's character was outlined in a 1939 interstudio memo by a story man:

The Duck is the most versatile of all the Disney characters, He can carry off any role with honors—except dumb roles or gentleman parts. . . . He is vain, cocky and boastful, loves to impose on other people and heckle them; but if the tables are turned, he flies into a rage. . . . It is his cockiness that gets him into most of his scrapes, because it is seasoned with foolhardy recklessness. . . . His most likable trait is determination. . . . The Duck never compromises. Regardless of the odds against him, he comes back again and again into the fray.

When attacking a problem, he may be either cocky, cautious or cunning—or all three by turns. He seldom flies into a rage at his first rebuffs; usually those defeats serve to bring out his cleverness.

He doesn't stay angry for long periods; even in his wildest rages, he can be completely and instantly mollified with a little gratification. . . . He is easily amused and laughs especially heartily when he thinks he has caused some person or thing discomfort.

TOP RIGHT: *Character sketches for Donald's debut, before the metamorphosis.*

The Advent of Donald Duck

"Who—me? Oh, no! I got a bellyache."

These were the opening lines for the debut of Donald Duck in *The Wise Little Hen*, a 1934 Silly Symphony. He was a supporting player, a long-beaked bird in sailor's cap and jacket, four feathers for hands and spiky tailfeathers.

He is first seen doing a sailor's hornpipe aboard a boat as the hen and her chicks seek help in planting corn. The duck feigns a stomach ailment to avoid work. He and lazy Peter Pig retire to the Idle Hour Club. They end up kicking each other when they are not invited to a luscious corn dinner prepared by the hen.

It was an inauspicious beginning, but clearly the duck had possibilities. They were realized in his next cartoon, *Orphan's Benefit*. Prophetically, he stole the picture from Mickey Mouse.

Mickey calls on Donald to help entertain the orphans. Donald insists on reciting "Mary Had a Little Lamb" and "Little Boy Blue" in his sputtering, half-understandable voice despite the jeers of his youthful audience. When the vegetables start flying, Donald explodes in a Vesuvian tantrum.

Audiences were convulsed by the foolish, bad-tempered bird, and he became a regular cast member in the Mickey Mouse series. He played a peace officer in *The Dognapper*, a peanut vendor in *Mickey's Band Concert*, a fireman in *Mickey's Fire Brigade*. Between 1935 and 1942, Donald costarred in twenty-six Mickey Mouse cartoons. In 1937 he became the second Disney character to star in his own series, portraying a Latin lover in *Don Donald*.

Donald Duck was first drawn by Dick Lundy. Jack Hannah, who later directed the cartoons, once said of Donald, "I could kill him sometimes. But he can be fun to work with."

The main limitation of Donald, said Hannah, was the voice (squawked by Clarence Nash). The words could not be understood by many in the audience. But the voice was so comical and fit Donald's explosive nature so neatly that other

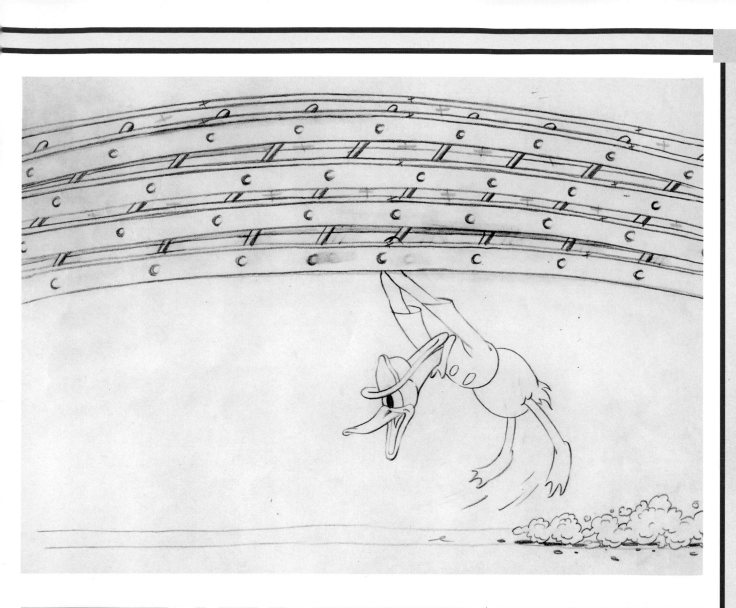

TOP: *By the time of his sixth cartoon,* Mickey's Fire Brigade *(1935), Donald Duck had become a major player (animation drawing).*

LEFT: *In* Orphan's Benefit *(1941), Donald reprised the role that helped make him famous.*

ABOVE: *Story sketch for* Don Donald *(1937), the duck's first starring role.*

ABOVE: *Story sketch for* Don Donald.

BELOW: *Animation of Donald in* The Wise Little Hen *caught his infectious jauntiness.*

storytelling devices were used: the dialogue was repeated by another character with a clear voice, or the plot was related in pantomime. Most of the payoff gags in Donald Duck cartoons featured action, not dialogue.

Donald's appearance changed after his debut. The long bill was shortened to a more expressive size. His angular figure was rounded to make him cuter and more maneuverable.

Donald Duck's versatility is demonstrated by the fact that he has appeared in four feature films, more than any other Disney character including Mickey Mouse. He also works better than the others when appearing with live actors; he doesn't seem out of place, as some of the other characters do. For instance, he frequently exchanged dialogue with Walt Disney on the *Disneyland* television show.

Over the years Donald Duck has enjoyed a steadier career than Mickey Mouse, whom he replaced as the studio's number-one comedy star. Mickey suffered an eclipse in the late Thirties. He had started his career as something of a scamp, but public pressure had softened his character, made him more of a leading actor than a comic. Animators were more comfortable with the easy comedics of Donald, Goofy, and Pluto, who had animal-like proportions. "What can you do with a four-foot mouse?" the artists pondered. Mickey also suffered from a lack of attention from his mentor. Walt Disney had loftier goals than dreaming up gags for Mickey Mouse.

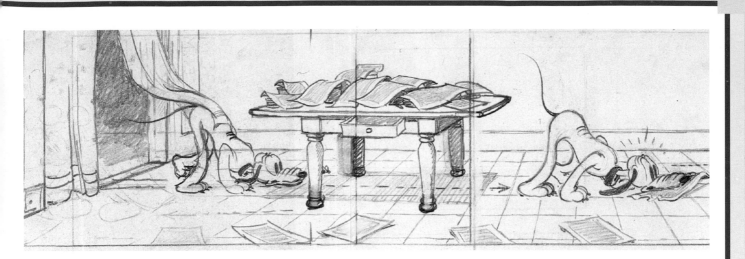

New Stars for the Disney Roster

Pluto made his debut in a brother act in *The Chain Gang*, a 1930 Mickey Mouse. He was one of a pair of bloodhounds chasing Mickey after an escape from a prison. What made Pluto's debut memorable was a closeup, something relatively novel in cartoons. The dog raced up to the camera, his panting mouth almost filling the screen. Audiences were startled and amazed.

Like the late Peter Pig, one of the hounds disappeared, but his partner showed up in another cartoon with Mickey Mouse, *The Picnic*. This time he was given a name, Rover. He threw the whole picnic into an uproar when he rampaged in pursuit of a rabbit while being tethered to Mickey's car.

Rover was so successful that Disney decided he could be a permanent foil for Mickey. But he needed a better name. Pal and Homer the Hound were proposed. Disney suggested Pluto, and the name stuck.

In his next film, *The Moose Hunt*, Pluto spoke. The event was not as auspicious as Greta Garbo's first words in a talkie. In the scene Mickey believes mistakenly that he will be forced to shoot his pet dog, and he pleads, "Speak to me!" Mickey is astonished when Pluto replies, "Kiss Me!"

The line brought a big laugh, but it was out of character.

"We've generally kept Pluto all dog," explained Nick Nichols, longtime animator of Pluto. "He usually keeps all four paws on the ground, and he doesn't speak, except for a breathy 'Yeah! Yeah!' and a panting, raspy kind of laugh. When he talks to other animals, he uses what I call garbage—a combination of growls, gurps and mutters."

His only other venture into dialogue came in *Mickey's Pal Pluto*, in which his good and evil selves debate his actions.

Walt Disney won an Academy Award in 1941 for the Pluto cartoon *Lend a Paw*, the studio's sixth Oscar in six years. Animators have nominated Pluto for another award: being the first cartoon character to break away from the old style of animation. He was not a flat figure that had been obviously drawn. He seemed as round and plump as an oversized sausage. He owed nothing to the Circle Formula or the Rubber-hose Method. He had his own size and shape, and he moved convincingly.

He could also reason, which may seem like a minor matter, but its value was overlooked for a long time. Early cartoon characters could think in elementary

TOP AND ABOVE: *Story sketches for* Playful Pluto, *in which he displays reasoning powers.*

BELOW: *Finished animation of* Pluto *in* Lend a Paw.

O.S. EXCLAMATIONS
GOOF BOWS

ABOVE AND BELOW: *Animation drawings of Goofy dancing with a mop in* Mickey's Birthday Party *(1942).*

TOP RIGHT AND OPPOSITE TOP: *Story sketches of the cake catastrophe for* Mickey's Birthday Party.

terms: a bright notion was symbolized by an electric light over the head. But these pioneering figures had little reasoning power; they merely reacted to outside forces. Only when cartoon characters learned to reason could they be entirely convincing.

The classic example of Pluto's reasoning was the flypaper sequence in the 1934 *Playful Pluto*, animated by the gifted Norm Ferguson. Sniffing along in his usual style, Pluto encounters a sheet of flypaper. His nose sticks to it. He figures he can get rid of the flypaper by holding it with his paw. Now his paw is stuck. He continues taking step after logical step, only to become further entrapped by the sticky paper.

Here is an analysis of Pluto's character, prepared as a guide for story men, animators, and comic-book artists:

"Pluto is best appreciated when he is not too smart. . . . In pantomime, his dumb, one-track mind is similar to that of Stan Laurel's. . . . Pluto is nervous and sensitive, easily startled. . . . His feelings are easily hurt when scolded, especially by Mickey. . . .

"He is foolhardy rather than brave. He might be termed a likable coward. . . . His loyalty to Mickey is a good asset. . . . Pluto will bark at anything strange, but he will retreat hastily when it makes a move toward him. . . . His natural facial expression, when not happy or angry, is sad and mournful."

Unlike Pluto, Goofy was a dog who spoke, though in a halfwitted gurgle, and assumed human proportions and costumes. Goofy's debut came in 1932 with *Mickey's Revue*. He was simply the member of an animal audience watching a musical show. Wearing pince-nez glasses and whiskers, he munched on peanuts and laughed. But what a laugh! It was deep-throated and convulsive, as delivered by the former circus clown Pinto Colvig.

Goofy evolved slowly. At first he was named Dippy Dawg, and he provided minor comic relief in such shorts as *The Whoopee Party*, *Touchdown Mickey*, and *The Klondike Kid*. He began as a genuine hayseed, the kind that Disney had known on his

THROWS CAKE O.S.

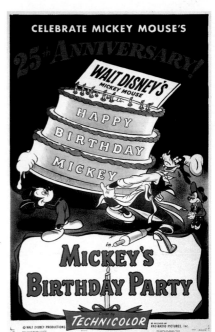

boyhood farm in Marceline, Missouri. Then he became a likable bucktoothed dolt, slow on the uptake but willing to go along with the schemes of Mickey and Donald. The tall lumpy hat remained, but the white vest was exchanged for a rumpled suit or overalls.

Art Babbitt is credited with elevating Goofy from bit player to star. The animator gave him a pattern of mannerisms and a loony, flat-footed shuffle similar to the walk assumed by black comedians. In a 1934 memo, Babbitt analyzed his protégé:

"Think of the Goof as a composite of an everlasting optimist, a gullible Good Samaritan, a halfwit, a shiftless, good-natured hick. He is loose-jointed and gangly, but not rubbery. He can move fast if he has to, but would rather avoid overexertion so he takes what seems the easiest way. . . .

"He very seldom, if ever, reaches his objective or completes what he has started. . . . Any little distraction can throw him off his train of thought. . . . His brain being rather vapory, it is difficult for him to concentrate on any one subject.

"Yet the Goof is not the type of halfwit that is to be pitied. He doesn't drool, dribble or shriek. He is a good-natured dumbbell who thinks he is pretty smart."

Through the Thirties Goofy proved an ideal scene-stealing foil for Mickey and Donald. Finally in 1939 he achieved star status in *Goofy and Wilbur*, a fishing adventure with a friendly grasshopper. On his own, Goofy became far more versatile, even though his lines were reduced to little more than the trade-mark laugh, yelps of pain and terror and the bashful "Gawrsh!"

Jack Kinney introduced a whole new career for Goofy with *How to Ride a Horse* in 1941. Kinney devised a formula in which a serious, slightly pompous voice (sketch artist John McLeish) narrated the various steps in learning to ride horseback. Goofy with mock concentration demonstrated the steps, always falling into comical predicaments. The juxtaposition of the straightarrow narrator and the terminally maladroit Goof was pure magic, and the How To series continued into the mid-Fifties, when the making of cartoon shorts came to a halt.

ABOVE AND OPPOSITE TOP: *Minnie in* Mickey's Rival *(1936).*

RIGHT: *Story sketch of the two sweethearts in* Mickey's Rival.

BELOW: *The mail brings portent of trouble in* Donald's Nephews *(1938).*

OPPOSITE BOTTOM: *A story sketch of Daisy Duck in her 1937 film debut,* Don Donald *(LEFT). In the same film, she dances the fandango while Donald plays guitar (RIGHT).*

Leading Ladies and Supporting Players

From *Steamboat Willie* onward, Disney required leading ladies, hence the presence of Minnie Mouse, Daisy Duck, and—for Pluto—Fifi the Peke and Dinah the Dachshund. They were necessary as objects to be wooed or rescued. But none of the female characters ever emerged as more than faintly defined ingenues. The cartoons were comedies, and audiences were less apt to laugh at the indignities that befell female figures (exception: Betty Boop). The fact that all the animators were male may have been a factor.

Minnie appeared in seventy of the 129 Mickey Mouse cartoons, often in brief roles, and in none of the feature films, except for a token appearance in *Who Framed Roger Rabbit*. Only in a few cartoons, such as *Mickey's Rival* and *The Nifty Nineties*, does she have a substantial part.

In the 1938 *Donald's Nephews*, Donald Duck receives a postcard from his sister Dumbella that she was sending her three "angel children" for a visit. Donald's delight turns to rage when Huey, Dewey, and Louie wreak havoc on the house with a wild polo match on tricycles. The nephews immediately became the perfect instigation for Donald's tantrums, and they appeared in twenty-four of the Donald Duck cartoons.

Two more nemeses for Donald were introduced in 1943 with *Private Pluto*. These were pesky chipmunks who were given names in their third cartoon: Chip an' Dale. With their round furry bodies, wide cheeks, and prominent teeth, they became popular enough to star in their own series.

A few early Disney characters faded from the scene. Clarabelle Cow and

Pegleg Pete was a superb heavy who predated Mickey Mouse, having appeared in both the Alice and Oswald cartoons. A combination of Wallace Beery and an alley cat (though he sometimes resembled a ferocious dog), Pete provided the first menace for Mickey Mouse, twisting Mickey's body like chewing gum in Steamboat Willie. *He served as a Mexican bandit, French trapper, evicting sheriff, bullying train conductor, always being trounced in the end by Mickey or Donald. Whenever a first-class villain was required, Pete was pressed into service, right up to 1990 in* The Prince and the Pauper.

Horace Horsecollar were engaging figures in the early Thirties cartoons, and they combined well together. Their pipestem legs and grotesque faces harked back to the Rubber-hose style of animation, and they were phased out in favor of more realistic characters.

The Animators Go to School

Except for a few studio-trained artists, most of the animators at Disney were self-taught cartoonists from the New York school. They brought zest and exhilaration to the Disney pictures, but their methods were the same that cartoonists had employed since the beginning of the medium.

Disney once remarked: "A lot of the artists who came to me from the East and had been in the business a good number of years were individualists. They insisted they not only draw, but they wanted to do the inking. They wanted to follow it to the last detail. I said, 'That's silly. You draw it and then we have people who can do the inking better than you can.' I had quite a time breaking that down."

Early in the studio's history, Disney concluded that he needed a new and different breed of animator to realize his plans for the future. He couldn't afford to start a school of his own, so in 1931 he arranged for his artists to attend classes at the Chouinard Art Institute in downtown Los Angeles. The studio paid the tuition. Many of the young men did not own cars, so Walt drove them to Chouinard. He returned to the studio for an evening's work, then drove back to the school and distributed the students to their homes.

"To do the things I wanted to do, I needed better artists," Disney told me in 1956. "A cartoonist is not the same as an artist. A cartoonist knows the shortcuts and tricks—how to do things in a hurry. His work might have been comic, but it wasn't convincing.

"The cartoonist had to learn about art. So I sent the boys to school. Some of

them hated it and wouldn't go along; most of those fell by the wayside as the studio progressed. But the top men at the studio today are largely those who went through the Disney school."

When a distribution contract with United Artists brought financial stability, the Disney Art School was established at the studio. Don Graham, a teacher at Chouinard, conducted two night classes a week. The opening class in the Disney sound stage on November 15, 1932, attracted twenty-five students. Attendance soon doubled, especially when word spread that Graham was using nude models for the life class.

The fledgling artists did not merely draw static figures, as they had at Chouinard. The models were told to move, and the drawings reflected the progressive poses. Graham knew nothing of animation when he arrived at the studio. He was given a crash course, sitting in the sweatbox for hours as Walt and directors explained aspects of making drawings move. Soon Walt and Graham were critiquing the work of new animators together. Graham began working at the studio full-time, teaching three days and two nights. Field trips were made to the nearby Griffith Park Zoo to sketch animals in movement. Classes were given on color psychology and action analysis. Frank Lloyd Wright, Alexander Woollcott, and other notables came to lecture.

In the six years since the loss of Oswald, the Disney staff had grown from six to 187, including forty animators, forty-five assistant animators, a dozen story and gag men, thirty inkers and painters, and a twenty-four piece orchestra. They were producing nine Mickey Mouse cartoons a year and eight Silly Symphonies. With all the training and instruction that had been going on, it was clear that Walt intended something bigger than the making of short cartoons. That was confirmed one day in 1934 when Walt said to Don Graham: "I need three hundred artists. Get them."

OPPOSITE: *Horace Horsecollar and Goofy in a failed adagio with Clarabelle Cow in* Orphan's Benefit. *Animation drawings.*

LEFT AND ABOVE: *Story sketches for* Mickey's Rival.

CHAPTER FIVE
SNOW WHITE AND THE SEVEN DWARFS

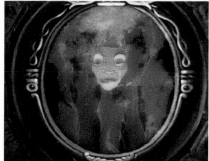

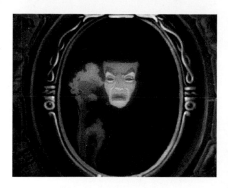

Launching the Animated Feature

One evening in 1934, the chief animators returned to the studio after a dinner at a cafe across Hyperion Avenue. Walt had been awaiting their return, and he seemed to be in a state of unusual excitement. "Come on into the sound stage; I've got something to tell you," he said.

They joined him inside on the bare stage and pulled up folding chairs as Walt stood under the light of a bare bulb. He began telling them the story of Snow White and the Seven Dwarfs. Each scene was acted out, beginning with the dwarfs arriving after a day's work to find Snow White in their cottage. He impersonated each of the dwarfs, hunching down to approximate their size and telling their individual idiosyncrasies. Then he was the wicked queen, eyes flashing as she demanded of the mirror, "Who's the fairest of them all?" The recital continued for two hours until the prince awakened Snow White with a kiss. Even the most hardboiled animators wiped away tears.

"That's going to be our first feature," Walt announced.

The idea for *Snow White and the Seven Dwarfs* had been gestating in Disney's mind for a few years. As a teenager he had been invited along with other Kansas City newspaper delivery boys to attend a performance of the silent movie *Snow White* starring Marguerite Clark. They gathered in the huge Convention Hall, where the movie was projected on screens in the four corners of the auditorium. Walt watched two of the screens, and the performance remained the most vivid memory of his moviegoing childhood.

Walt had long yearned to escape the constrictions of the eight- or nine-minute cartoon, to tell a fully developed story as the other Hollywood studios did. The Snow White fairy tale offered all the elements: romance with an attractive heroine and hero; menace from an evil villainess; comedy and heart with the dwarfs; a happy ending to a timeless folklore story familiar to audiences around the world.

PRECEDING SPREAD: *Picturesque background watercolor of the dwarfs' cottage in* Snow White and the Seven Dwarfs *(SPREAD). Closeup film frame of Snow White (INSET).*

TOP LEFT: *Film frame of Snow White peering in a window of the Dwarfs' cottage.*

ABOVE: *"Magic mirror on the wall. . . ." Film frames.*

ABOVE AND OPPOSITE TOP: *Film frames of* Snow White and the Seven Dwarfs.

Animation drawings of Grumpy (BELOW) *and Doc* (OPPOSITE BOTTOM).

"The figures of the dwarfs intrigued me," Disney recalled in later years. "I thought it was a good plot with wide appeal. It wasn't too fantastic. You can't have too much in a picture that is beyond the realm of your audience's experience."

Disney's decision was economic as well as artistic. Mickey Mouse was an international celebrity as famous as Charlie Chaplin or Greta Garbo, but he wasn't paid as well as his fellow stars. Theater owners allowed only a few dollars for cartoon shorts, no matter how high their quality. Even a huge hit like *Three Little Pigs* brought the studio less than $60,000.

Furthermore, the Disneys had only shorts to sell. Big studios like MGM and Paramount could offer cartoons at a loss as a service to customers of their feature pictures. The Disney studio could not have shown a profit except for the license fee for sales of toys and other products with the Mickey Mouse imprint. Roy Disney was well aware of the dwindling economics of short-subject production, but he was cautious about Walt's plan. So was Walt's wife Lilly. Walt expected *Snow White* to cost $500,000, a huge burden for the small company (the final cost was three times that amount). As usual, he had his way.

Don Graham began the search for the artists Disney needed. Recruiting ads were placed in newspapers up and down the West Coast, then across the nation. Graham spent three months in an office in the RCA Building in New York, poring over portfolios.

Three hundred artists converged on the Hyperion Avenue studio from all over the United States. Unlike the early animators, many had attended four years of college. Some were highly trained as architects and commercial artists who could not find work in Depression America. Disney admitted later that the economic slump proved a boon for the studio; without it, he could never have recruited artists of such high caliber.

The arrivals were sent immediately to school. They were drilled in the drawing of characters, the function of the animation camera, the making of in-betweens (the transitional drawings between those of the animator and his assistant). For two weeks they spent every day drawing in life classes. Then they devoted half a day to drawing, half to the intricacies of production. They were also encouraged to attend night classes, which had grown in attendance to one hundred and fifty. Those who

showed promise after eight weeks of training were assigned to work in the animation department one day a week. The days increased until the newcomers worked full-time.

Walt held regular story meetings to perfect the *Snow White* script. This was something new for the story men: devising an eighty-three-minute movie with brand-new characters instead of inventing gags and business for the studio's stable of cartoon stars. The clarity of Disney's vision is demonstrated in his comments on the scene of the Queen, disguised as the old witch, visiting Snow White at the dwarfs' cottage:

At the time the menace comes in, Snow White should be doing something that shows she is happy and that she is trying to do something nice for these little men. That's the time the menace should strike. It's most powerful when it strikes when people are happy. It's dramatic. . . .

She's taken aback when she first sees the Queen, but [when] there's a lunatic around somewhere and he approaches you, you have a funny feeling. It's nothing you can put your finger on. You wouldn't have the police come, but you'd be on your guard.

That's the point we ought to bring out with the animals. They are dumb, but they have a certain sense like a dog who knows that somebody is not a friend. When the birds see that old witch they know that everything is not right and they're alarmed and back out of the way, retreat quietly. It has just dampened everything.

But when the birds see that the vultures have followed her, that tells them something that even a human won't recognize.

Some of the thought processes that went into animating the dwarfs are illustrated in studio meeting notes:

Dave Hand: There is a hundred feet of the dwarfs walking home from the mine. They are singing the "Hi-Ho" song. We have closeups of the dwarfs in the musical sequence, and we want all their characteristics. George will bring out some of the points about what the dwarfs are doing and the way they are walking. George Stalling: The march home should be a spirit and not a play thing. There is no showoff; the dwarfs do this every day. Doc is leading. He whistles and struts along, waving his hand like a baton. Grumpy takes it as a matter of routine. He turns his head and spits, then goes right back to the song. Happy has a rollicking, rolling movement that is all rhythm. When he comes to a tree stump, he hops over it in a graceful manner. Sneezy is plodding along. Maybe his nose is twitching, maybe he slaps at it. Bashful is walking along in a dreamy attitude, as though he is thinking of something that is unusual to him—a dream, perhaps. Sleepy is almost walking in his sleep, dragging his feet but keeping pace. His pick gets caught in his clothes and forces him to walk on his toes. Dopey tries to keep in step, skips to keep in step, then stumbles and is out of step again.

Seven Dwarfs for Snow White

Disney realized from the beginning that the dwarfs themselves were crucial to the success of *Snow White and the Seven Dwarfs*. Snow White was a charming but standard heroine. The Prince appeared only at the beginning and end of the picture. The Stepmother was a fairy tale villainess. The dwarfs would need to provide most of the comedy and human interest.

The ancient fairy tale offered little help. The dwarfs were phantom figures with no definition. One play version named them Blick, Flick, Glick, Snick, Frick, Whick, and Quee.

Disney assigned the story department to devise seven engaging, easily recognizable characters. The natural thing was to select names that were descriptive. Among the suggestions: Jumpy, Deafy, Wheezy, Baldy, Gabby, Nifty, Swift, Lazy, Puffy, Stuffy, Tubby, Shorty, and Burpy.

Through a process of elimination, the seven finalists were chosen. Those with the obvious characteristics were fairly easy: Grumpy, Happy, Sleepy, Sneezy, and Bashful.

"For the leader, we needed a special kind of personality," Disney commented in 1956. "He was one of those pompous, bumbling, self-appointed leaders who tries to take command and then gets all tangled up. We gave him the name of Doc, since it was a good handle for a person in authority.

"Dopey was the toughest of all. The boys just couldn't seem to get him. They tried to make him too much of an imbecile. Dopey wasn't an imbecile. Finally I thought of a way to put him across: Make him a human with dog mannerisms and intellect.

"That solved it. You know the way a dog will be so intent on sniffing a trail that he doesn't see the rabbit right in front of him—and when the rabbit scurries away the dog does a delayed take? That's the way Dopey was. We made him able to move one ear independently of the other, the way a dog could shake off a fly. And when Dopey had a dream, he pawed with his hand the way a dog does while sleeping.

"But he had to do one thing really well; otherwise he'd just be stupid. So we had him do a clever little slaphappy dance at the dwarfs' entertainment. That let him show off."

The extra effort on Dopey produced results. He proved to be the most beguiling of the dwarfs.

Once the characters of the dwarfs were established, the faces followed with little difficulty. The name dictated the facial expressions to the artists: Happy's face was wreathed in a smile, Grumpy wore a perpetual scowl, Sleepy was droopy-eyed, etc. All had broad cheeks, bulbous noses, white beards (except for Dopey), and wore caps.

The big problem came in animating the dwarfs. Human figures had always proved difficult for animators; now they were drawing ill-formed humans as well. Notes from a meeting of the directing animators illustrate the thought processes in animating the dwarfs:

Dave Hand: "I would like to get an expression of opinion whether we should drive toward the human angle of the dwarfs walking, or whether they should swing from side to side working with their hips."

Bill Tytla: "On account of the pelvis condition, dwarfs are inclined to walk with a swing of the body."

Fred Spencer: "Dwarfs seem to walk with a little waddle. I think we should establish some kind of walk but not make it repulsive."

Fred Moore: "I think we should use a quick little walk, try to work out some pattern where we could get away from the usual way of covering ground."

As the dwarfs began to take physical form, they were fitted with voices befitting their characters. Billy Gilbert, famous for his sneezing routine in vaudeville and movies, was a natural for Sneezy. Roy Atwell, a radio comedian who specialized in mixed-up language, played Doc. Happy was veteran actor Otis Harlan, and Bashful was Scotty Mattraw. The versatile Disney hand, Pinto Colvig, played both Grumpy and Sleepy.

"We tried many voices for Dopey," Disney remarked later, "and every one of them killed the character. So we decided not to let him talk. It wasn't that he *couldn't* talk. He just never tried."

Some of the story men argued that the scene in which Snow White woke up to discover the dwarfs was too long.

"Maybe it is," replied Disney. "But we've got to take the time to have her meet each dwarf individually, so the audience will get acquainted with them. Even if we bore the audience a little, they'll forget it later because they'll be interested in each dwarf."

OPPOSITE LEFT AND ABOVE: Snow White *film frames.*

OPPOSITE RIGHT AND TOP LEFT: *Animation of the homeward march.*

ABOVE: *Animation shows the personality of Snow White.*

TOP RIGHT: *Inking instructions on Dwarf animation.*

OPPOSITE: *Film frames of Snow White's escape through the forest.*

New Tools: Live Action, Multiplane Camera & Effects

From the beginning of animation, the principal figures were anthropomorphic animals and caricatured human beings. Little attempt had been made to present the human form as it really was. The Disney animators faced a problem in making Snow White seem like a real girl.

"It was easy to animate animals," Disney observed. "The audience wasn't familiar with the fine points of how animals move, so we could give a semblance of animal motion and it would be convincing.

"Humans were different. Everyone knows how humans stand and walk and move their heads. If we couldn't duplicate that, we wouldn't have a convincing picture.

"So we tried making movies of live actors doing the things that the animated figures would do. Then the animator could study the film and use it as a guide for his drawing.

"After all, the animator couldn't think up everything in his head. Even such a simple matter as rising from a chair was important. In the old days, a cartoon figure would simply rise to an erect position and walk away.

"But that isn't how people move. By studying live-action film, the animator could see that the figure leaned forward in the chair, placed his hands on the chair arms and pushed himself into a standing position.

"The important thing is to use live action as a guide and not a crutch. When we first started using it, some animators tried to copy the live action exactly. Their work was stilted and cramped.

"The fact is that humans can't move as freely and gracefully and comically as we can make animated figures move. We're not in the business of duplicating live action."

In the 1934 Silly Symphony, *The Goddess of Spring*, an attempt had been made to

portray the goddess Persephone as a realistic girl. The animation was awkward and unconvincing. "We'll get it next time," Disney said confidently.

For *Snow White*, the studio photographed a lithe young dancer, Marjorie Belcher—later known as Marge Champion—whirling and dancing and walking in a costume like the heroine's. Billy Gilbert and other voices of the dwarfs performed before the camera in the flat-footed dance.

The best animators followed Disney's thinking and used live action as a guide. Most of them preferred scenes in which their imaginations could run rampant without concern for lifelike human action. But with the animated feature requiring greater realism, live action became imperative as a reference point.

"No matter how good they are, actors can seldom give you what you want," observed animator Frank Thomas. "You can talk to them and get them thoroughly immersed in the character, but when they do the action, it's not what you have in the back of your mind."

Milt Kahl agreed: "The best use of live action is for ideas—little pieces of movement that an actor does and which do not occur to you. For instance, a couple swirling around on a dance floor. The live action tells you how they move in and out, how the girl's dress twirls, how they move their heads."

For scenes of rapid or intricate movement, photostats of the movie frames were made so the animator could study them closely. Some kept a moviola by their desks so they could repeat the scene. No matter what device was used, the ultimate interpretation of the scene was through the mind and feeling of the animator as expressed with pencil on paper.

Walt Disney continued using the Silly Symphonies as a proving ground for the advancements he needed for the full-length animated film. To compete with live-action producers, his camera needed to be as fluid as any on a movie set: to dolly in

Disney put the multiplane camera (ABOVE) to the test in a Silly Symphony. He chose a subject called "The Old Mill," which he described as "just a poetic thing, nothing but music. No dialogue or anything. The setting of an old mill at sunset. The cows going home. And then what happens in an old mill at night. The spider coming out and weaving its web. The birds nesting, and then the storm coming up, and the windmill going on a rampage. And with morning the cows come back, the spider web was all shattered, and all that. It was just a poetic thing."

The Old Mill was the most successful Silly Symphony since Three Little Pigs. It won an Academy Award as the best cartoon of 1937 and provided Disney artists an invaluable tool for the first animated feature.

BELOW: Effects animation provides sparkle for the diamonds.

and out of a scene, to photograph foreground actors and background scenery with total realism.

The photography of cartoon backgrounds had changed little since the days of Raoul Barré and Winsor McCay. Drawings of characters were piled like pancakes on scenes of farms or forests or wherever the action took place, and photographed with a stop-action camera. As long as cartoons remained unsophisticated, the system worked satisfactorily. But as Disney sought to match the reality of live-action movies, new methods were needed.

"Our trouble was that we couldn't control the elements at infinity," explained John Hench. He cited the example of a scene with haystacks in the foreground, a farmhouse on a hill with a big moon behind it. As the camera moved past the haystacks and toward the house, the house got bigger, and so did the moon. Said Hench: "We could make the foreground elements bigger, but we couldn't keep the moon the same size."

Another problem. The audience couldn't detect the lack of depth as long as all parts of the picture remained still. But when the foreground trees swept out of camera range as the camera moved in, the trees were exposed as undoubtedly flat.

The solution: the multiplane camera.

As designed by Disney craftsmen, the camera towered fourteen feet and cost $70,000. The camera was stationed above, as with customary animation photography. But instead of layers of art work piled on each other, they were separated onto several glass frames. On the bottom layer could be a row of trees. On the next, a fence. The next might contain the animated layer, perhaps a Prince and Princess walking arm-in-arm. On the top layer, some shrubbery.

The camera could pull in closer and the foreground shrubbery would drop out of the scene. The couple could walk off-screen, and the camera move in further, past the fence and into the trees for a closeup of an owl.

The camera could also be used for a woodland scene with a waterfall. Since the animation of the waterfall required special effects done on a separate frame, the other, static elements of the picture could be placed on separate planes.

Each plane was lighted individually, the lighting adjusted to assure the same colors with each exposure. Bulbs burn blue at their height, red as they wane; so their life span was charted, and the bulbs removed before they reddened.

As part of the preparation for *Snow White*, Disney established the animation effects department. Scenes of action that are taken for granted in live-action movies—waterfalls, forest fires, lightning, rainfall—are far beyond the skills of even the most gifted of animators. Disney needed to portray such things in order to make features dramatic and convincing.

The Disney researchers went to work. They experimented with colored gels, camera diffusion (blurring focus), filming through frosted or rippled glass, and scores of other techniques. Some of their discoveries were astonishingly simple. Others were too technical to explain to the layman.

Longshot (LEFT) and closeup (TOP) film frames of the housecleaning scene (ABOVE) from Snow White illustrate how animators used the multiplane camera to achieve depth.

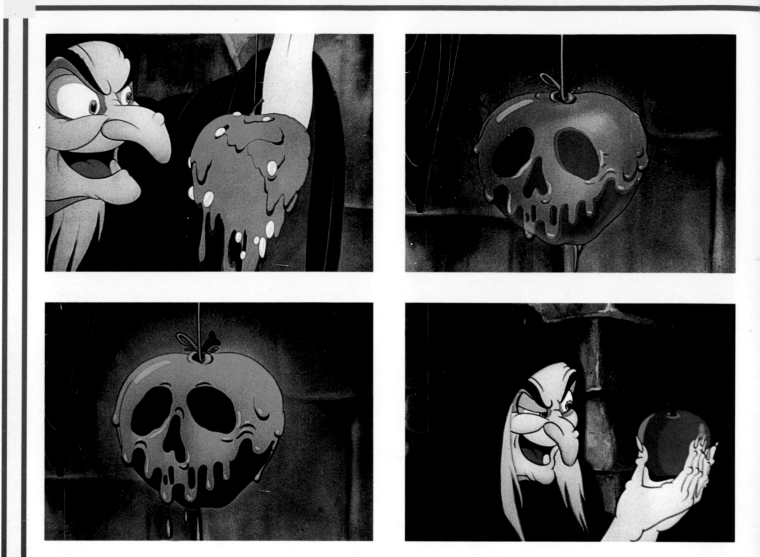

A *November 1936 story conference concerned the scene of the Witch preparing the poisoned apple:*

Walt: The thought just struck me on the buildup of the music to where she says, "Now turn red, etc." Where it starts you might go into innocent, sweet music while she is saying something about how innocent it looks. The music changes as the apple changes and could stay that way until she says, "Have a bite." It would be a good contrast.

Dave Hand: You mean the innocence of the apple or of Snow White?

Walt: The apple. You have seen the poison seeping into it and the buildup of the hocus-pocus around it. Then some innocent little theme there, coming back to the heavy music after she says, "Have a bite."

Richard Creedon: Admiring the apple as if she'd like to eat it herself—"Pink as a maiden's blush."

The Old Mill, a Silly Symphony, provided the showcase for the discoveries. The animation effects men gave it everything they had: lightning, rain, ripples in water, clouds, sun rays, firefly glow. These things brought fascination to an essentially plotless short subject. Part of the effectiveness of *Snow White* was due to the animation effects: the sparkling jewels in the mine, the horrid concoctions of the witch's brew, the soap bubbles in the washing scene.

"Our business is to present something in an unreal way to make it seem more real," explained Dan McManus, an animated effects veteran. "If you make a pillar of flame the way it really is, it wouldn't look like the real thing. We have to create it as the eye thinks it *should* look."

Lightning, he pointed out, is not convincing if it is drawn exactly as it appears in a photograph. By exaggerating the bolt and filling the screen with intermittent white frames, the effects artist can make his lightning more dramatic than nature's.

Shadows had long posed a problem for animators; the early artists simply ignored them. But shadows were necessary for realism and for dramatic effect.

"Shadows are a lot of trouble," commented effects artist John Reed. "But they are useful. They help create mood. And they lend the illusion that characters have depth instead of being two-dimensional.

"To make shadows, you first of all figure the origin of light. Then you calculate

in what direction and at what angle the shadow will fall. The shadow is done in two ways: by using transparent paint or by painting the shadow black and double-exposing the frame, first with the shadow and then without."

Josh Meador began his Disney career in the effects department with *The Old Mill* and continued through most of the classic films. One of his assignments was to find a way to show mud pots breaking and splashing in the "Rite of Spring" segment of *Fantasia*. He began by stirring an ungodly mess of oatmeal, mud, and coffee grounds in a vat. Air hoses sent bubbles up through it, and the action was captured by high-speed cameras. The individual frames were processed on cels and dyed red against a yellow background. Animation was added to create more splashes and broaden the action. All this was photographed against backgrounds with controlled light intensities. Thus, for a few fleeting seconds on the screen, that audience saw convincing replicas of primeval convulsion of the earth's surface.

Rain had always been drawn in cartoons until the Disney effects department discovered that slow-motion filming of water falling was more convincing. The sprinkles of water were photographed against a dark background and superimposed on the picture. The same with snow. It was really bleached cornflakes photographed against a black backdrop.

Walt: *Something to show how tempting the apple is, how tempting it would be to anyone she offered it to. . . . It would be part of her sales talk here. The apple has just changed from this terrible thing in blowfly colors and the skull to a beautiful red. There wouldn't be too much of it, just enough for contrast.*

OPPOSITE: *Effects add to the horror of the poisoned apple.*

ABOVE: *Using the candle as light source provides dramatic effect.*

No words can describe its beauty, its charm, its glow, its tremendous appeal to the heart of man!... Nothing like it has ever been seen before!... It is so utterly different from everything the screen has ever known—so refreshing, so wonderful, so deeply thrilling...that every man, woman and child in the world owes it to himself not to permit anything to keep him from seeing it!

Walt Disney's
Snow White
and the
Seven Dwarfs
in
TECHNICOLOR
Adapted from
GRIMM'S FAIRY TALES
RELEASED BY RKO RADIO PICTURES

THE MOST DARING ADVENTURE IN SCREEN ENTERTAINMENT SINCE THE BIRTH OF THE MOTION PICTURE!

ABOVE: *The Disney Studio took special care with its first feature release, even with the press book.*

BELOW: *The dwarfs peering over the cliff as the witch falls to her death.*

"Disney's Folly"

As Snow White pushed into its third year of production, costs continued to mount, and the studio's bankers became increasingly restive. The film trade debated whether audiences would sit still for a feature-length cartoon; it was one thing to amuse them with eight minutes of gags, another to attempt a fully developed plot with serious overtones. There were predictions that "Disney's Folly" would plunge the Disney company, which was forever in hock to the Bank of America, into the bankruptcy court.

Walt Disney continued pressing forward with almost demonic energy. Nothing escaped his scrutiny. He insisted on testing each sequence before it was assigned to animation. Storyboards that portrayed the action in sketches weren't enough. He had story sketches filmed on what became known as a "Leica reel" so they could be viewed in sequence on a movie screen. He also looked at "pencil tests," films of rough animation. He auditioned singers for the leading roles.

Music was important to Disney. Aside from trying to play the violin as a boy, he had no musical education. Yet he had an uncanny ear for what would appeal to the public. He rejected early attempts at songs for Snow White. They were Tin Pan Alley tunes designed for diversion from the story, following the formula in Thirties musicals. "We should set a new pattern, a new way to use music," Disney insisted. "Weave it into the story so somebody doesn't just burst into song."

The entire Disney studio worked furiously to complete *Snow White and the Seven Dwarfs* in time for release at Christmas 1937. When Walt viewed the completed film, he noticed a disturbing detail. Something had gone awry in the animation or the camera work so that the Prince shimmied slightly when he leaned over Snow White's glass coffin. Walt told Roy that he wanted to fix the defect; the repairs would cost several thousand dollars. Roy, who had borrowed all he could, decreed, "Let the Prince shimmy." And so the Prince shimmies to this day.

Snow White and the Seven Dwarfs triumphed beyond even the dreams of Walt Disney. Critics praised it to the skies, and it made more money than any film in 1938—$8 million, at a time when the average movie ticket cost twenty-three cents, a dime for children. Defying scoffers who said people would not sit still for eighty-three minutes of drawings that moved, audiences shuddered at the fearful Witch, delighted in the dwarfs, especially Dopey, and cried when Snow White was awakened by the Prince's kiss.

With the release of *Snow White*, Walt at last had the wherewithal, as well as the talent, to thrust the art of animation to greater heights.

TOP: *Film frame of the happy ending.*

BELOW: *Snow White's delight as she watches the dance of the dwarfs.*

CHAPTER SIX
EXPANSION AND WAR

PRECEDING SPREAD: *Detail from the milkweed ballet of "The Nutcracker Suite," in* Fantasia. *Expanding the role of Jiminy Cricket* (INSET) *proved vital to the plot of* Pinocchio.

ABOVE: *Boy actor Dickie Jones provided the voice for Pinocchio.*

BELOW: *Cliff Edwards (Ukulele Ike) was ideal as Jiminy Cricket's warm, cautionary voice.*

Pinocchio

As the money flowed in from *Snow White and the Seven Dwarfs*, Walt Disney resisted the cry of distributors and theater owners: "Give us more dwarfs!" He used his newfound prosperity to commence with new animated features. *Pinocchio* came first.

It seemed like a natural: an internationally recognized story, a puppet hero who could only be realized in animation, a host of colorful adventures to choose from. With all the pioneering work they had done on *Snow White*, the story men and animators should have had smooth sailing with *Pinocchio*.

For a time it seemed that way. The sprawling tale by Carlo Collodi was trimmed to manageable length, the major characters were designed, the sequences storyboarded, and animation began. Six months later, Disney halted production.

"It isn't working," Disney said. He recognized the lack of endearing characters that had made *Snow White* such an instant success. To remind the audience that Pinocchio was a puppet come to life, he had been animated with simple, almost automated movement, and his face lacked expression. Without a conscience, he performed bad deeds with total innocence. He had none of the boyish humanity that would induce sympathy in his many travails.

Pinocchio was redesigned to make him rounder and more boylike. His nature was altered so that he did bad things only when influenced by evil companions. Because Pinocchio was more or less a blank character, he needed to be surrounded by lively, flamboyant figures. The most important invention was Jiminy Cricket.

Collodi had made the cricket an incidental character who tried to advise Pinocchio to change his ways and then was crushed under the puppet's foot. In the movie, Jiminy Cricket now played a major role as the boy's conscience, trying to steer him back every time he took a wrong turn. Ward Kimball animated Jiminy,

TOP: *The thrilling and dangerous delights of Pleasure Island, in* Pinocchio.

ABOVE: *Walt Disney gave a vivid performance acting out all the characters on a storyboard.*

OPPOSITE: *Effects animation added greatly to the realism of the underwater scenes.*

making him an appealing sage instead of an ugly insect and using carefully selected camera angles so he wouldn't seem tiny. Voiced by Cliff Edwards, who sang the hit songs "When You Wish Upon a Star" and "Give a Little Whistle," Jiminy provided the unifying element for *Pinocchio.*

The Disney artists made ample use of the new toys that had been developed for *Snow White.* The multiplane camera facilitated an opening scene for *Pinocchio* that matched the intricate camera movements of the most skilled live-action directors. The scene sailed over the rooftops of the sleeping village, employing as many as twelve planes. But when the scene ran up a bill of $25,000, Disney blew the whistle and cautioned against such intricate camera work in the future.

Disney was determined that *Pinocchio* would be an even greater achievement than *Snow White,* and he devoted all of his energies to the new production. During a March 1938 story meeting, he expounded on the sequence in which Pinocchio is swallowed by the whale:

"Pinocchio should use every ounce of force he has in his swimming to escape the whale [Monstro]. This should be built to terrific suspense. It should be the equivalent of the storm and the chase of the Queen in *Snow White.* . . .

"The old man [Geppetto, already swallowed by the whale] should get excited

when the whale goes after the fish. When the fish start coming in, he could look toward the whale's mouth and say, 'Tuna!' Pinocchio could be swimming with the fish, and [Monstro] swallows them all. As the old man is fishing inside the whale, he pulls out one fish after another, and finally pulls out Pinocchio without realizing it. The cat [Figaro] sees Pinocchio, gets excited and meows to the old man, but the old man goes on fishing. Finally, Pinocchio calls, 'Father!' The old man recognizes who it is and shouts, 'Pinocchio! My son!'

"We can get comedy out of the whale sneezing with Pinocchio and Geppetto inside. They should react in a certain way—it would be the equivalent to the hiccups in a giant's mouth. . . .

"The underwater stuff is a swell place for the multiplane, diffusing and putting haze in between, with shafts of light coming down. I would like to see a lot of multiplane on this."

The second Disney feature was released in early 1940, and its technical marvels were commended by critics. But it lacked the sentiment and human appeal of *Snow White*, and theater business was disappointing. The start of the war in Europe had wiped out 45 percent of the Disney market, and that contributed to the million-dollar loss on *Pinocchio*, which had cost a staggering $2.6 million.

TOP RIGHT AND OPPOSITE: *Animation drawings and finished film of* The Sorcerer's Apprentice.

ABOVE: *Baton ready, Leopold Stokowski visits the Hyperion studio to meet with Walt and his staff. With studio musicians Frank Churchill* (LEFT) *and Leigh Harline* (RIGHT).

Fantasia

Mickey Mouse had hit a slump, expectable in the careers of movie stars. By the late Thirties his eminence in cartoons had been eclipsed by more surefire Disney comics—Donald Duck, Goofy, and Pluto—as well as other studios' stars such as Popeye and Porky Pig.

Mickey was a throwback to the early years of animation, the time of the Circle Formula and the Rubber-hose Method. He had been rehabilitated in the mid-Thirties by the gifted Freddy Moore. Moore applied the "squash-and-stretch" technique to Mickey, making him more boyish. The body became more pearshaped so it could express emotion; a sunken chest denoted dejection. The head became more flexible; at last Mickey had cheeks. The eyes were placed for better expression. The only thing left unchanged were his ears. Animator Ward Kimball observes: "No matter which way he turns, the ears remain the same. He can make a 360-degree turn and the ears will float in the same position. They're always round, like bowling balls."

Moore changed Mickey's wardrobe as well. No more the two-button shorts and outsized brogans. Now Mickey was dressed in a suit and tie and jaunty hat. The new look made Mickey more accessible but less funny. He had become a supporting player in his own cartoons while his onetime second bananas did the funny stuff.

In 1938 Disney found a new vehicle for his first star. He decided to make a cartoon of *The Sorcerer's Apprentice*, a fairy tale which had been made into a poem by Goethe and a concert piece by Paul Dukas. Disney had been attracted to the music when he heard it at Hollywood Bowl, where he had season tickets. He had started schooling himself in classical music, which he had never found time to listen to before.

Disney bought the rights to the music and cast Mickey as the apprentice whose tampering with his master's powers causes disaster. The short would be done entirely in pantomime; Walt had suspected that his own squeaky voice had contributed to Mickey's decline.

The Sorcerer's Apprentice developed beautifully—in fact, too well. It had cost

Disney poured more care and expense into The Sorcerer's Apprentice than he had given any short cartoon. Special attention was devoted to the use of color, even the absence of color. The scene in which Mickey misuses the magical powers begins with normal colors. Then the broomsticks begin fetching the pails of water with alarming persistence, and Mickey battles furiously to halt them. He finally hacks them to pieces, and the scene turns to a deathly black and white, which in Technicolor has overtones of dark brown.

Mickey shuts the door behind him with great relief. Then the music begins to thump, like the sound of a revived heartbeat. When the door is opened, a bright yellow shaft of light cuts through the gloom, signifying that life remains in the hacked-up brooms. On they come, marching inexorably forward in the sunshiny glow.

ABOVE: *"Rite of Spring" in* Fantasia *drew praise from critics and scorn from the composer, Igor Stravinsky.*

TOP RIGHT: *Parents complained their children were terrified by the "Night on Bald Mountain" sequence.*

$125,000, which it could never recover if released as a short. What could be done? The answer began when Disney met Leopold Stokowski at a restaurant.

"I understand you are doing *The Sorcerer's Apprentice*," said the famed conductor. "I would love to conduct it for you. I will do it for nothing."

Stokowski came to the studio the next day and became excited when he saw the work that had been done with Mickey and the *Apprentice*. Out of the enthusiasm of Disney and Stokowski came the idea for *Fantasia*, an anthology of serious music illustrated by animation. As the project grew, musicologist Deems Taylor came from New York to act as liaison between the two creators.

As Stokowski explained at the time: "In making *Fantasia*, the music suggested the mood, the coloring, the design, the speed, the character of motion of what is seen on the screen. Disney and all of us who worked with him believe that for every beautiful musical composition, there are beautiful pictures. Music by its nature is in constant motion, and this movement can suggest the mood of the picture it invokes."

Disney and most of the creative staff on *Fantasia* were not students of classical music. They brought to the compositions their own unbridled imaginations, devoid of reverence for the musical score. They first listened to the music and developed storyboards on how the action might take place, allowing their imaginations to soar while keeping the spirit of the compositions. Afterward the music was edited to fit the animation. Such tampering with the classics later brought vituperation from music critics and especially from Igor Stravinsky, the only living composer represented in the score. He never forgave Disney for the editing of "Rite of Spring." As late as 1962 he was complaining about the alterations in the score, adding, "I will say nothing about the visual complement, as I do not wish to criticize an unresisting imbecility."

Some of the selections immediately suggested pictorial themes. Beethoven's *Pastoral Symphony* became a merry romp with fauns, centaurs, centaurettes, and

Bacchus, interrupted by thunder of the gods. "Rite of Spring" was pictured as a fearsome prehistoric scene with monsters battling and the earth taking form with titanic convulsions. Ponchielli's *Dance of the Hours* suggested a comic ballet with ostriches, hippos, elephants, and alligators.

Toccata and Fugue in D Minor by Bach was different.

"Here we were dealing with pure music," Disney explained. "There was no story, nothing to go on but our own imaginations. So we would play the music over and over and try to see what images were created in our minds. Perhaps a great crash of music would sound like an ocean wave crashing against the rocks. Then another, and another."

Disney listened to the full symphony orchestra as led by Stokowski in the studio sound stage, then heard it on the playback. The recording was pale and tinny by comparison. He instructed his sound department to develop a multiaural system which could approximate the sound of an orchestra in a concert hall. The result was Fantasound, which recorded the music with several microphones and broadcast it on an equal number of speakers. Thus Disney presaged the era of stereophonic sound in recordings and movies by fifteen years.

Except for "The Sorcerer's Apprentice," all of the music was recorded at the Philadelphia Academy of Music, which had the ideal acoustics. The cost of the music alone amounted to $400,000, and the entire film ran $2.2 million at a time when the average live-action film cost less than a half-million. Theater chains resisted the expensive installations of sound and projection equipment, and *Fantasia* had a limited release in its original form. Eventually the distributor cut the film from two hours to eighty-one minutes, and it played on the lower half of double bills. Without a foreign market, Disney suffered a huge loss, eliminating any plans for *Fantasia* II. Two decades later, a new generation of filmgoers embraced *Fantasia*, with its flights of pure fancy, as a psychedelic trip. Today *Fantasia* is considered by many to be Disney's greatest achievement in animation.

TOP LEFT: *Beethoven's Sixth (Pastoral) Symphony provided inspiration for a vision of Mount Olympus.*

ABOVE: *Story sketches for Bach's Toccata and Fugue in D Minor.*

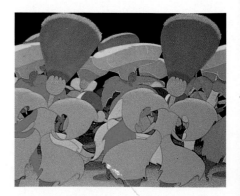

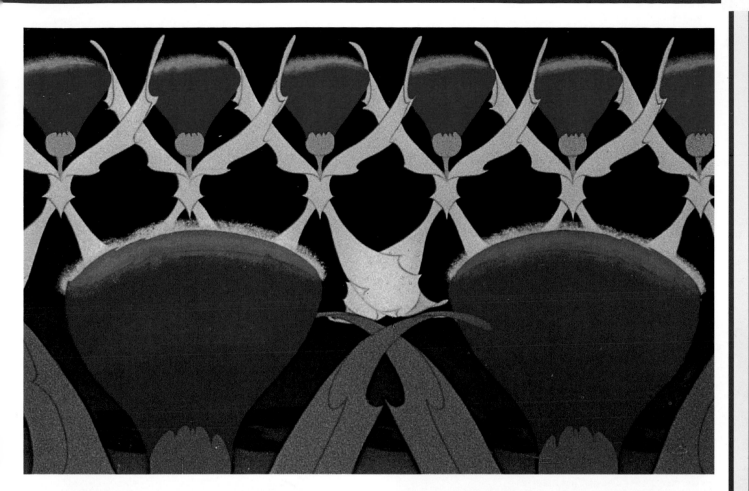

OPPOSITE LEFT: *Leaf and blossom patterns for "The Nutcracker" section.*

OPPOSITE RIGHT AND ABOVE: *The Orchid Girls and Thistle Boys perform a Russian dance in "The Nutcracker Suite."*

LEFT: *Animation of the Mushroom Dancers, depicted as Chinese rice peasants.*

In an early story meeting, Disney outlined his thoughts about the Bambi characters.

"When it comes to the animation, we can do a lot with the rabbit. He has a certain mannerism that can be drawn. We might get him to twitch his nose [he ended up thumping his foot]. . . . I don't like to have us get off the track too much to show his life. Everything should be done through Bambi. . . . The owl ought to be a silly, stupid thing. He is always trying to scare people. I like his crazy screech, as it is described in the book [by Felix Salten]. . . . I would hate to see any of the characters too straight. You would want that in Bambi's mother. You would want Bambi more or less straight in a way. The comedy would come from him as a kid through his questions and his curiosity. The rest of the characters I would like to see come out of life. . . . I would like the Old Stag to say what he has to say in a direct way, and in such a voice that Bambi is unable to answer him. What he says will be sort of final. That can be put over through the voice. . . . I like Faline's character in the book. She is clever and understands things. Bambi asks a lot of questions which she can answer. If we build her up in that way, we will be able to get a lot of stuff over when she and Bambi get together."

ABOVE: *Disney studies art work in the early stages of* BAMBI.

TOP RIGHT: *Model sheet of the mischievous Thumper, who came close to stealing the show.*

OPPOSITE: *Animators captured the movements of deer by studying the animals at the zoo and the studio.*

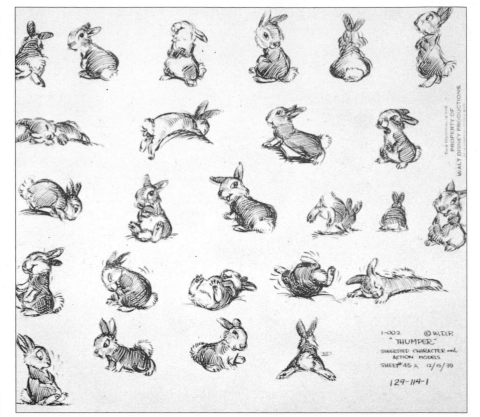

Bambi

The third production in the wake of *Snow White*, *Bambi* presented special challenges: the story was far more serious than any the studio had yet undertaken, even tragic, with the death of the deer's mother; the entire cast consisted of animals, and they had to be animated in a natural manner, in keeping with the serious theme of the story. Cartoon characters would destroy the drama.

Disney brought to the studio the painter of animals, Rico LeBrun, who lectured on the structure and movement of animals. Nature photographer Maurice Day spent months in a Maine forest, recording the animals and the changing of seasons. A zoo was established at the studio so animators could study fawns, rabbits, ducks, owls, and even skunks closeup.

Even though no humans appeared in *Bambi*, live action of human figures was used for reference by animators. Two championship skaters were photographed for the sequence in which Bambi and Thumper skate on a frozen pond.

Despite Disney's hopes to "start moving on the thing and not drag it out too long," *Bambi* could not be hurried. Unaccustomed to drawing natural animals, expert animators could each manage no more than eight drawings daily, which amounted to half a foot of film, compared to the normal rate of ten feet a day, or less than a second of film vs. over thirteen seconds.

The multiplane camera contributed to the reality of *Bambi*. The opening shot, as designed by Dick Anthony, was a marvel. The camera roamed through the forest glade, passing trees that seemed amazingly round. The scene of the owl flying through the trees was a masterpiece.

The rain sequence employed color to great advantage. It begins with the young Bambi getting dampened with raindrops as he nestles near his mother. The drops begin to grow in number, and the colors of the forest take on the shadowy gray of rain as the animals scurry to cover. The shower continues and then diminishes. The rain stops, and we see drops fall from a silvery leaf into a forest pool. Reflected in it is a gorgeous rainbow.

Bambi struggled through production and finally reached the screen in August 1942, after America had gone to war. Audiences were seeking more exciting entertainment, and some critics decried Disney's venture into realism. Another crushing loss for the Disney studio.

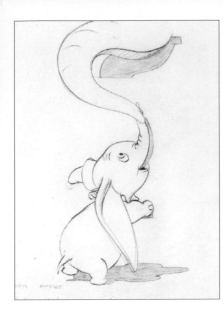

Economizing: *Dumbo*

One day in the studio parking lot, Disney encountered one of his gifted young animators, Ward Kimball. Walt expounded the plot of a proposed feature, *Dumbo*. Such a recital usually took half an hour or more. This time it was three minutes. That's how simple and straightline *Dumbo* was.

The story of an ugly-duckling baby elephant who redeems himself by learning to fly, *Dumbo* seemed ideal for an inexpensive animated feature. Disney assigned Ben Sharpsteen as supervising director with instructions to avoid the indulgences of *Pinocchio*, *Bambi*, and *Fantasia*.

Sharpsteen took his work seriously. Instead of the customary ten feet of work from animators, he insisted on twenty, or more. He prowled the animators' offices, urging them on and banning any frills. He even riffled through their drawings at night, eliminating any in-between work that might slow down production. Ward Kimball had drawn a clever sequence in which a crow nodded in cadence to the music. Sharpsteen discarded the in-between movement, and the crow's head merely turned. Despite the crash schedule—or perhaps because of it—the animators responded with inspired work. *Dumbo* possessed an exuberance that the previous features had lacked. Because it's set in a circus, the film exploded with great flashes of color. But an abundance of reds, yellows, and greens would be too jarring for the eye, so contrasts were made.

One effective scene is staged in silhouette. It pictures the shadows of the circus clowns against the canvas wall as they remove their makeup and costumes. Another sequence shows the elephants and roustabouts struggling in the rain to set up the circus tent. All is gray and murky. Then the sun emerges, and the midway becomes alive with bright colors, the bustling of ticket buyers, the sounds of calliopes and barkers. The sun-drenched colors dramatize the awakening of the circus after the grayness of the rain.

Sharpsteen's economies resulted in a feature that was sixty-four minutes long, ten to twenty minutes short of the customary length. The RKO distributor urged Disney to make it longer, but he refused, explaining that the fragile story could not be stretched. Besides, an additional ten minutes might run a half-million dollars, which the studio couldn't afford. *Dumbo* cost $800,000 and returned an equal amount in profit.

The New Studio, the Strike, and the War

During the expansion of the late Thirties, the Disney Studio on Hyperion Avenue became jammed with more than a thousand workers, triple the number it was first designed for. Production units of *Pinocchio*, *Bambi*, and *Fantasia* as well as the still flourishing shorts were tumbling over each other. Disney was forced to move the *Bambi* unit to a rented building on Seward Street in Hollywood. *Bambi* animators half-seriously called themselves the Foreign Legion, and caricatures of the men in legionnaire uniforms reached Walt. He was not amused.

Roy Disney agreed with his brother that a new studio was necessary. In 1938 they put $10,000 down against the $100,000 purchase of fifty-one acres of flatland on Buena Vista Street in Burbank. Despite the losses on *Pinocchio*, *Bambi*, and *Fantasia*, the Disneys found a willing lender in A. P. Giannini of the Bank of America.

Walt plunged into the planning of the new studio with the thoroughness he applied to feature cartoons. He even examined the design of chairs for the animators. The Animation Building was to be the hub for all operations, connected

Opposite left: *Bill Tytla's animation of the baby Dumbo captures the character's endearing qualities.*

Opposite right and above: *Finished animation.*

to Ink and Paint, Camera, and Cutting by underground tunnels. The Animation Building would be three stories with eight wings on each floor, connected by a long corridor. The wings were isolated from each other, and some animators complained that such a plan eliminated the collegial atmosphere at the Hyperion studio, where animators mingled easily with each other and with workers in other departments. On the day before Christmas 1939, the exodus from Hyperion to Burbank began. The new studio opened at the worst of times. The war in Europe had started four months earlier.

Strife would soon come to the Disney Studio itself. Walt had planned the Burbank facility to be a workers' paradise, but many of them considered it less than that. Many of the newcomers were dissatisfied with their salaries, the tedium of their work, and the impersonality of the studio.

By the end of the Thirties, all of the talent and crafts at the Hollywood studios had been organized in guilds and unions. At Disney, two unions battled each other and management to organize the workers. One evening, Walt gathered his employees for a remarkable performance in which he traced the sacrifices he and Roy had made to get the studio started, the expansion after *Snow White*, the collapse of the foreign market. He explained how he had rejected easy solutions of abandoning features, cutting salaries, selling control of the company.

He even touched upon his own lack of accessibility: "It's my nature to be democratic. I want to be just a guy working in this plant, which I am. . . . However, I realized that it was very dangerous and unfair to the organization as a whole for me to get too close to everybody."

His pleading failed, and on May 29, 1941, a picket line appeared at the studio. The strike was bitter and acrimonious, shattering the benign image the Disney studio had presented to the world. Frustrated and angry and unwilling to

compromise, Walt accepted the U.S. government's invitation for a goodwill tour of South America in June of that year. He took along animators and story men, and the trip resulted in two lively features, *Saludos Amigos* and *The Three Caballeros*.

When Disney came back from South America, the strike had been settled by government conciliation which made the studio a union shop. Bitterness remained on both sides, and the intimacy and trust Walt had shared with his animators was gone forever.

On the afternoon of December 7, 1941, a few hours after the Japanese had bombed Pearl Harbor, the United States Army moved into the Disney studio. For eight months, it was used as a supply depot for the antiaircraft installations in the mountains surrounding Los Angeles. Walt abandoned plans for features of *Peter Pan*, *Alice in Wonderland*, and *Wind in the Willows* and turned to training films. The first was for the nearby Lockheed Aircraft Corporation, *Four Methods of Flush Riveting*. It was a success, and orders followed from Canada, U.S. Navy Air, the Agriculture Department, U.S. Army, Treasury Department, and others.

Subjects ranged from *Aircraft Carrier Landing Signals* to *Defense Against Invasion*, a health film. Donald Duck was recruited to persuade Americans to pay their taxes. He also gave Hitler the Bronx cheer in *Der Fuehrer's Face*. Disney made one propaganda feature for general release, *Victory Through Air Power*, which promulgated Alexander de Seversky's theories of aerial bombardment.

The war work helped keep the studio doors open at a time when little income was coming from theaters. The training films also interested Disney in a wide range of technical matters not concerned with entertainment and proved that he and his animators could make complex matters understandable to the general public. But they were "lost years," as Roy Disney later remarked. The Disney studio emerged from the war heavily in debt, with little prospect of recovery in the future.

OPPOSITE LEFT: *"I've seen a peanut stand, I've seen a rubber band. . . . When I see an elephant fly. . . ."* Animation drawings by Bill Tytla.

OPPOSITE RIGHT AND TOP: *Dumbo's* expressive face could show sorrow and elation.

CHAPTER SEVEN
THE POSTWAR
FILMS

The Anthology Features

After the war, Roy Disney once remarked, "We were like a bear coming out of hibernation; we were skinny and gaunt, and we had no fat on our bones." The new films reflected that.

The acrid aftertaste of the strike remained, and the company was deeply in debt. Unable to finance a new feature like *Snow White* or *Pinocchio*, Disney launched a series of economical films that brought little glory but much-needed income to the studio.

Make Mine Music was a pop-music vaudeville show with the talents of Dinah Shore, the Andrews Sisters, Nelson Eddy, Jerry Colonna, Benny Goodman, and others. Walt liked the "Peter and the Wolf" episode, but he realized the rest of the film offered no great challenge to his animators.

Disney had long wanted to make a feature based on the Joel Chandler Harris *Uncle Remus* stories he had loved as a child. Because he lacked the money for an animated feature and because of his growing conviction that he needed to move into live-action films, he decided to combine cartoons with a human story about life on a Southern plantation. James Baskett as Uncle Remus told his stories before actual sets painted to look like cartoon backgrounds. After the footage was edited, animators added Br'er Fox, Br'er Bear, and other creatures.

Released in 1946 as *Song of the South*, the film had a modest success. Its importance was largely historical, as a portent of live-action things to come.

In his last major effort to revive his first star's career, Disney reinstated *Mickey and the Beanstalk*, which had been suspended during the war. Donald Duck and Goofy were cast in supporting roles, but again they dominated the comedy. For the first time, Walt Disney was not the voice of Mickey Mouse. Grumbling that his voice was too hoarse, he said to sound effects man Jim MacDonald, "Why don't you do it?"

Mickey and the Beanstalk was combined with a Sinclair Lewis fable *Bongo* for a 1947 release as *Fun and Fancy Free*.

Melody Time in 1948 offered another musical smorgasbord with pop performers; it was noticeable for the raucous "Pecos Bill" episode. The following year brought the last of the anthologies, *The Adventures of Ichabod and Mr. Toad*.

PRECEDING SPREAD: *Detail of the interior of Lady's home in* Lady and the Tramp *(SPREAD).* Romance blossoms between the mismatched couple *(INSET).*

OPPOSITE: *The castle in* Cinderella. *It later inspired the castle at The Walt Disney World Magic Kingdom in Florida.*

TOP LEFT AND ABOVE: *Joel Chandler Harris's* Uncle Remus *stories provided rich comedy for* Song of the South.

Disney on the Fairy Godmother sequence:

"The carriage should be dainty. The wheels shouldn't be enough to hold the weight. We should feel that it's a fairy carriage. . . . Cut out all the excessive dialogue and work on some new dialogue for Cinderella in counter to the melody while she is crying. Have her run out and hit the spot, and as she is saying this, let the animals come up and get closer. Have them gather around in a sympathetic manner. They don't know whether they should approach her or not. . . . Have the miracle happen at the end of the song. "The dream that you wish will come true" is where we start to bring the Fairy Godmother in. She materializes because she is there to grant the wish. The voices come back at Cinderella. Her faith is being thrown back at her. Everybody has gone through a 'the hell with it' feeling."

ABOVE: *Cinderella leaves the ball in her "dainty" carriage.*

TOP RIGHT: *Cinderella's gown.*

Cinderella **Restores the Glory**

The long dry season at the Disney studio ended with *Cinderella*. Work had started on the story before the war, along with *Peter Pan* and *Alice in Wonderland*. Walt had been unable to instill warmth into the characters in *Peter* and *Alice*, but he found *Cinderella* to possess the same qualities as *Snow White*: an engaging heroine in Cinderella, valid villainesses in the guise of the stepmother and the ugly sisters, comic relief with a set of house mice, a well-rounded story with a happy ending.

Disney assigned all of his key story men, directors, and animators to *Cinderella*, and he took part in every story meeting. The directing animation was done by the brilliant Norm Ferguson as well as the "Nine Old Men" (a play on Franklin Roosevelt's epithet for the arch-conservative Supreme Court) who helped create all of the Disney classics from *Snow White* on: Milt Kahl, Frank Thomas, Ollie Johnston, Eric Larson, Les Clark, Marc Davis, John Lounsbery, Woolie Reitherman, and Ward Kimball.

The mice and the cat Lucifer were the inspired creations of Ward Kimball. Walt, who often cast cats as heavies, was dissatisfied with drawing proposals for Lucifer. One day he was visiting Kimball's full-scale railroad train and saw the house cat, a smug, rounded calico. "There's your model for Lucifer," Disney said.

When *Cinderella* was released in June 1950, it was welcomed as Disney's first full-length feature in eight years. With a few dissenters, critics were generally enthusiastic. The postwar generation, many of them with young families of their own, found in *Cinderella* the same kind of euphoric entertainment they had discovered with *Snow White* in their own youths. *Cinderella* had the same comforting message: that good will triumph over evil. And a rollicking song, "Bibbidi Bobbidi Boo," added to the film's popularity. *Cinderella* became Disney's biggest moneymaker, eclipsing even *Snow White*.

Alice, Peter, Lady and the Tramp

Of his unsuccessful *Alice in Wonderland*, Walt Disney told me in 1963: "I think Alice got what she deserved. I never wanted to make it in the first place, but everybody said I should. I tried to introduce a little sentiment into it by getting Alice involved with the White Knight, but they said we couldn't tamper with a classic. So we just kept moving it at circus pace."

No classic ever seemed so ideal for the Disney treatment, and none proved so unworkable. From 1933 on, Disney had tinkered with *Alice*, at times fashioning it for such actresses as Mary Pickford and Ginger Rogers. He bought rights to the John Tenniel illustrations but found they were too intricate to use in animation, except for character design. In story sessions before and after the war, Walt failed to rise to his customary storytelling passion. He simply wasn't enjoying it. Nor did his animators when *Alice* went into production. Productivity sagged, along with their spirits.

"Alice herself gave us nothing to work with," remembers Marc Davis. "You take a nice little girl and put her into a loony bin, and you have nothing. If she had had her cat with her, anything. But she had nothing to work with other than facing

TOP: *Alice in Wonderland was technically proficient, but the characters were cold and unappealing.*

ABOVE: *Disney and studio veteran Wilfred Jackson in a story session.*

one nut after another, one insane person or thing. And that was right through to the end."

"Walt blamed it on us," adds Ollie Johnston. "We blamed it on him. He said, 'You guys didn't get any heart into it; it was too mechanical.' He was right, though it wasn't necessarily our fault. It was everybody's, I guess. Anyway, it has become a cult picture, and now they ask us, 'What were you guys "on" when you worked on *Alice*?' "

Disney was attempting the impossible: to please the Lewis Carroll purists and produce a popular entertainment. British critics assailed the liberties he had taken, and American audiences failed to respond. *Alice in Wonderland* lost a million dollars, wiping out the profit from *Cinderella*.

Peter Pan had been owned by Disney since 1939, and he made several attempts at an animation treatment of the James M. Barrie play. Finally in 1951 he agreed to a story line that closely followed the play, and animation began.

The Nine Old Men and Norm Ferguson (on his last Disney film) realized they could no longer have the benefit of Disney's close participation. He had launched live-action filming in England to make use of frozen funds—money earned in the country that could not be taken out in the tight postwar economy. He was making early preparations for a venture into television. And a new kind of amusement park was forming in his mind. "We knew the moment Walt climbed onto a camera boom, we'd lost him," says Frank Thomas.

Disney still attended storyboard sessions, though his comments were more succinct. Samples: "We don't have the right crocodile yet, it's out of character. . . . Watch so as not to get Hook's teeth too big. . . . Rebuild the Tick Tock scene of Hook. Get expression of fear in his eyes. I don't like the hair-raising. . . . We want to make the music a little more important. I think music will tie it together."

On *Peter Pan*, the animators once again had the use of live action as a guide. As Frank Thomas recalls: "It helped us, and we didn't have to use it if we had a better idea. A lot of stuff we did entirely on our own."

"*Peter Pan* had good imagination and very good characters, and you could get involved in it," adds Ollie Johnston. "Maybe there was less involvement [by Walt] with Peter Pan, but he was the motivation for the picture, so that didn't matter much. Certainly you were involved with Captain Hook and to a lesser extent with Mr. Smee, and a lot with Tinker Bell."

The multiplane camera contributed to some of the best scenes in *Peter Pan*. The first flying sequence over the rooftops of London and around Big Ben required twenty levels of paintings.

The technical innovations and long period of development contributed to the $4-million cost of *Peter Pan*. It was scorned by the Barrie loyalists, particularly for its portrayal of Tinker Bell as a Marilyn Monroe kind of nymphet. But families flocked to the movie, and it restored the Disney reputation, which had been tarnished by *Alice in Wonderland*.

After tangling with two classics, Disney enjoyed working on an original story he could fashion to his own liking. *Lady and the Tramp* dated back to 1937, when it began as a story about a sedate cocker spaniel. In 1943, Disney bought an unpublished short story by Ward Greene about a rowdy, whistling mutt and a lovely, demure cocker spaniel. Not until 1953 did the story take form. It was especially appealing to Walt because it was set in small-town 1910 America and it concerned dogs.

Disney's storytelling skill is illustrated in a meeting about the sequence in which the Tramp kills a rat about to attack the baby at Lady's house.

"Lady's barking, trying to get Jim's [the father] attention, then you see the light coming, his shadow coming up—she's waiting when the door opens. She barks, starts up the stairs, he tries to grab her, says, 'Girl what's the matter?' Jim Dear chains Lady to a dog house out in the rain because of her barking. She has to get Tramp's attention instead.

"She says, 'A rat!' Tramp says, 'Where?' She says, 'Upstairs in the baby's room!' He says, 'How do you get in?' She says, 'The little door in the back.' He runs right through the door in the back. . . .

"It's quick, short things. He'd go right in there. We have this guy cautiously coming up the stairs—remember, he's an *intruder*. He doesn't know which door it is. Then he picks up the scent, and he comes in the room, and there's the baby's crib. We get suspense for a moment. The baby's crib and it's dark. He starts looking around the room, and suddenly he sees two eyes glowing over there. He begins to growl and his hair bristles. You see the form move, and he runs over there.

"It has to be like two guys fighting in the dark and not knowing where the other guy is. A hell of a realistic fight there. We can do it in the shadows from the window onto it—shadow forms against silhouette forms, against the light. Certain lighting effects will make it very effective."

"*Lady and the Tramp* was tough to animate because the dogs were like the deer in *Bambi*: you had to do a realistic, believable animal," says Frank Thomas. "You had

TOP LEFT: *The flying sequence in* Peter Pan *over nighttime London was a masterpiece of camera work.*

TOP RIGHT: *The legendary Nine Old Men who animated the Disney classics: (front, left to right), Woolie Reitherman, Les Clark, Ward Kimball, John Lounsbery; (rear) Milt Kahl, Marc Davis, Frank Thomas, Eric Larson, Ollie Johnston.*

ABOVE: *The demure cocker spaniel; radio actress Barbara Luddy supplied the voice.*

to have the joints in the right place in the leg, and they had to keep their weight, and you had to keep the right distance from the front leg to the back leg."

Another challenge of *Lady and the Tramp* was using CinemaScope for the first time in an animated feature. Developed by 20th Century-Fox and introduced with *The Robe*, CinemaScope used special lenses to compress filmed images which were then spread out on a wider than normal screen during projection. Layout artists almost had to reinvent their craft. Animators had to remember that they could move their characters across a background instead of the background passing behind them. Scenes could be played with fewer cuts because more characters could be fitted into the broad screen. But the screen had to be filled lest dull patches appear. The result was greater realism but fewer closeups, and hence less involvement with the audience. Despite such drawbacks, the appealing characters and sentimental story of *Lady and the Tramp* found a wide, appreciative audience.

Sleeping Beauty Awakens

Sleeping Beauty ventured boldly into uncharted territory and proved an expensive failure. "I sorta got trapped," Disney admitted afterward. "I had passed the point of no return, and I had to go forward with it."

The film was developing during the mid-Fifties when Disney was enmeshed in Disneyland, the *Mickey Mouse Club*, *Zorro*, and *Disneyland* television shows, and a full program of live-action movies. The *Sleeping Beauty* story men and animators often waited weeks before Disney could meet with them.

The style for *Sleeping Beauty* originated when John Hench observed the famed unicorn tapestries at the Cloisters in New York. Hench bought reproductions

of the tapestries and showed them to Disney. "Yeah," said Walt, "we could use that style for *Sleeping Beauty.*"

Disney assigned Eyvind Earle to paint the backgrounds. Earle had once applied for a job at the old Hyperion studio. Turned down, he spent eleven years in New York building a reputation in the art world. Hired at Disney in 1951, he rose fast as a background painter. For *Sleeping Beauty,* Earle used the best of pre-Renaissance art for inspiration—Dürer, Bruegel, Van Eyck, Botticelli, as well as Persian art and Japanese prints. Earle's landscapes were stylized in primitive technique. "The trees are squared, and everything else carries out the horizontal pattern," he observed at the time. "The hedges, the rocks, the lines of the horizon, all are horizontal. The primitive style never tilts things."

The backgrounds were stunning to the eye but hellish for animators.

"The gothic style was impossible to work with, it was so austere," recalls Frank Thomas. "You couldn't get any life into your characters or your animation. You had to stay within that style."

The animation of the good fairies called for special attention. "I found that when old ladies move, they bounce like mechanical toys," Thomas explained. "They paddle, paddle, paddle on their way. They stand straight, and their arm movements are jerky. Their hands fly out from the body. The reason for all this is that they're afraid to get off-balance, afraid they will fall."

Sleeping Beauty was in production longer (three years) and cost more ($6 million) than any previous Disney feature. The film lacked the humor and personality that Walt could usually endow. It had impressive design and a titanic dragon fight for a climax, but critics called *Sleeping Beauty* pretentious and audiences were unmoved. The film lost money on its first release.

TOP LEFT: *Eyvind Earle's landscapes dominated the style of* Sleeping Beauty.

TOP RIGHT: *Frank Thomas and Ollie Johnston strove to enliven* Sleeping Beauty *with the three good fairies, Flora, Fauna, and Merryweather. Thomas spent time at the supermarket observing rotund old ladies, usually at the dog-food counter, and he also found a model in his children's babysitter.*

ABOVE: *Live action of actors provided a guide for animation of the* Sleeping Beauty *kissing scene, which was less chaste than the one in* Snow White *(page 77).*

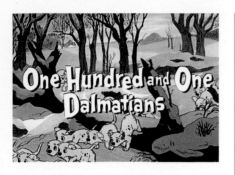

ABOVE AND RIGHT: *The spots in* 101 Dalmatians *were an animator's nightmare until Xerox helped provide a solution.*

BELOW: *A press book page from the merchandising campaign for* 101 Dalmatians.

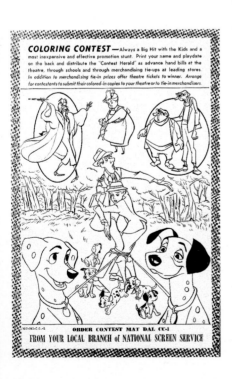

Walt Disney's Last Films

101 *Dalmatians*, released in January 1961, marked the introduction of xerography to the Disney studio. The movie probably couldn't have been made without it. Based on the book by Dodie Smith, it was a landmark in other ways: it was the first Disney animated feature in a contemporary setting; it was the first created by a single story man. Bill Peet was a gifted, headstrong artist and a superb storyteller. He fashioned the 101 *Dalmatians* story on his own, counting on Disney's inattention.

After the Xerox copier appeared on the market, Ub Iwerks, who had developed many technical innovations, adapted Xerox to animation. He fashioned a huge machine that copied drawings onto an electrically charged plate and then onto cels. The technique was perfect for a film in which dozens of spotted dogs appeared on the screen at once. The animators could draw a small group of dogs, and the camera could repeat the group to fill the scene. If the process was done adroitly, the repeats would not be noticed.

Since xerography copied an animator's drawings, for the first time the work could be seen immediately, without the intervention of outlining by an inker. There was one serious drawback: the Xerox machine could not duplicate the animator's delicate lines that endowed unique character; the figures had to be outlined in severe black. Disney believed it was a step backwards to the primitive Twenties before animation had acquired a more sophisticated, elegant look.

But audiences sensed a different, more contemporary appearance in the animation, and 101 *Dalmatians* earned far more than its $4-million cost.

The Jungle Book was the last animated feature in which Walt Disney took part. After the disappointing *The Sword in the Stone*, a fantasy about Merlin and the young Arthur, Disney was determined to give his animators a chance to do their best work. Larry Clemmons was one of the four story men he assigned to the film. Disney

handed him a copy of the Rudyard Kipling book and instructed him: "The first thing I want you to do is not to read it."

The story was built around the Kipling characters, eliminating many of the figures and situations in the 1942 *Jungle Book* movie with Sabu as Mowgli. For years the animators had been drilled in the importance of a clear story line, and Milt Kahl expressed their concern in a meeting with Disney. "You can get all bogged down with these stories," he counseled Kahl. "It will be all right."

Disney was counting on the characters to carry *The Jungle Book*. After hearing Phil Harris perform at a Palm Springs benefit, Walt decided to cast the band leader-singer as the bear Baloo.

"Harris didn't think he could do it, and neither did we," admits Ollie Johnston. "But Walt said he could. After Harris put the lines of dialogue in his own vernacular, why, it just came to life. You know, that deep voice, the friendly attitude the guy has. It was just a pleasure to work with that voice."

Other voices inspired the animators: Sebastian Cabot as Bagheera, the sophisticated panther, Louis Prima as the scat-singing monkey, King Louie, George Sanders as the purringly evil tiger, Shere Khan. As he acted out each role, Walt seemed to be enjoying his sessions with the animators. At the end of one productive meeting he commented: "You guys ought to have me down here more often. I'm the least-paid gag man in the studio."

The Jungle Book was released in October 1967, a year after Walt Disney died. It was a rousing success, with surefire musical numbers such as "The Bare Necessities" compensating for the meandering plot. It was a fitting climax to the Walt Disney era of film animation. During thirty-eight years, Disney and his artists had raised the simple cartoon to the level of rare creativity, producing more than four hundred short cartoons and twenty-three features, of which ten are likely to be seen for generations to come.

TOP LEFT AND ABOVE: **The Jungle Book** *was the last animated film in which Walt Disney participated. The unique voices added greatly to the film's charm.*

BELOW: *"Whoso pulleth out this sword . . . is rightwise King of England."* **The Sword in the Stone.**

CHAPTER EIGHT
THE FILMS WITHOUT WALT

Carrying on the Tradition

The remaining members of the Nine Old Men, along with a few newcomers, continued the string of successes with *The Aristocats* and *Robin Hood*, both competent films though no trailblazers. *The Rescuers*, released in June 1977, was a more impressive achievement, and a proper valedictory. It was the last joint effort by veterans Milt Kahl, Ollie Johnston, and Frank Thomas. As directing animators, they were joined by a newcomer, Don Bluth. Other young recruits, including John Pomeroy, Ron Clements, Glen Keane, and Gary Goldman, were among the character animators.

Walt Disney had acquired the rights to a series of stories by Margery Sharp about an International Rescue Aid Society operated by mice from the basement of the United Nations Building. A screen story had been developed from one of the stories, about the captive of a totalitarian government in a Siberia-like stronghold. Frank Thomas recalls Walt abandoning the project with the comment, "Hell, the politics is pushing our entertainment."

After Disney's death, at least three of the Sharp stories were explored as feature subjects. Finally, a plot was developed about a little orphan girl named Penny who is kidnapped and held in a southern bayou by the villainous Madame Medusa; only someone as small as Penny could enter a cave where a prized diamond had been hidden. Bianca of the Aid Society chooses a shy janitor, Bernard, to help her rescue the girl. Both characters resembled real mice, unlike the cartoony Mickey Mouse. Their characters were enhanced by the voices of Eva Gabor and Bob Newhart.

A pigeon was originally proposed as transportation for the two mice. Then Frank Thomas remembered film taken for the *True Life Adventures* of albatrosses in their hilariously ungainly takeoffs and landings. Captain Orville, brilliantly animated by Ollie Johnston, became the most memorable character of *The Rescuers*. The wryly humorous voice was supplied by Jim Jordan, radio's Fibber McGee.

Madame Medusa was the creation of Milt Kahl. His fellow animators recall that Kahl set such a high standard that his assistants couldn't duplicate his work,

PRECEDING SPREAD: As with Robin Hood, Oliver & Company told a classic story with animal characters. The reworking of Oliver Twist made use of contemporary language and music (SPREAD). Confrontation of Toon star and private eye in Who Framed Roger Rabbit (INSET).

OPPOSITE AND BELOW: After long being relegated to villainous roles in Disney films, cats became the heroes in The Aristocats.

TOP LEFT: The Rescuers became a worthy climax to the careers of Disney's Nine Old Men.

ABOVE: Between Errol Flynn's and Kevin Costner's versions came Disney's Robin Hood.

ABOVE AND RIGHT: *The successful* The Fox and the Hound *concerned a fox cub and a puppy who become friends, then find themselves enemies because of the ways of nature.*

BELOW: *Milt Kahl's Madame Medusa followed the Disney tradition of classic villainesses, but her fear of mice diminished her menace.*

and he was forced to draw almost all of Madame Medusa himself. The voice was supplied by Geraldine Page, whom Thomas considers the best of all Disney voices. She had a habit of standing before the microphone, leaning from one foot to the other, then racing around the edge of the studio and returning to the mike to bellow her lines.

Medusa took her place alongside the Witch of *Snow White*, Maleficent, and Cruella De Vil as a classic Disney villainess. Yet Medusa's menace was diffused by one simple scene. When she leaped onto a chair upon seeing the mice, she became a comic villainess, dangerous but less threatening.

The climactic moment in *The Rescuers* comes when Penny, Bianca, and Bernard search frantically for the diamond as the tide rises inside the cave. "But there's hardly any tide in the bayous," someone pointed out in midproduction. After considerable debate, the sequence was animated as written. "Who cares?" said one of the animators. "It's just a cartoon."

The tidal discrepancy went unnoticed by the crowds who patronized *The Rescuers*. Milt Kahl retired after finishing his work with Madame Medusa. Thomas and Johnston developed the characters and animated one sequence for the next feature, *The Fox and the Hound*, then both retired. The new generation took charge.

The Black Cauldron

Four years in production at a record cost for an animated film, *The Black Cauldron* was anticipated as a giant step forward for Disney animation. The adaptation of Lloyd Alexander's *Chronicles of Prydain* promised to offer bold new art by Disney's young generation.

The Black Cauldron came at a time when the Disney management was in turmoil. Film revenues were declining, and the company was seeking to make films for a mature audience, since teenagers scorned anything with the Disney label as

"kid stuff." More threateningly, corporate-raider wolves were circling the faltering company, sniffing for a kill.

In 1979, Don Bluth led a group of young animators out of the studio, declaring that Disney no longer upheld the principles established by its founder. Bluth established his own production company, and his defection had a devastating effect on morale among the young Disney artists. The news signaled trouble within Disney to the public at large, and a flurry of articles speculated on the fall of the House That Walt Built.

Production of *The Black Cauldron* was split into several units, some of which did not communicate with others. There was no strong, guiding hand. Andreas Deja, then a young animator newly arrived from Germany, recalls, "It was a stormy period of change, transition from the old guys to the new guys. There were some guys supervising us who didn't know how to make it happen. Looking back on my drawings for *The Black Cauldron*, I know that I had done many, many better things than those that ended up on the screen." Another new recruit was John Musker, who recalls the general feeling that *The Black Cauldron* would give the new breed "something they could shine on. But once production was rolling, a lot of the younger people believed it was misguided. It was getting too dark, without enough fun aspects. Just too stodgy in many ways. Then it became lethargic in terms of its development, a kind of wavering. A lot of the younger people lost hope in that movie."

Deja had been assigned to conceptual drawings, teaming with Tim Burton, a CalArts graduate with a seemingly inexhaustible imagination. Their efforts never reached the screen.The management gave him complete freedom, Burton remembers.

"I enjoyed that," he says, "but there was the feeling they'd say, 'This is wonderful, but let's not show anybody.'

"I think the company was really at odds with itself. They had this feeling of moving into the future and contemporizing, but they didn't know how to do it. There was a foot in the past and a foot in the future and no firm footing in either. *The Black Cauldron* was one of the things that steered me out of animation."

After attempting a couple of short films, Burton left Disney to become director of *Beetlejuice*, *Batman*, and *Edward Scissorhands*.

Top left: *The grotesque creatures of* The Black Cauldron *contributed to the film's lack of acceptance.*

Top right: *Taran was a credible hero for* The Black Cauldron, *but his adventures proved too labyrinthine for audiences.*

Above: *Spooky conceptual painting by James Coleman.*

Top: *The new Disney management, headed by Michael Eisner (here introducing the Sunday night television show), injected new life into the animation program.*

Above: *Early conceptual art for* The Black Cauldron *by Guy Vasilovich and Ruben Procopio.*

Opposite top: *Gurgi was a furry mammal of undetermined species, part hero, part coward.*

Opposite bottom: *The good creature, Gurgi, rescues Taran in* The Black Cauldron.

A New Regime and a Rebirth

As *The Black Cauldron* was nearing completion in 1984, the Walt Disney company underwent a corporate upheaval that resulted in the appointments of Michael Eisner, who had been president of Paramount Pictures, as chairman and Frank Wells, former vice chairman of Warner Bros., as president. The new regime was voted at a meeting of the Disney board on September 24, 1984, and the winning participants met afterward at the Lakeside Golf Club in Burbank for a champagne celebration. Eisner spoke to Roy E. Disney, who had been a prime mover in the change of management.

"Well," said Eisner, "now that this is over, what would you want to do?"

Disney, who had little time during weeks of frantic negotiations to contemplate the future, replied impulsively, "Why don't you give me the Animation Department? Because I'll bet I'm going to be the only guy around here that has any understanding of how it works and what the processes are and who the people are."

Although Roy had never worked in Animation, he had certainly been around it all his life. As the son of the cofounder and nephew of Walt, Roy had spent much of his childhood and his adult life at the Burbank studio. He had made nature films and television movies for the company, and he believed he could help in Animation, drawing on his experience in story and editing. Also he could act as liaison between his friends in Animation and the new, unknown management.

Roy Disney screened the almost finished *The Black Cauldron* and said inwardly, "Oh, God, we've got a problem here." Jeffrey Katzenberg, former production head at Paramount and now chairman of Walt Disney Pictures, had the same reaction. Katzenberg was admittedly unschooled in animation. His entire expertise lay in live-action movies, a totally different discipline. When he suggested that *The Black Cauldron* needed editing to relieve the darkness of the film, the animation people were horrified.

"We can't edit the picture," one of them declared. "It's seamless. It's been made from storyboard to story reel to finished animation, and the seams simply go from one part to another. It's not as if you have coverage that allows you to jump from one place in a movie to another and skip over."

Katzenberg heard their arguments and replied: "Bring the film into an editing room and I will edit it." He removed two or three minutes from the finished film.

Word spread swiftly that the new head of production was actually editing an animated feature. The Philistines had entered the temple! The morale among animators, already at a low ebb, plunged further.

When finally released in July 1985, *The Black Cauldron* was praised by some critics as a brave effort to seek new Disney ground, but others found it dark and forbidding, as did the moviegoing public. Its failure after four years of intense though unguided effort depressed the studio's animators.

Why *The Black Cauldron* failed so spectacularly is still a matter of painful conjecture at Disney.

"It was the most complicated animated movie at its time; it was beautifully done," says Michael Eisner. "But then, I would have spent less time worrying about animating on 70mm and made sure the story worked. . . . It advanced the art of animation, but that art is only as strong as the word. Whether you're in Sophocles' time or the Elizabethan theater or Gilbert and Sullivan or Andrew Lloyd Webber, you've got to have a story and emotion and characters."

Roy Disney agrees: "Story was really the number-one problem. I thought for the first third of the movie it worked pretty well. Then they got to something called the Fair Folk and the main characters got into a cave, and the story just completely stopped going anywhere."

"It was really an admirable attempt at a misguided idea," adds Jeffrey Katzenberg. "The idea, as I learned later, was to make a somewhat darker and therefore more adult movie that would perhaps widen the audience for these films. In fact, it made the fatal error of ignoring its primary audience, which is kids. These [animated] films are not made for kids; they're made for the kid that exists in all of us."

Disney animation artists were further disheartened when management decided to move the entire animation department out of the Animation Building to make room for management and live-action production. Animation assumed quarters in a warehouse two miles away in Glendale.

"So we were moved out of the old studio, and all the traditions were removed at that point," recalls Glen Keane, then a rising young animator. "There was no morgue [storage for past drawings and paintings] to look at, not really unless you drove down to Burbank. There were no more beautiful windows with nice oak trees outside and squirrels running around the college campus.

"We were in a warehouse with wires twisting all around. You got the feeling that 'Boy, we'd better make this thing work. If not, this is it.' It was probably a good thing. It was the equivalent of a kid being let independent by his parents: he doesn't

TOP AND OPPOSITE BOTTOM: *Early conceptual art for* The Black Cauldron *by James Coleman.*

ABOVE: *The sentiment in* Oliver & Company *comes when the Fifth Avenue Jenny adopts the kitten Oliver.*

need their full support anymore." Members of the Animation Department feared the expensive failure of *The Black Cauldron* would prompt the new management to sharply curtail production.

Says John Musker: "I think there was some pressure from certain parts of management just saying, 'These movies cost a lot and they don't return their investment. Here's a movie like *The Care Bears* that didn't cost very much, and it made a lot of money.' I think certain people were saying, 'You really should spend less on these movies and try to get a better profit margin.'" There was also a concern among animation people that Disney's corner on fantasy had been taken over by George Lucas, Steven Spielberg, and other young filmmakers who made startling use of innovative special effects.

"Even *The Black Stallion* could have and should have been a Disney movie," cites John Musker. "There was a feeling at the studio that here were a lot of young people who we thought were really talented, yet there was kind of a lid on them. They admired the films of fifty years ago—*Pinocchio, Snow White,* and all those—but there were restrictions keeping that type of film from being made."

Ron Clements suggests another frustration at that time: "There was a stigma about animated films: that they were strictly for kids. We were in our early twenties, and others in our generation were not even aware that Disney was still making animated features. They certainly wouldn't consider going to such films."

Shortly after the new regime had taken over, Roy Disney learned that two bright young directors, John Musker and Ron Clements, had managed to get themselves removed from *The Black Cauldron* and were preparing another feature, *Basil of Baker Street*, a Sherlock Holmes story told with mice. Roy admired what they had done, and he brought Eisner and Katzenberg to see the storyboards.

Katzenberg had seen a storyboard for action scenes in live-action movies, and Eisner had been familiar with storyboards when he was in charge of children's programming at ABC Television. But never had they experienced an entire film told in sketches pinned to boards. They walked from one wing of the building to another to review the boards, which had been left idle for six months awaiting a decision. Eisner and Katzenberg agreed with Roy's enthusiasm for the project. "Let's go with it," they said. And so *Basil of Baker Street*, which became *The Great Mouse Detective*, began production amid vast uncertainty and with a depleted and demoralized staff.

ABOVE: **The Great Mouse Detective** *borrowed its hero and locale from Conan Doyle.*

Roy Disney and Jeffrey Katzenberg began revitalizing the studio's animation, launching a search for new talent that matched Walt's enlistment of artists for *Snow White*. The Animation Department grew from one hundred sixty people to more than six hundred. The company announced that henceforth Disney would release a new animated feature every year, something that Walt had striven for after *Snow White* but could never achieve. No more would the studio put its entire resources into a single film for a three-year period. Two or three projects would be under way at the same time, assuring a yearly release. Budgets would be tight and schedules stringent.

Disney and Katzenberg felt the need for a full-time manager of animation. Katzenberg outlined the qualifications: "Someone who would be able to serve the artists really well, who was going to be very sensitive to talent, who would recognize, as I did from the beginning, that these are not engineers or technicians, they are artists."

After an extensive search, Eisner, Disney, and Katzenberg decided on Peter Schneider, a bright, wiry thirty-five-year-old who had produced plays in London and Chicago and worked for the Arts Festival for the 1984 Los Angeles Olympic Games. Like Katzenberg, he had no background in animation, but he was a quick learner.

The Great Mouse Detective, released in July 1986, proved a happy surprise, filled with humor and inspired animation, and helped immeasurably by the voice of Vincent Price as the archvillain Ratigan. Disney animation appeared to be recovering from the trauma of *The Black Cauldron*.

The recovery was confirmed with the 1988 release, *Oliver & Company*, directed by George Scribner. The story, based on *Oliver Twist* with dogs and a kitten as Fagin's gang, was the first out-and-out comedy among the Disney features. *Oliver & Company* proved that Disney animation could appeal to the teenage crowd. The songs were in the contemporary style, and voicing the characters were such pop stars as Bette Midler, Billy Joel, and Cheech Marin. But despite its success, some Disney animators considered it "another talking dog-and-cat movie."

TOP: *For his scenes with Roger, Bob Hoskins worked with mimes and puppeteers; the animation was added later.*

ABOVE: *Movie magic: Bob Hoskins drives a cartoon car with a cartoon passenger along a real-life boulevard.*

OPPOSITE TOP: *The torchy Jessica Rabbit is described as having "more curves than Mulholland Drive."*

Who Framed Roger Rabbit

The previous Disney regime had bought Gary K. Wolf's whimsical book, *Who Censored Roger Rabbit*, about a movie cartoon character with a real life of his own. Several film treatments were attempted, but the task of combining animation with real-life action seemed impossible. The new management revived the project in 1986 and proposed a coproduction with Steven Spielberg's Amblin Entertainment.

Spielberg sparked to the proposal, but with the proviso that the animation and live action be totally integrated. "If Roger comes into a room and sits down on a big chair," he said, "you should see the cushion go down and a puff of dust. When he sits at a desk, you should see the pencil move and the phone rattle. The action should be completely interactive. The characters should have interactive lighting affected by the environment."

A large order, considering the state of technology. From *Song of the South* on, animation had always been added to live action that had been shot with a stationary camera. But Robert Zemeckis, who had been enlisted by Spielberg and Disney as director, had more ambitious ideas. Peter Schneider recalls: "There were two mandates that Bob Zemeckis brought to the movie: To make this [illusion] work, you must have the cartoon character hold something that is real; second, the camera must move as it does in a live-action movie."

Zemeckis began searching for an animation director who could fulfill his requirements. Then one night in the St. James Club in London, he met Richard Williams, a London-based Canadian who had supplied cartoons for the *Pink Panther* movies and had won an Academy Award in 1972 for *A Christmas Carol*.

"You know," said Zemeckis, "I can't stand the way in *Pete's Dragon* and *Mary Poppins* that those cartoon characters seem pasted on top of the frame."

"I couldn't agree with you more," said Williams. "Forget about the animation. Shoot a modern movie, move the camera, do all the things you'd do if you were shooting *Back to the Future*. We'll make it work."

Their task seemed impossible. The cartoon characters would need to be changed subtly with every camera movement. Zemeckis was certain it could be accomplished with his "one-two punch"—Richard Williams and Industrial Light and Magic. George Lucas's ILM would put the cartoon characters in the frame, darken them and put light patterns over them and perform other optical miracles. A thirty-second test convinced Disney executives, and the project, now called *Who Framed Roger Rabbit*, became a "go" production.

After completion of live-action photography, the Disney animation crew, directed by Dick Williams, took over. There were twenty-five principal animators and a hundred others, enlisted from England, America, Europe, and Australia, in London, creating fifty-six minutes of animation. Another crew in California provided an additional ten minutes.

The vastly complicated production suffered several production slowdowns and cost overruns. In October 1987, Jeffrey Katzenberg summoned the major figures in

the *Roger Rabbit* animation to New York for some tough give and take. The filmmakers returned to their tasks with new resolve, and the fall 1988 release date was met. *Who Framed Roger Rabbit* provided a huge moneymaker and a great leap forward for the animated art. The final sequence, in which the major characters from all the cartoon studios join for a celebration, will remain a landmark of animation.

Triumph: *The Little Mermaid*

Hans Christian Andersen's "The Little Mermaid" dated back to the late Thirties at the Disney studio. Roy Disney recalls that during the *Fantasia* period Walt mulled a feature that would be composed of vignettes based on the Andersen tales. Kay Nielsen, the art director of the "Night on Bald Mountain" sequence of *Fantasia*, created art work and storyboards for "The Little Mermaid," but the Andersen project was abandoned. Fifty years later, some of Nielsen's art work appeared in the shipwreck scene of Disney's *The Little Mermaid*.

Shortly after the new management took over, twenty members of the Animation Department were summoned to a meeting with Michael Eisner, Jeffrey Katzenberg, and Roy Disney. Each was asked to come with three ideas for an animated feature.

Ron Clements had browsed in a book store and came across a collection of Andersen stories. His suggestion of "The Little Mermaid" sparked immediate enthusiasm. The subject was also welcomed by animators. At last they were free from the constraints of gravity; their characters could swim and dive and twirl in the

Top: **The Little Mermaid** *allowed animators to free characters from the restrictions of gravity.*

Above: *Broadway actress Jodi Benson's voice in* The Little Mermaid *helped make Ariel (shown here with Flounder) a spunky heroine.*

water. The underwater ambience seemed inviting, with castles and shipwrecks and a whole civilization under the sea.

John Musker and Ron Clements wrote and directed *The Little Mermaid*, and the producers were Musker and Howard Ashman, who also wrote the lyrics to Alan Menken's songs. Ashman proved a giant contributor to *The Little Mermaid* and later to *Beauty and the Beast*. He was a Broadway craftsman whose most notable success had been *The Little Shop of Horrors*. Jeffrey Katzenberg had admired *Little Shop of Horrors* and had tried to buy the film rights to the Ashman-Menken show. Failing that, he invited Ashman and Menken to work at Disney. Ashman wrote a song for *Oliver & Company*, then he and Menken joined *The Little Mermaid*.

The film required extensive special effects to create the underwater atmosphere. The young animators had worked mostly with animal characters, so much live-action filming was required to key their drawings to human movement. The production schedule was stringent, but deadlines were met. *The Little Mermaid* was a thundering success, selling $84 million worth of tickets in the United States and Canada alone, a record for the first release of an animated feature. Americans bought eight million of the videocassettes.

It was another milestone in rebirth of Disney animation. Musker, Clements, and company had proved that the new breed could create an entertainment that would be embraced by all ages.

The Rescuers Down Under

After the massive outlays of talent, time, and money for *Who Framed Roger Rabbit* and *The Little Mermaid*, Disney theorized that it was time for a simple, inexpensive feature, like the prewar *Dumbo*. A sequel to the 1977 hit, *The Rescuers*, appeared a likely candidate. The company owned the Margery Sharp stories, and no character development would be needed for the two leads, Bernard and Miss Bianca.

Writing began in 1986, with the story set in Australia. *The Rescuers Down Under* proved to be no *Dumbo*. The huge success of recent Disney animated features decreed that future films would need to be major productions. Although Bernard and Miss Bianca had been established, the rest of the characters had to be created.

A new team was formed for *The Rescuers Down Under*. Tom Schumacher, like Peter Schneider, had spent most of his career in theater. He was brought to the studio as producer. Hendel Butoy and Mike Gabriel were given their first directing jobs. Both had come to the studio as animators in the late Seventies.

The Rescuers Down Under benefited from the exotic landscapes and animals, researched by a production team that visited Australia. It also marked the first extensive use of computer technologies which provided unlimited color and more freedom of camera movement. The film was a disappointment at the box office, but it contained stunning visual concepts and superb animation.

As the world entered the last decade of the century, Disney animation had acquired a confidence reminiscent of the *Snow White* era. The situation was similar: young artists with a sense of exploring fresh and exciting vistas, armed with new technologies that made anything seem possible. The Nineties generation was ready for its greatest challenge.

TOP: *Bernard's proposal to Miss Bianca is interrupted by a sudden assignment in Australia.*

ABOVE: *The casting of voices was all-important. Bob Newhart and Eva Gabor agreed to return for the lead roles. But Jim Jordan, hilarious as the voice of the albatross Orville in The Rescuers, had died. A mimic was tested but he lacked the inimitable Fibber McGee quality.*

"Then Roy Disney came up with the idea that Orville would have a brother, Wilbur," says Tom Schumacher. "That solved it, and we thought John Candy would be ideal for the role. He agreed to do it."

BOOK TWO
THE MAKING OF BEAUTY AND THE BEAST

PROLOGUE
ANATOMY OF A MOVIE SCENE

PART TITLE: *Early concept drawing of Beast by Andreas Deja.*

PRECEDING SPREAD: *Mysterious background painting of the lair where Beast hides his enchanted rose. Finished animation (INSET) depicts the rose shimmering within its bell jar.*

ABOVE: *Han's Bacher's conceptual sketch captures the menace of Beast's lair.*

Walt DISNEY
Feature Animation
Beauty and the Beast

Production No. 0254
Sequence No. 11
Scene No. 2
Same as_____

From Printed Word to Finished Film

More so than any other kind of filmmaking, animation is a long and intricate process requiring the talents of scores of artists before the original concept reaches fulfillment on the screen.

The following pages illustrate the path of that journey, which may take months to complete. The result is 80 seconds of finished film. The process is repeated again and again until all the elements, including 120,000 drawings and 1,295 painted backgrounds, are gathered into 75 minutes of entertainment called Beauty and the Beast.

SCRIPT

Sequence 11, as written by Linda Woolverton:

Interior—The Beast's Lair

Belle's eyes go wide as she takes in the sight that lies before her. It's the Beast's lair: dark, dank, filthy, strewn with broken furniture, cracked mirrors, torn, tilted portraits, doors torn from their hinges, wall sconces encrusted with old wax, shredded curtains, gnawed bones, a matted pile of bed coverings, and ripped clothing. Dusty winter light filters in through an open window where gnarled tree vines have grown inside. They creep along the filthy carpet and spread their fingers up the walls.

It's a horrific sight . . . a violent uncivilized place where the Beast has lived with his own filth and self-recrimination. Belle shivers with equal parts disgust and

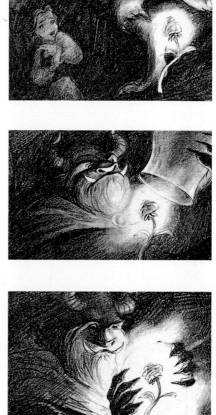

Storyboard sketches by Chris Sanders.

trepidation. She glances up at a small portrait that has been raked by razor-sharp claws. It appears to be the portrait of a young boy. She looks closer. There's something about the eyes.

But then, she catches a glimpse of something near the window that sparkles with a strange, unnatural light. The Rose sits under a bell jar on a table in front of the open window. It still shimmers with enchantment.

Belle approaches the Rose with wide-eyed wonder. Its sparkling delicacy seems very much out of place in this filthy room. Belle grows closer. The Rose is drooping. More petals have fallen to the bottom of the jar.

There's a *creak* outside the window. But Belle is entranced by the Rose and she doesn't hear it. Fascinated, she reaches out toward the jar . . .

as a huge clawed hand grips the sill of the open window.

Belle carefully lifts the jar . . .

as the Beast climbs up over the edge. He stops . . . shocked at the sight of her there.

Belle gazes with awe at the shimmering Rose. She reaches out . . .

The Beast's eyes fill with fear.

Her fingers are extended out to touch one soft velvet petal . . .

He roars and jumps over the window ledge. Belle backs away fearfully as the Beast covers the Rose protectively with the bell jar. As he sees that the Rose is undamaged, his fear begins to abate and fury rises up in its place. He glowers at her . . . eyes burning with rage.

STORYBOARD

Working from Linda Woolverton's script, Chris Sanders depicts the action in a series of sketches. He concentrates on building the sense that Belle is invading a forbidden place. She enters Beast's creepy lair, and the feeling of suspense pervades Sanders's drawings. As Belle approaches and admires the enchanted Rose, Sanders creates a peaceful moment—"the calm before the storm." Belle's calm is shattered by the crashing entrance of Beast. His tirade and her frightened response is played in closeups to maximize the drama. Sanders completes the sequence in seventy drawings, occupying a storyboard and a half.

TOP: *The "blue sketch" tracing of the animation serves as a guide for camera moves and composition.*

ABOVE: *Kirk Wise directs Paige O'Hara as Belle and Robby Benson as Beast in the Disney Studio's Stage B.*

VOICES

We move to a recording session at the Disney Studio in Burbank, Stage B, where the words of Cinderella, Captain Hook, Cruella De Vil, and dozens of other Disney characters have been spoken by actors. Usually the actors deliver their dialogue singly. But because Sequence 11 is so critical in the plot of *Beauty and the Beast*, both Robby Benson, the voice of Beast, and Paige O'Hara, who plays Belle, have been called for the recording session. They stand opposite each other before microphones, as in the days of radio drama.

Kirk Wise, who is codirector of *Beauty and the Beast* with Gary Trousdale, explains the dramatic intensity of the scene and its importance to the structure of the film. He signals the actors to begin.

> Beast: Why did you come here?
> Belle: I'm . . . I'm sorry.
> Beast: I warned you *never* to come here!
> Belle: I didn't mean any harm.
> Beast: Do you realize what you have done?
> Belle: Please . . . stop!
> Beast: Get out! Get out!

Wise urges O'Hara and Benson to more emotional heights, and they respond with full force. After ten takes, the recording session is over.

Layout

A story reel has been prepared, combining Chris Sanders's story sketches, the dialogue by Robby Benson and Paige O'Hara, and a temporary track of mood music. Thus Sequence 11 can be viewed on videotape as it will appear after animation. Fred Craig, a member of the Layout Department, prepares a "workbook," which details the staging of the sequence—camera angles, lighting, effects, etc. Craig works closely with Glen Keane, who is animating Beast, to capture the full drama of the confrontation of Beast with Belle. It is played mostly in closeups, without many camera angles. Craig completes his work, drawing 225 sketches.

Live Action

In a side room off the warehouse of the Imagineering Building on Flower Street in Glendale, Belle is entering the Beast's lair. Belle is portrayed by Shari Stoner, an actress who works in improvisational theaters. She provided the visual imagery for animators of Ariel in *The Little Mermaid*, and she is doing the same for Belle in *Beauty and the Beast*.

Gary Trousdale is directing Shari in Belle's movements as she enters the dark room and sees the Rose. The actress is dressed in Belle's costume. The set is bare except for a table on which the bell jar will stand. On the blank walls are painted grids which will measure the movement for the animators. The live-action scenes, which can be printed out frame by frame, are not copied by the animators but provide inspiration for movement.

Trousdale and the camera operator consult the layout sheets to determine the position of the video camera. The director shows Shari the story sketches to explain the action. The playback of the dialogue between Belle and Beast is repeated three times so the actress can memorize the lines.

"Action!" Trousdale calls. Shari walks up to the table and pantomimes the lifting of the bell jar. She recoils when she hears the enraged Beast: "Why did you come here?" The scene continues until Trousdale calls "Cut!" The scene is repeated and replayed on a video screen until the director's needs are satisfied.

Top left: A *layout drawing.*

Top: A *live action sequence where Shari Stoner acts out Belle racing from Beast's lair.*

B-89

89

Belle and Beast before and after cleanup.

ANIMATION

Glen Keane faces a staging problem. Beast first appears in the scene at the window; how can he seem to have just arrived there? Keane's solution is to have Beast's cape swirl. The animator dons a cape and swirls it in the hallway of the Air Way building. For a better view, he asks his fellow animator, Geefwee Border, to model the cloak. Keane draws the movement, adding a grace and flow to the heretofore "animal-like guy."

Keane must coordinate his work with that of Mark Henn, three thousand miles away. Henn is drawing Belle at the Disney-MGM studio in Florida, in full view of the thousands of visitors who daily watch the animation process from behind windows. The animation studio was opened in April 1989 as a tourist attraction and a future base for the production of animated features.

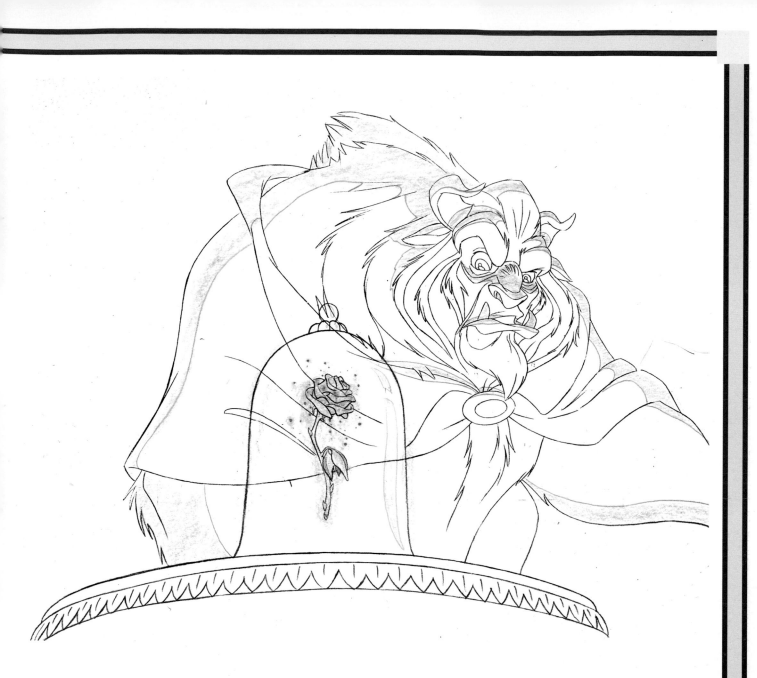

Keane makes his drawings of Beast and scribbles in the figure of Belle. Henn does the reverse, and the pair exchange their work by overnight courier.

Beast is the dominant figure in the scene, and Keane must pace his character's rage. At first, Beast's only concern is the Rose. With the "ticking time bomb" safely under the bell jar, he turns his attention to Belle. She is apologetic and frightened, and Henn must time her reactions to Beast as he mounts into a violent, screaming rampage.

CLEANUP

After the animation is approved by directors Wise and Trousdale, it is handed over to Cleanup. Bill Berg, in charge of the cleanup of Beast, works closely with Glen Keane, trying to capture the drama of Keane's rough, fluid drawings. Berg refers to model sheets and sculptures to make sure Beast conforms to how he looks in other sequences. Berg cleans up the key drawings and draws the important in-betweens. The rest is done by his eleven assistants. Renee Holt, who is in charge of Belle, goes through the same procedure with Mark Henn's drawings.

Special effects' drawings of tone mattes on Beast and magic effects on the rose.

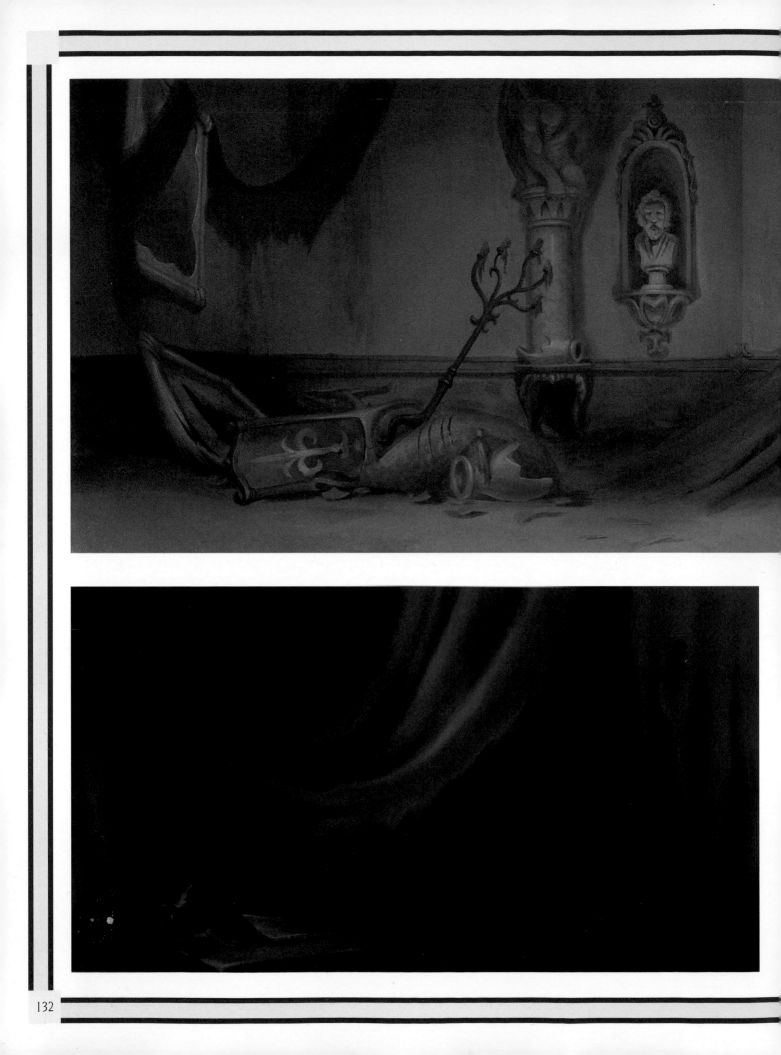

BACKGROUND

After the colors for Beast's lair have been agreed upon, Donald Towns is assigned to paint the background. He consults with the head of Background, Lisa Keene, and they agree on a soft "Bambi-ish, indoor look." Towns paints the room with an eye toward a mystery, none of the features crisp and sharp. The scene is dark, with only the rose and moonlight from the window for illumination.

Towns bears in mind that the castle had once been a beautifully elegant place, and that can be seen in the room's arch and moldings. But years of occupancy by a boy turned beast have left the place completely trashed, with disarray and broken furniture everywhere.

EFFECTS

Randy Fullmer animates the Rose, as well as its effects. A soft glow is applied to indicate the Rose's magical power. Fullmer outlines the shape of the Rose and enlarges it, applying a blurry image that makes it seem like a light source. He gives the bell jar an outline that creates a slightly different glow from the Rose. Since the Rose is partially illuminating the room, Fullmer adds the glow to surfaces of the walls and furniture.

Until now, the Rose has been seen in progressive stages of decay. But as Belle approaches, the Rose responds emotionally, as if Belle represents hope for Beast. Fullmer also animates light around the Rose to indicate its magical qualities.

Background paintings of Beast's lair.

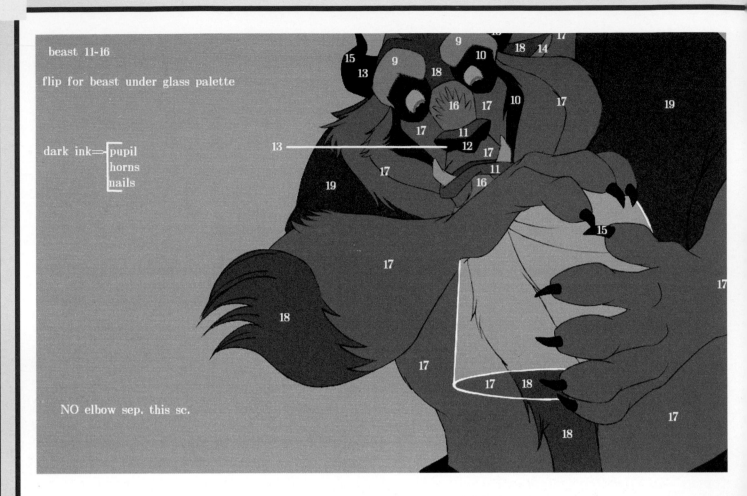

beast 11-16

flip for beast under glass palette

dark ink⟹[pupil
           horns
           nails

NO elbow sep. this sc.

A color model marked-up with Beast colors, in preparation for painting.

ANIMATION CHECK

Janet Bruce oversees the checking of all the elements of the scene. Among the questions to be answered:

Are all the camera moves executed as planned in the layout?

Are the lines in place on Belle and Beast so the color can be properly applied?

Do the effects levels work with the characters?

Do the characters work against the environment, so everything registers?

Does the background fit with all the other elements?

Are the contact points coordinated, so Belle doesn't walk through furniture and Beast doesn't stick his hand through the bell jar?

COLOR MODEL

Karen Comella, color model supervisor, and Brian McEntee, art director, select the colors for Belle and Beast. They consider the circumstances: it's a night scene, with an element of menace; there are two light sources—moonlight is streaming in from the window, and the Rose emits a warm light.

Masculine colors of blue and red dominate the Beast's lair, but they are muted and somber because of the darkness. Having become part animal, Beast is dressed in earth tones, his body brown, his torn cape and trousers reddish brown, a blood-red lining inside the cape. His eyes are "Paul Newman blue," hinting of the Prince within the bestial body.

Belle is designed to be freshly beautiful, not made-up. She wears a simple peasant costume, blue skirt, white blouse. The Rose is a glowing, pure red.

COLOR, CAMERA, SCORE

After Karen Comella and Brian McEntee agree on the colors, they are applied by artists in the Paint Department. This is done by computer with an incredibly wide-ranging palette. The characters, backgrounds, effects, and other elements of the scene are combined in a computer.

The compilation is checked for color inconsistencies and other glitches by the final checker, Hortensia Casagran, then printed on 35mm film.

Finally, Alan Menken composes a musical background featuring the Beast theme and records it with a full orchestra.

The result of all this effort and artistry is inserted into the work reel, which is growing by accretion with each week of production. In the beginning, the work reel consists only of story sketches which convey a rough approximation of the Beauty and the Beast *story. As rough animation is completed, it takes the place of the story sketches. Then comes the cleanup animation and finally, the color. The process continues until* Beauty and the Beast *takes the form that will be seen by audiences throughout the world.*

Completed animation in full color.

CHAPTER NINE
FROM LEGEND TO FILM

"Beauty and the Beast" Through the Ages

Scholars have traced the "Beauty and the Beast" theme in the ancient folklore of three continents. "Animal groom and [human] bride stories have varied as widely across time and culture as versions of the Cinderella theme," writes Betsy Hearne in the comprehensive *Beauty and the Beast: Visions and Revisions of an Old Tale*. The legend of Cupid and Psyche might have originated in fourth century B.C. Greece. In *A Midsummer Night's Dream*, Shakespeare drew comedy from the spectacle of Titania, Queen of the Fairies, falling in love with Bottom the Weaver, whose head had been transformed into an ass's.

"Beauty and the Beast" was a favorite tale at the French court in the mid-seventeenth-century, and Gabrielle de Villeneuve included it in a book in 1740. It was followed by another version by Madame Le Prince de Beaumont, printed in France in 1756 and in England in 1783. This became the version most widely known. The basic plot:

A successful merchant who has lost his fortune goes in search of a reported valuable cargo in a port city. His three daughters talk about the riches he may bring home. The elder sisters greedily yearn for lavish gifts. Beauty, the pure-hearted younger daughter, wants only a rose.

Heading home after his fruitless mission, the father loses his way in a storm and encounters an enchanted castle where he stays overnight. Before leaving, he cuts a bough from a rose bush as a gift for Beauty. The master of the castle, a ferocious, animal-like Beast, suddenly appears.

"I have saved your life by receiving you into my castle," he roars, "and in return you steal my roses, which I value beyond anything in the universe." He decrees that the father must pay for his transgression with his life—or a daughter.

PRECEDING SPREAD: *In this conceptual painting, moonlight captures Belle's father at the top of a cliff. Inset features finished animation of Belle as she sings in the village.*

OPPOSITE: *The life of the Prince before the curse is illustrated by stained-glass windows in a prologue. Designed by Mac George.*

ABOVE: *A conceptualization of the Prince's castle by Hans Bacher.*

ABOVE AND RIGHT: *Vance Gerry's story sketches inspired the stained glass prologue.*

OPPOSITE: *The immensity of the castle is portrayed in an early watercolor.*

BELOW: *Andreas Deja's early sketch of Belle and Beast dramatizes their relationship.*

Over her father's protest, Beauty agrees to live with the Beast. She is at first repelled by Beast, who asks every night at dinner if she will marry him. She declines, but gradually she perceives goodness behind the fearful mask. She sees in a magic mirror that her father is seriously ill. Beast reluctantly allows her to go, warning that he will die within a week if she does not return.

Beauty's selfish sisters delay her return to the castle until it almost too late. She arrives to find Beast near death from pining for her. Beauty tells him of her love, and the Beast is transformed into a handsome prince.

"A wicked fairy had condemned me to remain under that shape till a beautiful virgin should consent to marry me," says the Prince.

Beaumont concludes: "He married Beauty, and lived with her for many years, and their happiness, as it was founded on virtue, was compleat."

Beaumont's version provided the model for two centuries of interpretations, including those by Charles Lamb, the Brothers Grimm, Walter Crane, Eleanor Vere Boyle, and Andrew Lang.

Operas, plays, novels and short stories have been written on "Beauty and the Beast." Psychiatrists have pondered over it. Bruno Bettelheim postulated that in the Greek myth "the highest psychic qualities (Psyche) are to be wedded to sexuality (Eros) . . . spiritual man must be reborn to become ready for the marriage of sexuality with wisdom."

In 1946 Jean Cocteau wrote and directed the film *La Belle et la Bête*, which he based on the Beaumont version. Fraught with symbolism, the lavish, surrealistic production was considered one of Cocteau's finest achievements.

Most younger Americans know "Beauty and the Beast" from the television series that appeared on CBS from 1987 to 1990. This time the beast was a deformed inhabitant of underground New York and the beauty was a successful lawyer.

Don Hahn, who was producing *Beauty and the Beast* in Disney style, cautioned his fellow workers: "Don't look at either the Cocteau or the television version. We'll make our own."

Top: *Belle in the opening sequence.*

Above: *Linda Woolverton amid illustrations of the creatures in her script.*

Script: A Disney Heroine Who Reads

Until the late Eighties, Disney animated features had always been conceived on storyboards, then they went directly to production.

"It's okay to do it that way if you've got a guy verbalizing the script," says Michael Eisner. "Walt Disney could do that. He carried everything in his head."

"He'd walk into a story meeting," adds Jeffrey Katzenberg, "and tell the whole movie from beginning to end—the characters, the dialogue, everything. Literally he was the script."

Michael Eisner, Jeffrey Katzenberg, and Peter Schneider reasoned that *The Black Cauldron* and other animated films since Walt Disney's death had suffered from a lack of direction which resulted in costly reworkings and delays. The problems could be alleviated, they said, by having a script first. Then it could be amended by storyboards and story meetings.

The script of *Beauty and the Beast* was written by Linda Woolverton, who had once created plays for a children's theater and had risen to executive in late-night programming at CBS. Against all advice, she quit to become a writer, working as a substitute school teacher to pay her bills. She managed to sell two young-adult novels to Houghton Mifflin and a couple of Saturday morning animation stories to Disney. After writing a couple of animation feature scripts for Disney, she was assigned to do a rewrite of *Beauty and the Beast*. Two and a half years later, she was still working on it.

First of all, Linda read all the "Beauty and the Beast" fairy tales. And discarded them.

"It's very difficult to take the originals and convert them into a story that works for the Nineties," she observed. "You have to consider what kids are like now in terms of sophistication, you have to make sure that your themes are strong, that people can relate to the characters, that the story isn't sexist.

"Belle is a strong, smart, courageous woman. She sacrifices herself for her father. There are great themes of passionate love in the story, almost operatic themes. She's a Disney heroine who reads books. It excites me. We've never seen that before."

The writer's first big hurdle was the middle of the second act, when Belle is confined to the castle. The solution: Belle stages an escape, encounters wolves in the forest and is rescued by Beast. There were other problems to be solved down the line, and they were thrashed out in story meeting after story meeting. Everyone seemed to have ideas, and it was Linda's job to assimilate them and interpret them creatively.

ABOVE: *Chris Sanders's story sketch depicts the wolves reacting to the appearance of Beast.*

BELOW: A *color model of the studious Belle.*

*F*rank Thomas remembers "When Walt became all wrapped up in the theme parks and live-action films, we tried to get him interested in animation again. Walt said, 'If I ever do go back, there are only two subjects I would want to do. One of them is Beauty and the Beast.' For the life of me, I can't remember what the other one was."

TOP AND ABOVE: *Key artists took a trip to Burgundy and brought back photos of buildings and interiors to help them depict eighteenth century France with authenticity.*

OPPOSITE TOP: *Hans Bacher's art captures the mood of the mob singing outside the enchanted castle.*

OPPOSITE BOTTOM: *Debbie Du Bois' depiction of the interior of Gaston's lodge.*

The Story Takes Shape

Ollie Johnston recalls, "Probably before *Cinderella*, Walt asked us to read "Beauty and the Beast" and come up with some ideas for it. The story guys may have done some work on it, but I never heard any more about it."

If there had been any work done on "Beauty and the Beast" during Walt's time, it is lost to history. Not a trace remains in the studio's seemingly infallible Archives. After the Eisner-Wells-Katzenberg team assumed control of the studio, "Beauty and the Beast" seemed a logical selection in continuing the Disney interpretations of classic fairy tales.

Two writers produced scripts, and neither qualified. Then Linda Woolverton produced a screenplay that seemed workable. Richard Purdum, an American-born animator who had made imaginative films in England, was hired to direct. Don Hahn, who had worked closely with Richard Williams on *Who Framed Roger Rabbit*, was assigned to produce.

Hahn spent ten weeks in London with Purdum, who created storyboards with his wife Jill. Hahn led ten artists, including animators Glen Keane, Andreas Deja, and art directors, to the Loire valley to soak up the atmosphere of French countrysides and chateaux. They returned with videotape, still photographs, sketches, and warm memories of elegant vintage wines.

Jeffrey Katzenberg viewed the story reels of the Purdums' work and declared that it was too dark and too dramatic. *The Little Mermaid*, which was approaching release, had been greatly enhanced by the songs of Howard Ashman and Alan Menken. Katzenberg invited Ashman, who had been coproducer as well as lyric writer on *The Little Mermaid*, and Menken to join *Beauty and the Beast*.

Ashman flew to Walt Disney World for the premiere of *The Little Mermaid*. He met with Katzenberg, Roy Disney, Peter Schneider, the Purdums, Linda Woolverton, and others and outlined his ideas for *Beauty and the Beast*. His suggestions were immediately embraced, and Woolverton spent weeks in New York with him, revising the script.

"Howard is really good at plot," says Woolverton. "He always said he was 'the simplicity police.' When things started getting too complicated and 'plotty,' he'd say, 'These movies have to be very simple, they must move simply.' He would always make us stop going off on tangents and come back to the purity of the source, the emotion of the source. Howard told us that every single scene, not just the ones you'd expect, but *every one* should have an umbrella of emotion over it, whether it's warmth or terror or love or drama or even comedy. Every single scene."

Richard Purdum, who had taken part in the revisions, came to the conclusion, "This is not the film I want to make," and he resigned amicably as director in December 1989. Katzenberg, who felt the studio had failed to develop new animation directors during its fallow period, chose Kirk Wise and Gary Trousdale, who had worked together in story, to succeed Purdum.

ABOVE: *The British butler turned mantel clock, Cogsworth.*

TOP RIGHT: *Mrs. Potts serves up tea and sympathy in Beast's castle.*

BOTTOM RIGHT: *Lumiere introduces the Busby Berkeley production number, "Be My Guest."*

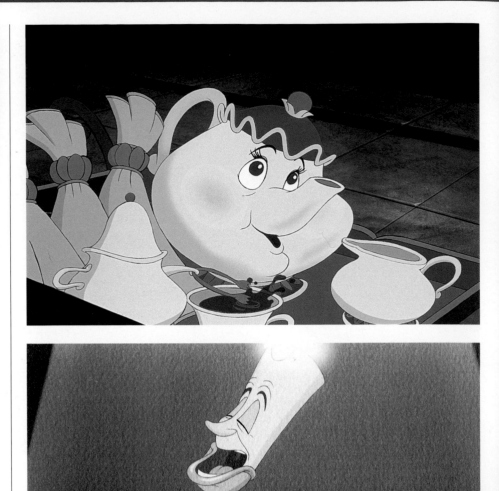

The major work on the *Beauty and the Beast* script was accomplished at the Residence Inn at Fishkill, New York, near Ashman's home. A workplace was set up in a conference room, which was filled with giant foam boards that had been found in a storage room. Sketches were pinned on the board, and Alan Menken played songs on a rented Yamaha piano keyboard. Don Hahn, Trousdale, and Wise flew from California to confer with Ashman and Woolverton.

Ashman solved the story's number-one problem: how to enliven the second act, when Belle and Beast are alone together in the castle. Ashman's solution was to make important characters out of the servants who have been reduced to inanimate objects by the sorceress's spell, principally, Cogsworth, the majordomo of the castle, who becomes a mantel clock; the cook, Mrs. Potts, now a teapot; and the main waiter, Lumiere, a candelabrum. They would provide comedy and music while helping to advance the plot.

Beauty and the Beast also needed a villain, someone to menace Belle and Beast alike. The two sisters had provided conflict in the fairy tale, but they had been

discarded in the film script. The fairy tale included suitors clamoring for Belle's hand in marriage, and they pointed the way to a solution. Gaston, the town muscleman bully, became the ideal protagonist. Thwarted in his plan to marry Belle, he is willing to send her father to an insane asylum, and in the end he gathers a mob to destroy Beast in the castle.

In the fairy tale, Belle's father removes the rose branches, enraging Beast to decree that the father must die—or sacrifice his daughter. The father returns home, and Belle volunteers to go to the castle. To activate the sequence, the plotmakers decided to have the father remain captive in the castle, and Belle goes there to substitute for him.

"We also had trouble with the rose," says Don Hahn. "Why would it tick off Beast so much? What is this guy, a gardener or something? So we changed the function of the rose to be a ticking clock, the hourglass, as it were. When Beast is cursed in the prologue, he gets the rose and the magic mirror. The rose is the symbol of the amount of time he has before he can love another and be loved in return. If the rose wilts and dies, he will remain a beast forever.

"And the magic mirror is his window to the outside world that he will never see, because he's cursed up on the hill in the castle."

The revised script met with the approval of Eisner, Katzenberg, Roy Disney, and Schneider, and preliminary production began in early 1990. The team of artists was assembled, and the work of animating Belle, Beast, Gaston, and a host of other characters started in July.

ABOVE: *The Magic Mirror proved an important device for furthering the plot. A story sketch by Bruce Woodside.*

BELOW: *The falling rose petals serve as a time clock ticking toward the doom of Beast. Drawn by Brian McEntee.*

The Storyboard Process

From the very beginning of the Disney studio, the story man was a vital and valued part of the creative process. He was part scriptwriter, part gagman, part actor, selling his wares with his own performance. He often illustrated his ideas with hastily drawn sketches or worked with a sketch artist, and the drawings were pinned to a board so they could be viewed in continuity. The first and best of the story men was Walt Disney.

Roger Allers was the story head for *Beauty and the Beast*. He trained as an artist at Arizona State University, roamed the world for a couple of years, then settled in Boston where he took a job with a small animation company.

From the Boston studio he went to Toronto and Tokyo and joined Disney in 1985. He was assigned to story work. Allers felt comfortable, having done story as well as animation in his previous jobs. His first Disney assignment was *Oliver & Company*.

"The tone of the story changed drastically while we worked on it," Allers recalls. "George Scribner's original idea was a lot rougher, a lot tougher. Fagin was kind of mean-spirited, and the dogs were really tough, and it was really a hard, hard film."

The Little Mermaid was an easier assignment. John Musker and Ron Clements had written a well-structured script with defined characters and themes. "When we went to storyboard it, we weren't hunting around a lot," says Allers. "The challenge really was to make it as entertaining as possible and to make it come alive.

"The songs were the backbone of the whole thing. In the very early days, Howard Ashman came and played the songs he and Alan Menken had written. He told us the ideas behind them, and it was so inspiring that everybody was jazzed up on the project."

In the beginning, Allers had little enthusiasm for working on *Beauty and the Beast*, which seemed to him bleak and forbidding. But again Howard Ashman provided the spark to fire imaginations.

"Howard said that [if based on the fairy tale] the movie was about two people having dinner," Allers recollects. "Every night at dinner, he asks her to marry him, and she says no. You can do that once, but after that, it's not very entertaining.

"So what do you do? For one thing, you have Belle come to the castle, rather than having the father come home, as in the traditional story. That helped energize it a bit. Then you have the inanimate objects who really want the romance to happen so they can be human again. They really help the story, because the Beast, in our version, is not a very expressive character in terms of words."

Allers and the story crew were responsible for taking the script pages and visualizing them with their own sketches. It is a vital, even crucial phase in the production process, since the scenes will be viewed for the first time as they will appear in the movie.

Walt Disney once described the qualifications for a story man: "The first thing is to have a good memory. A good story man never forgets a situation. Everything should be related to human experience in storytelling. An incident that happened to you years ago might be usable in a cartoon sequence. Screenwriters as such have never been of much use to us. Nearly all of our story men started as artists years ago. They think in terms of pictures. That's how we tell our stories, not with words."

TOP: As story head for Beauty and the Beast, Roger Allers not only draws the sketches but acts out the storyboard himself.

OPPOSITE: Belle's escape from the castle is depicted in Chris Sanders's story sketches. Beginning with top left, the sequence progresses from top to bottom.

Brenda Chapman grew up in a small Illinois town that had no movie theater, so in her youth she had scant knowledge of Disney animation. She studied art in junior college, aiming for a career in advertising. In a roundabout way she heard about the training for animators at CalArts. She enrolled, and in her third year she made a short film that impressed the Disney studio, not for her animation but her sense of story. She was hired as a story trainee, working with Roger Allers on a short Little Mermaid sequence. Brenda's work expanded on Beauty and the Beast. Among her assignments: part of Belle's opening song, the scene where Belle bandages Beast's wounds after his fight with the wolves.

"Basically you're putting a written idea into visual terms and seeing how you can make it play emotionally and finding the places to express the humor that's latent in the characters," explained Allers. That meant collaborating closely with Linda Woolverton on every scene.

"For the scriptwriter it must be frustrating to be reworking and reworking," said Allers. "I guess that's what the storyboard process is. That's why we put our sketches up with little pins, because it all comes down, lots of times. You rework it, and rework it, and craft it."

Roger Allers is not only storyboard artist; he must also be pitchman and actor. He must present his work either on the storyboards or on reels, which may include dialogue and songs.

"I think most people who go into animation in some way or another are born actors," he observes. "Even though they couldn't get up and perform in front of people, they are closet actors. You have to be an actor to get into your roles. A good story person must feel the characters from the inside out. You have to get attitudes that express the character. To do that, you have to feel within yourself—what would your attitude be if you were cursed to stay a clock all your life?"

Major alterations were required during the scripting period.

Ashman and Menken had written a song "We'll Be Human Again" for the objects to sing as Belle and Beast are falling in love. The storyboards promised an entertaining sequence, but the spotlight was on the objects instead of the title characters. "We'll Be Human Again" was junked and replaced with "There May Be Something There That Wasn't There Before," in which Belle and Beast tell of their feelings for each other.

"Be Our Guest" was planned as a rousing number to be sung by the objects to the first visitor to the castle, Belle's father, Maurice. But Maurice was a peripheral character, and when story man Bruce Woodside pointed out that the song should be directed to Belle, everyone agreed. Back to the storyboards.

Beast was originally conceived as a quiet, monosyllabic, morose character. He needed to acquire a larger personality, to express himself more fully.

Gaston was first portrayed as a broad, comical figure. In the early scenes he was the butt of jokes. Jeffrey Katzenberg suggested that Gaston had to be treated seriously, otherwise his villainy would lack conviction.

Brenda Chapman is one of a growing number of women who now work in story at Disney. She shares an office with Roger Allers. They collaborate frequently since they started working together on *The Little Mermaid*. "It's really wonderful to get in on the beginning of a project," Brenda commented. "It's like a blank page that you start on, and by the time the animators come in, it's all figured out. It's like putting together the pieces of a puzzle."

Like Allers, Brenda creates her own sketches.

"Back in the old days, there was a story man and a story sketch artist who interpreted his ideas," Allers observes. "Not anymore. Today the story person does both functions."

YOU.. YOU CAME BACK.

MAYBE IT'S BETTER THIS WAY

YOU'LL BE ALRIGHT.

...SEE YOU ONE LAST TIME

Chris Sanders's storyboard sketches for Beast's dying scene.

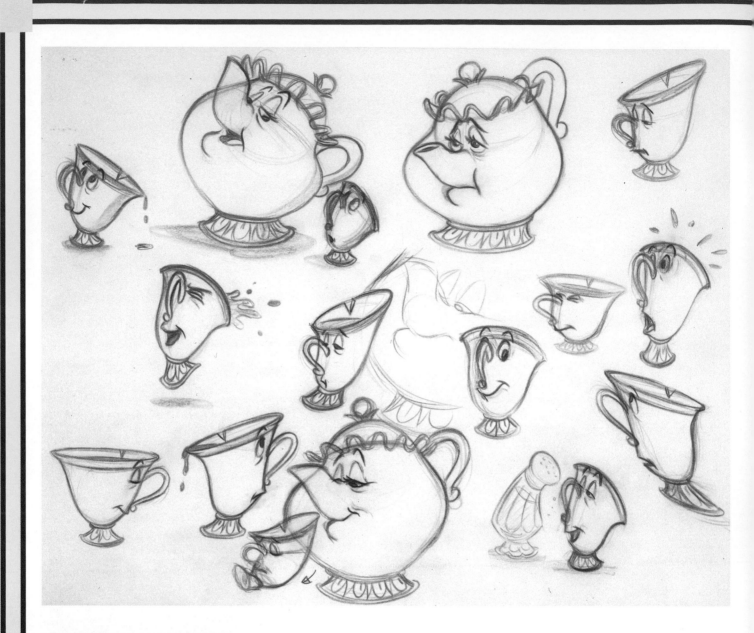

TOP: *Early Dave Pruiksma character designs for Mrs. Potts and Chip.*

ABOVE: *Dave Pruiksma pours a cup of tea for Bradley Pierce, whose unique voice inspired the expansion of the role of Chip.*

Story Meeting: The Emergence of Chip

It has the aura of a college seminar, rather than a meeting of the major figures of a Hollywood production. Jeffrey Katzenberg is the professor, the only one of the thirty participants who is wearing a coat and tie. He stands at the head of the violet-walled conference room in the Air Way building. Instead of a blackboard, he has an oversized video monitor.

This is one of dozens of story meetings held through most of the production of *Beauty and the Beast*. Some are attended by a handful of directors, animators, and story people. In some all the major figures in the production take part, including Katzenberg, Roy Disney, Peter Schneider, and, occasionally, Michael Eisner.

The meeting is scheduled for 7:30 in the morning, and most of the participants are there early, chatting around the breakfast table. There is an air of theatricality in the room: the meeting is being taped by a crew from the ABC-TV news magazine show "20/20" for broadcast when *Beauty and the Beast* opens in theaters across the nation.

Katzenberg takes his place beside the video monitor, and the others settle in the rows of chairs before him. He discloses a new development: the role of Chip, the china-cup son of Mrs. Potts, will be expanded. In previous versions of *Beauty and the Beast*, he was given a single line and hovered in the background. Then one of the boys auditioning for the voice, Bradley Pierce, overwhelmed his listeners.

"It's such a great voice, we want to have many more moments with Chip in the film," Katzenberg enthuses. "Who's animating him?" David Pruiksma is identified. "You're going to have a lot more work to do."

As the meeting progresses, Chip's role expands: When Maurice is served tea, Chip should be his cup. . . . Chip could run off at the mouth like a precocious child who is overjoyed at having a visitor in his house. . . . Maybe Chip could be coming along behind Mrs. Potts, imitating her as she starts to sing her verse of the song. . . . Perhaps Chip could replace the Music Box as the stowaway when Belle leaves Beast to go to her father's side. (This was done, and the Music Box was relegated to the cutting-room floor.)

Katzenberg conducts the meeting in a show-and-tell manner, beginning at the start of the *Beauty and the Beast* tape, which is mostly story sketches and small amounts of animation, together with the dialogue and music tracks. He runs the tape for a minute or two, then pauses for comments. There is much give and take from his listeners, some jocular, some serious.

The meeting occupies most of the morning and includes a wide range of comment from Roy Disney, the producer; Don Hahn; the directors, Kirk Wise and Gary Trousdale, and others. Two days later, Don Hahn's assistant, Patti Conklin, distributes the condensed meeting notes to all the participants. Among the items:

"Only the Beast's back should be visible during the prologue. The Beast's posture must communicate despair, anguish, loneliness.

"Can there be some funny business happening between Belle, the old washerwoman, and the sheep in the scene around the town fountain?

"After Maurice sneezes on Cogsworth, Cogs. should use his clock hands to wipe his face clean. He could potentially use them like windshield wipers.

"The music accompanying Belle's approach to the castle is crucial. It must convey the ominous, tentative mood of the scene.

"Although Belle has a hard time looking into Beast's ghastly visage, her strength and courage allow her to hold her ground.

"Gaston's hairy chest should be more like a lumberjack's—less sensual.

"When Beast says, 'I've never felt this way about anyone,' it should be clear that he is literally amazed at the new emotions he is experiencing.

"Cut at least twenty seconds out of the Love Montage song's overture.

"Get the dead air out of the various scenes in the mob fight. The individual segments are all great, but they need tightening.

"[At the end] Could a moment be invented for Chip to say, 'I saved him'?"

ABOVE: *Roger Allers describes the storyboard for, left to right, Gary Trousdale, Roy Disney, Kirk Wise, Jeffrey Katzenberg, and Don Hahn.*

BELOW: *Roger Allers's story sketches capture the relationship of Mrs. Potts and Chip.*

CHAPTER TEN
THE ELEMENTS OF ANIMATION

PRECEDING SPREAD: *Preproduction sketch by Hans Bacher visualizes the menace that faces Maurice and Belle in the woods* (SPREAD). *Full-color animation of Lumiere* (INSET).

ABOVE: *Early versions of the story included a sequence where Gaston and Lefou rode off to the "Maison de Loons" and bargained with Mr. D'Arque to commit Belle's father. The sequence was cut in favor of a simpler version that took place late at night in Gaston's pub. Preproduction sketch by Hans Bacher.*

H oward Hughes started his around-the-world flight from there. Hollywood stars once stood in the doorways of Ford Trimotor planes and waved for photographers before departing on the four-stop flight to New York. Now the runways are gone, and all that remains of the Glendale Airport is the modest stucco control tower. The rest is an industrial development, filled with sprawling, faceless one-storied buildings.

Across from the old control tower on Air Way is a Disney building, one of five in the area. At one time it housed the Disney printing plant. Later it was used for the California animation of *Who Framed Roger Rabbit*. Then in late 1989 the building was completely gutted to accommodate the production of *Beauty and the Beast*.

Now the building is a violet labyrinth of partitions, with windowless offices around the walls. Every partition, every wall, is adorned by mementos that only artists can collect. Along the ceiling run the exposed air ducts that blow cool air during the sweltering San Fernando Valley summer.

The maze of work spaces gives a helter-skelter appearance to the place, but within the span of eighteen months the artists therein would produce an entertainment that might be seen over the years by a billion people. There are 370 men and women making *Beauty and the Beast*, and forty-three of them are animators. They are the actors of the production.

Production: The Unity of Vision

At a towering six feet five, Don Hahn is the only person at the Air Way building who can gaze over the partitions that honeycomb the central area. That's only fitting, since Hahn is the producer of *Beauty and the Beast*. As he describes the job, he is "cheerleader, counselor, artistic colleague."

"I'm also the film's advocate," he adds, "meaning I go to bat for it in all areas:

with management, with marketing, with consumer products. To be the spokesperson, the host, the representative of the movie, to all areas of the company. There has to be a single person who can look out for the interest of the movie.

"I don't want somebody down at the parks, for example, doing a float or an emporium window or a walk-around character that doesn't reflect what the movie is. I don't want to walk into a store and pick up a coloring book that's terribly drawn, or read a story that doesn't reflect what our *Beauty and the Beast* is, or hear a music box that plays the wrong notes. All of which could happen."

Asked to define what the producer does, Hahn replies modestly, "Probably not very much, but he is responsible for a lot.

"I enjoy working with artists and trying to focus everyone's talents on a common creative goal. It's like being a symphony conductor, where you don't necessarily know how to play everybody's instrument, but you can collaborate with the players to make great music."

He explains that his artistic side might say to an artist, "Have you thought about a shadow here? Do you like the way this layout works?" But as producer he might say, "Is this sequence getting too complex? Can we finish it in time?"

"I rely heavily on my associate producer, Sarah McArthur, to be the production side of me," he says. "The animators and department heads report directly to her to make sure that all the production, the flow of footage, the numbers and budgets, are going on schedule."

Hahn also deals with the voice talents and the music, acting as liaison between the West Coast and Howard Ashman and Alan Menken in the East. He spends a typical day viewing film tests; talking to lawyers, agents, executives, and artists; and looking at dolls, plush animals, Mrs. Potts teapots, Cogsworth clocks, and other merchandise to assure that *Beauty and the Beast*, on screen and off, has a unity of vision.

TOP: *Brian McEntee's color sketch for the "Be Our Guest" finale.*

ABOVE: *Like most of the new generation working on* Beauty and the Beast, *producer Don Hahn was fascinated in his youth by Disney. His major interest was Disneyland, which he haunted—"I knew the location of every bathroom, every drinking fountain." He studied music at Cal State University Northridge, played percussion in local bands, and came to Disney to work on Pete's Dragon in 1976. He rose from cleanup artist to associate producer of* Who Framed Roger Rabbit *in London. "I really enjoyed being associate producer on Roger," says Hahn, who is thirty-five.*

ABOVE: *Kirk Wise grew up in Palo Alto and was introduced to drawing by his father, who had been an art student and high school cartoonist. Kirk learned the rudiments of animation in a community center course that used cutouts or clay models for films on super-8mm.*

In high school Kirk heard about California Institute of the Arts (CalArts), at Valencia, north of Los Angeles; endowed by the Disney family, the school provided training for those interested in animation. Kirk studied for four years, and he began animating at Disney on The Great Mouse Detective. *After a year's layoff, he came back to the studio to animate on* Oliver & Company.

"But I discovered that being an animator wasn't exactly my niche; it never came easily to me," Kirk says. He gravitated toward the story department, where he eventually joined forces with a schoolmate from CalArts.

TOP RIGHT: *The storytelling moves visually from fall to winter to spring. Here is Gaston's pub under the first-snows-of-winter background by Greg Drolette.*

Direction: The Disparate Partners

No codirectors could be more unalike.

Kirk Wise, who is twenty-seven years old, once considered being an actor, and still could be. The Wise office is neat and uncluttered. A bulletin board with pictures of animals, comic strips, sketches from *Beauty and the Beast*. A bust of Belle, portraits of the Beast. A large television set and a VCR, tools of today's director. A series of rose pictures, petals falling. A desk devoid of nonessentials.

Gary Trousdale's desk in the adjoining office is a mound of esoterica. The prominent feature is a model of a medieval castle complete with toy soldiers—"I keep it here because I have a three-year-old at home," he explains. Seated in a director's chair is a lifesize paper skeleton. Murals of mountain scenes adorn the walls. Trousdale, who is thirty, looks like a mountain man with his camouflage pants, red shirt, bushy beard, and long red hair joined in a ponytail.

The disparate directors seem to work in perfect tandem. They collaborate on some things and specialize individually in others. Wise directs the actors in voice-recording sessions, explaining the emotion of the scene. Wise spends much time with the animators and with the art director, Brian McEntee, on color models. Trousdale oversees the live-action filming that is used for reference by the animators and works with layout effects and computer graphics. Both are concerned with storyboards, editing, and background.

"A lot of directors are more comfortable with just splitting the movie into sequences and saying, 'Okay, you do this part, and I'll do that part,' " comments Wise. "Gary and I do better when we collaborate; we like splitting up the areas of production more than splitting up the movie."

And if they disagree?

"We hash it out and argue about it until we come to an agreement. Or sometimes we'll bring in a third party, like Roger Allers, the head of story, to be the arbitrator."

What does an animation director do?

"It's like those circus guys who have a bunch of plates spinning on the top of

sticks," Gary suggests. "To keep all the plates spinning takes a lot of running from stick to stick, and occasionally picking up the pieces."

"What a director does in animation is very similar to the director in live action," Kirk theorizes. "Except that you're dealing mostly with artists instead of actors. Typically we work with the story people trying to develop a sequence. We're shown storyboards, and we critique. I'll often make thumbnail sketches to get across what I mean. Gary and I try to give our main creative players a lot of rope, a lot of room to play around, and we try to guide the story but not just make the artists our own hands. It's really important that all get a chance to contribute their best work."

There's a major difference between animation and live action, as Kirk points out: "In live action they shoot a lot of film and then cut it after the fact. We don't have a lot of outtakes and extra footage left over."

Animation is such an expensive process that discarding a completed sequence would be catastrophic. Hence storyboarding is all-important. The editing of a feature is done on the storyboards, then in story-sketch reels.

Whereas live-action directors spend much of their days developing scenes with Julia Roberts, Tom Hanks, and the like, directors of animation deal with a different breed of actors. They are the animators, who create acting performances with their drawings.

"When we hand out a group of scenes," Wise says, "I talk a great deal about the intent of the scene, what is the emotional moment in context with the entire sequence. We'll go through the storyboard and talk about each shot.

"There's a lot of pantomime and acting in these meetings. We stand there and say, 'Well, maybe Belle should do something like this: walk around the rose slowly, hesitate for a minute, and reach out to touch it, but change her mind.' I tend to be sort of physical and animated. That's where my acting in high school comes in handy. I think you'll find that a lot of people in animation have had some acting experience or are just naturally 'hammy' people.

"If the animator knows what the intention is and doesn't stray too far, it usually works out great. The greatest thing comes when an animator takes whatever ideas you have and will 'plus' them. That's been happening a lot on this show."

BEAST :

Arrrrgh!!

TOP: *Beast's cry of anguish as portrayed in story sketches.*

ABOVE: *Robby Benson expressed unexpected intensity in his voicing of Beast.*

Voices: Listening to Actors with Closed Eyes

"Aaahwooah!"

"Eeeouwaah!"

"Waahoaaya!"

Three screams of agony, carefully spaced. They are uttered by Robby Benson, responding to the instruction of the director, Kirk Wise: "Now we need an inarticulate cry of pain, as though you were stabbed in the back. Which is exactly what happened."

Wise sits in a darkened control room of the BMG recording studios on West 44th Street in New York City. He faces Benson, who stands before a microphone in a soundproof studio big enough to hold a symphony orchestra. The actor is the lone figure in the studio, and his concentration is palpable. He seems to be experiencing the torturing pain as Beast is stabbed during the climactic battle with Gaston.

The recording session moves on to the scene where Beast is apparently dying from his wounds. Benson gasps the words to Belle: "At least I get to see you one last time." As with all dialogue, he delivers three interpretations, each with a shade of difference.

"That was good," Wise calls from the control booth. "Let's try it again, and this time stress 'one last time,' which is more important."

After several more readings, Benson seems emotionally exhausted, and Wise calls for a break. The actor walks into the corridor for a cup of coffee. He is thirty-three now, but he still has the youthful look and shy manner that attracted young admirers in films like *Ode to Billy Joe* and *Ice Castles*.

"This kind of recording comes easy to me," he says. "When I was young, I dubbed the children's voices in a lot of foreign films. Everything from *War and Peace* and *The Garden of the Finzi-Continis* to *Godzilla vs. Gamera*. I also did one cartoon, but nothing in the past few years. I'm more excited about [*Beauty and the Beast*] than just about anything I've ever done."

"The casting of the voice for Beast was the most difficult we've had," says Jeffrey Katzenberg, "because it requires such a extraordinary balance. When the film starts out, you see this huge beast who seems like an old character, but underneath he's a kid. A twenty-year-old boy, yet he's this huge ferocious animal.

"Now how do you be a ferocious animal on the outside and inside your heart and gut you're a twenty-year-old? In fact, he's been locked inside a castle for ten years, so in many respects he's a ten-year-old—very impatient, spoiled, which is why the spell was cast on him."

Katzenberg and the production team listened to dozens of voices, but none possessed all the desired qualities. Robby Benson seemed the least likely candidate. After all, his screen image was that of an earnest but immature young man. Yet he invested Beast with a power that was totally unexpected.

"If someone had mentioned Robby Benson to me, I would have laughed at them," Katzenberg admits. "But I have learned from the animation people to ignore the physical persona of a voice you're considering. If you can listen to a voice and not know the embodiment of that person, then you can judge.

"Right now I'm driving Glen Keane nuts. Glen [who is animating Beast] is dying to meet Robby, and I want to hold him off as long as possible. I want Glen to keep his own concept of Beast."

The casting of Belle's voice was not as difficult, though it also required a lot of searching. Wise and Trousdale heard the auditioners with eyes closed because they didn't want their judgment affected by the physical appearance of the actresses. One of those trying out was Paige O'Hara.

"Our ears perked up, our eyes opened, and it was like, 'Hey, not bad,'" recalls Wise. "She had some little hitch, some little tone that made her unique. There was, I think, a little bit of Judy Garland. The more we listened, the more we found she was a really strong actress, equally adept with the light comic scenes as with the very dramatic and heartfelt scenes. She was able to whip up real tears at the drop of a hat."

Others had favored casting Jodie Benson, who had shone as the voice of Ariel

TOP: *The confrontation of Gaston and Beast in three story sketches by Vance Gerry.*

ABOVE: *Paige O'Hara provides youthful vivacity for the voice of Belle.*

At various recording sessions. Beneath or next to each individual pictured is an illustration of the character for which that person provided a voice.

ABOVE: *David Ogden Stiers (Cogsworth), Angela Lansbury (Mrs. Potts), and Jerry Orbach (Lumiere) join in the rousing "Be Our Guest" number.*

OPPOSITE: *At top, bluster and mindless bravado mark Richard White's interpretation of Gaston (RIGHT), while Jesse Corti delivers the dialogue of Gaston's weaselly underling, Lefou (LEFT). At bottom is Rex Everhardt, who gives voice to Belle's inventor father, Maurice.*

in *The Little Mermaid.* Ashman argued that Ariel was more the all-American-girl kind of voice, whereas Paige had the vocal quality of a classic fairy tale.

Casting Mrs. Potts was simple; it was a foregone conclusion that only Angela Lansbury could play the cook turned teapot. Howard Ashman wanted a Maurice Chevalier kind of voice for Lumiere, the candelabrum. Many actors were tested, and Ashman favored Jerry Orbach, whose work he had known in such shows as *42nd Street.*

Cogsworth, the stuffy majordomo turned mantel clock, seemed to be a British type, and several English actors were tested. Then David Ogden Stiers, the pompous officer of television's M*A*S*H, proved to have the pinched quality for the role. Richard White, an opera and stage singer who often starred in *Carousel,* became the villainous Gaston. Jesse Corti, a veteran of *Les Misérables* and *Jesus Christ Superstar,* was cast as Lefou, Gaston's clownish minion. Other major voices are Broadway actor Rex Everhardt as Belle's father, Maurice, and comedienne JoAnne Worley as the wardrobe.

Kirk Wise explains the preponderance of stage-trained actors: "Actors in the theater are required to project more, and that's what is needed in animation."

TOP: *Angela Lansbury provides the voice of Mrs. Potts in the ballad "Beauty and the Beast."*

ABOVE: *Born in Baltimore, Howard Ashman had studied at three universities before trying his luck in the New York theater. At first he worked as a performer and writer of advertising jingles. In 1978, he acquired rights to Kurt Vonnegut's book, God Bless You, Mr. Rosewater, and engaged Alan Menken as composer. The show was staged at the WPA Theater, where Ashman was artistic director. Next, Ashman and Menken wrote the smash hit Little Shop of Horrors.*

Music: "Tale as Old as Time, Song as Old as Rhyme"

Angela Lansbury has come to New York to record songs for *Beauty and the Beast*. The centerpiece is the title ballad, which Mrs. Potts sings as Belle and Beast fall in love. The recording studio is BMG, where Arturo Toscanini once conducted the NBC Symphony—also, Angela recalls, where she recorded the cast album of *Sweeney Todd*.

The conductor, David Friedman, has assembled an orchestra of sixty musicians, New York's finest, enlisted from the city's major orchestras. Gathered before Friedman are the concert masters of the Philharmonic, the Metropolitan Opera, the City Opera, and the City Ballet.

The delegation from California includes Don Hahn, Kirk Wise, and Baker Bloodworth, production manager of *Beauty and the Beast*. The central figures in the control booth are lyricist Howard Ashman and composer Alan Menken. Joining them is Danny Troob, who has orchestrated the music.

Ashman talks confidentially to Miss Lansbury about the scene in which the song takes place. It is a crucial time, when the palace objects finally see the chance to regain their human lives. "Mrs. Potts is the one to express their hopes that the spell can be broken," he says. "She is very warm and motherly."

Miss Lansbury, cozily dressed in a red blouse and brown corduroy slacks, listens intently and then takes her place in the isolation booth for singers. She takes out Ben Franklin glasses and studies the long, connected music sheets. She is concerned that her hands are shaking out of nervousness and the sheets will rustle.

"Don't worry about any noises," Ashman says assuringly over the microphone. "We can eliminate them later. We just want to get the orchestra into your rhythm."

He nods to Friedman in the studio, and the conductor gives the downbeat. The warm, richly orchestrated music begins. Shoulders hunched, Miss Lansbury awaits her cue. Then she begins. Afterward, conductor Friedman looks to Ashman and asks, "Too slow? Too fast? Indifferent?" Ashman replies, "I think it would be more interesting if the orchestra would sit on it a little bit. Pull forward at the first string entrance. By and large, go from A to M without going to Z."

Friedman seems to understand the instructions, and the song begins again. Afterward, he explains to Miss Lansbury: "On the first take I was tight and the orchestra was tight, and you were loose. Next, the orchestra was light and you were light. This time we'll be light and you can be tight."

"Okay," she answers.

Recording continues, with a number of false starts. Finally on take twenty-seven, everything goes right. Ashman's eyes are closed, and tears form at the sides. He turns to Menken, and they nod to each other. Friedman dismisses the orchestra, and Angela takes a break before the chore of repeating a few lines of the song which will be inserted into the final version.

"It's a lovely ballad," she says, "but when I heard it, I said, 'Oh, I can't sing that. I really don't have that kind of vocal equipment. I'm an actress who sings.' I felt I didn't have the sound that the song required.

"Howard didn't want the sound; he wanted all emotion and the drama behind it. He was very, very helpful, and he took away all my fears about not having a real balladeer's voice."

Playing a cartoon character in bits and pieces over a period of months is not difficult for her, she says.

"It's inherent in the words, in the pictures, in the character. I did a great deal of radio, and I think a lot of that training comes in handy.

"I see Mrs. Potts as Mrs. Bridges, the cook of *Upstairs, Downstairs*, who was played by Angela Baddeley. I used her a lot in my mind's eye and in my ear, too. I couldn't use her gravelly voice, but I could borrow her attitude, her pride in her job, her sense of what's right and what's proper. A little bit of cockney, but not so much that it would be unintelligible.

"Oddly enough, I'm borrowing also from Mrs. Lovett [in *Sweeney Todd*]. When she talks, she's that kind of comfy lady, even though she likes chopping up people's bodies and putting them into pies. Regardless, she had some of that very dear kind of London gutter qualities."

During another intermission in recording, Alan Menken sits in an adjoining studio and talks about his musical collaboration with Howard Ashman:

"Like every creative relationship, it has its tensions, but very healthy tensions. We have developed very much of a brother relationship. Howard is a perfectionist, he's driven to get exactly what's in his head, and he always wants it yesterday. I'm very quick, so I give it to him as close to yesterday as I can.

"But I'm somebody who will sit at the piano and let fly. It's fortunate that Howard will just let me go, find what he likes, and then write to it. Or he will write a lyric, and then it comes with a good deal of forethought in terms of how I'm going to set it.

TOP: *Mrs. Potts and back-up singers add warmth to the chilly castle.*

ABOVE: *David Friedman directs an orchestra filled with star symphonic musicians.*

TOP: *Finished animation of Belle in opening sequence.*

ABOVE: *Lyricist Howard Ashman, orchestrator Danny Troob, and composer Alan Menken listen in the control booth. Menken is a New Yorker who entered New York University as a premed student and graduated in music. He began writing words and music to songs at BMI's Lehman Engel Musical Theater Workshop, and some of his work was played in showcase performances.*

"We're a year apart; we both have a Jewish background, a derivation of Eastern European and German. We both like pop music and rock 'n' roll. Howard has the sense that we're very much in the same mold, but our functions are entirely different, though compatible. Howard is a director/librettist, I'm a composer/arranger. We're very much a four-armed animal when we're working together."

Menken explains how he and Ashman wrote the songs for *Beauty and the Beast*. First Ashman devised with the writer and directors where songs were needed to further and enhance the plot.

The opening song, "Belle," sung as Belle strolls through the village, needed to be energetic and charming, yet classical in nature. Menken sought inspiration from Bach and Haydn with a little bit of Mozart. He worked out a rhythmic vamp on the piano, then a beat and a melody. Ashman contributed lyrics, and they taped the song. They reworked it until "Belle" was completed.

About the title song of *Beauty and the Beast*, Menken comments: "Simplicity is the key. It's very simple emotion, it's very short, and it has a very simple arc to it. The song is sung in the foreground by Angela Lansbury as the teapot while Belle and the Beast waltz in the background. Angela reflects all the objects' feelings about Belle and the Beast coming together. They've been waiting for years for Beast to fall in love and be loved so they can stop being household objects and become human again.

"It's amazing. The simpler the song, the more impressive the accomplishment. I'm so in awe of Howard's lyric writing in general, and the lyric of this song shows

The waltz of Belle and Beast is a climactic moment, depicted here in a sketch by Roger Allers.

what he can do. It's minimal, it's specific, and it has an emotional simplicity to it. Amazing."

Unlike many composers who contribute only songs to films, Alan Menken prefers to compose the musical score as well. He did so with *The Little Mermaid*, and he is repeating with *Beauty and the Beast*. As he devises musical themes, he records them on tape with his synthesizer and sends them to animators of the scenes—"they cherish them for inspiration as they draw."

As the animation reaches completion, Menken's work of scoring really begins. He writes music for individual sequences and feeds them to his orchestrator, Danny Troob. The orchestrations are returned for Menken's approval. Menken then supervises the recording with a full orchestra in California. It's a huge job. Songs occupy twenty-five minutes of *Beauty and the Beast*, perhaps five minutes of the film are without music. The rest of the seventy-five-minute running time is wall-to-wall musical score.

"Music is of tremendous importance in animation," Menken emphasizes, "not only in sustaining the film as a musical, but also supporting the fantasy, which is the very essence of these films."

Tragically, Howard Ashman died on March 14, 1991, in New York of complications resulting from AIDS. Almost to the end, he was making comments on script changes and approving song recordings played to him by telephone.

Top: Brian McEntee planned Belle's colors to fit the mood of the scenes.

Above: Art Director Brian McEntee headed in the direction of his life's work at an early age, like most of those in the Air Way building. When he was a child, his older sister illustrated fairy tales for him with her own drawings. His instincts led him to the CalArts animation school, then to apprenticeship with Eric Larson at the Disney studio. He started work as an in-betweener on The Fox and the Hound, but discovered that layout and art direction interested him more. After serving as art director on an independent film, McEntee returned to Disney to work in visual development and art direction.

Opposite: In two separate scenes, Belle's coloring allows her to stand out from the backgrounds. Painting of village by Donald Towns; castle interior by Hans Bacher.

Art Direction: "They Should Be Lighted Like Bette Davis"

"The thing I like most is using color to enhance the scene. If you can use color to present the characters in a particular mood or setting, to kind of 'plus' the acting, that's real exciting. When you see it work, you get an emotional response. It goes beyond being visual and becomes more alive."

Brian McEntee is a thirty-three-year-old artist with brushed black hair and oversized dark-rimmed glasses. His workroom is surrounded by sketches of the *Beauty and the Beast*, cathedral interiors, castles, ribald caricatures contributed by his colleagues, and a drawing of a dying rose.

The layman thinks of color in films as conveying certain moods. McEntee theorizes: "To me, color *relationships* are the most important thing. If you have dynamic color relationships, it says something different from subtler relationships. If you're working in a blue color scheme or a red color scheme, how you relate those colors to each other and the values of those colors can set a different mood."

McEntee didn't start work on *Beauty and the Beast* until the story and songs had developed. "I don't believe in imposing a style on a film," he explains. "This is such an emotional film and the visuals are so important to the story. I wanted to know what the film was about before we started saying, 'Okay, this is what the design will be.'"

As *Beauty and the Beast* took form, McEntee found inspiration in a fifty-year-old movie *Bambi*.

"What's wonderful and kind of amazing about *Bambi* is that it feels very real and yet it's very simple," he says. "You look at it, and it's just deceptively simple because they didn't use any tone mattes [subtle shades and shadows on the character], they didn't use even contact shadows [shadows on the ground] most of the time, but their values—the character value, the background value, and the transitions—worked so well that it looked rich. It looked as if there were more production values on *Bambi* than on any other picture."

The art design of *Beauty and the Beast* is seasonal, McEntee points out:

"In the beginning of the film it's autumn, so we have predominantly warm colors. When Belle first reaches the castle, we move into cooler colors with the onset of winter. Later it starts to warm back up.

"It's almost like a dovetail effect, because we start off with warm colors in the background and Belle in blue. She's the only one in blue in the whole sequence. For

two reasons: for legibility, and because she is different from the others in the village. It says something about her character, that's she's blue, she doesn't fit.

"Then she gets to the castle. It's dark and scary somehow, not a happy moment. She's in blue, and everything's blue. After she's been in the castle for a while, she has a change, and she's in a warm costume. The castle is still very coolish, and gradually she warms it up. So we go through a kind of dovetail of progressing of color: from her being cool to warming, then from warming to cooling [when danger comes to the castle]. Then back to warming at the end. It's spring again, with a full release of color."

McEntee confesses his fondness for "a certain cartoon aspect to color—I don't want to do reality. I like pushing a color. After all, animation is caricature. If you animate directly from the rotoscope of live action, it isn't very interesting. But if you push it, if you caricature, then all of a sudden it becomes very interesting. The same way with color. If you push it a little further than reality, then you have something special."

Intensifying the character colors is especially vital when they are played against a gloomy castle interior or the bleakness of the forest.

"The characters are what the eye is supposed to see," McEntee reasons. "They are the actors. Just as they used to work on lighting Bette Davis when she was in a big starring role, so it is with animated characters."

Layout: Putting the Fun Back In

Ed Ghertner, the layout supervisor, shares an office with Brian McEntee, the art director. They work hand-in-hand to create the look of *Beauty and the Beast*, fashioning everything from village carts to Beast's castle.

Right now Ghertner is building the castle. He displays some of his preliminary drawings, remarking, "They don't give enough detail; we're trying to give it a more baroque, French look. Also I'm splitting the backgrounds for the castle into several levels. When Maurice enters the gates and turns to see the castle, it will have tremendous depth like a multiplane shot.

"This is the first picture that we've done in a long time that has separate locales, where we can put mood into each one, rather than have the whole picture

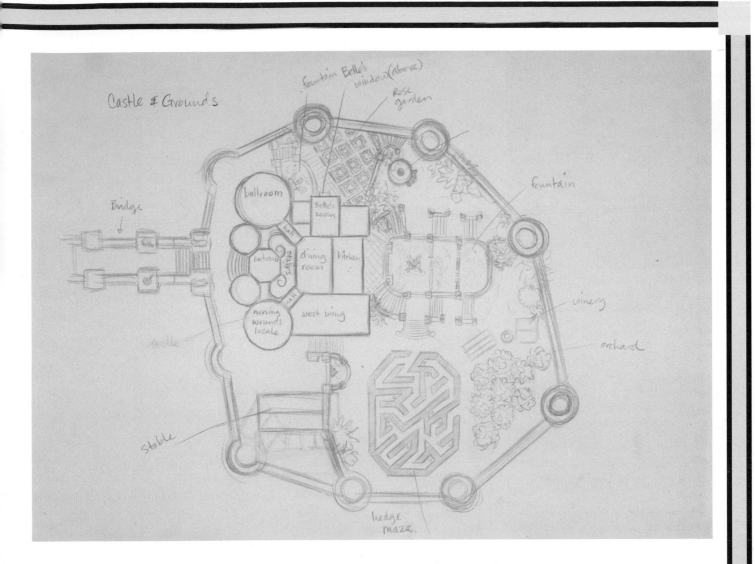

Castle & Grounds

Production planners even supplied a floor plan of the castle.

resemble one painting. We have Belle's house; Maurice's workshop; the tavern, where Gaston does his plotting; and the castle.

"The challenge in having so many different things to design in layout is to make the setting match the emotions of the characters. Everything has to be in balance, especially with the magical theme of this picture. We don't want it to be gothic, but there must be gargoyles, and it must have an emotional look."

Ghertner has strong ideas about layout, especially perspective and staging. "There is a tendency in this business of putting the horizon in the middle of the field, which makes everything look flat," he expounds. "Or trying to do a down shot so you can get more characters in a scene. That's a lazy man's way of staging.

"For the castle objects like Cogsworth and Mrs. Potts, we're going with a low horizon, to put the audience on the same level with the characters. When you start disassociating the camera angles from the characters, your audience becomes a third party. You tend to alienate them from the picture."

Ghertner deplores the trend toward more realism in animated films: "To me they've lost character; they're almost like documentaries. I don't think that's what people want to see. Our layout has been trying to mimic live action, and some of us would like to reverse that trend. On *Beauty and the Beast* we're doing it. We use stage lighting. Layout has become formularized, and I think it lost a lot of its sense of fun. I think there's a possibility of putting the fun back in."

TOP: *Glen Keane analyzed a host of wild animals, from wolves to a gorilla, before arriving at his concept of Beast.*

ABOVE: *Animator Glen Keane, who draws Beast, has an open, freckled face, brown hair, and a look and manner that is more Huck Finn than Godzilla. Drawing is in his blood. His father, Bil Keane, created the syndicated comic strip "The Family Circus." Growing up in Arizona, Glen decided not to follow in his father's footsteps but to pursue the more traditional art of painting. "But at CalArts I discovered animation, or it discovered me," he says, "and well, it just felt right. I've always been kind of a ham actor inside."*

Animation: Enter the Actors

GLEN KEANE: A MAN AMID BEASTS

He labors in a bestiary, surrounded by creatures that would chill your blood. A gorilla glowers from the wall. A lion stares menacingly, ready to pounce. A bear stands ready to crush an intruder with its paws. The head of a buffalo hangs over the room, along with a boar with fierce-looking tusks. A bearskin is spread against a wall. A walrus and a tiger add to the collection.

All these contribute to what Glen Keane calls "an evolutionary mess"—Beast.

The evolution took place over the period of a year. When Keane realized he would be animating Beast, he began studying zoo animals. During preproduction work in England, he visited the London Zoo almost every day on his walk to work. Keane became fascinated with Boris, a large, fierce mandrill, a species of baboon. "I just fell in love with the facial structure," he recalls. He also found inspiration from his daily visit to the wolves.

Keane had a productive encounter with Caesar, a six-hundred-pound, distinctly antisocial gorilla at the Los Angeles Zoo. The attendants warned Keane that Caesar disliked visitors and would try to scare him. Keane relates:

"There were bars between me and him, and he looked at me and just raced at the cage and bang! he slammed against the doors. I had my sketchbook out, trying to draw him, and he looked at me again, and he raced and bang! hit the bars and stared at me, expecting me to run away. I kept imagining how I would feel seeing this huge animal [in the wild]; that's how Belle must feel with Beast. I got that inspiration from being there next to him."

With the help of Boris and Caesar and a host of other creatures, Beast began to take form. Keane worked closely with sculptor Ruben Procopio on a model that provided a three-dimensional view of the character.

"That's finished the way he's going to look in the picture," Keane says, appraising the foot-high statue. "But in order to reach that point, the first challenge was to design a beast that felt real, felt like a real animal from earth. It was easy to design an alien. It's easy to come up with a crazy conglomeration of tusks and horns and appendages that make him beastly.

"But can you design something that looks like God created him as an animal here on earth? The only way to do that was to study animals that were around. The animal that most inspired me was the buffalo. There seems to be an incredible power and size in a buffalo. But he has very sad, cow eyes that say there's a gentleness inside of him.

"If you look at Beast, you'll see the beard and muzzle stem from the buffalo, as well as the feeling in the eyes. The gorilla, though, has a great, expressive brow, and we used this for Beast. We went for a very lionlike mane around the neck. Then we borrowed the tusks from that boar up there on the wall, also the hair on the nose. The little hair on the neck is from the ibis; it can come up and down. If he's angry, or if Belle is soothing him, it raises up. At one point, she's binding his wounds and she hurts him a little bit. Ugh! his hair all stands on end. The horns on his head are just something we gave him ourselves. He's got a big tail like a wolf's, and his body is generally like a bear, but with a wolf's legs."

Keane went directly from CalArts to the Disney studio in 1974, when Ollie Johnston, Frank Thomas, Milt Kahl, Eric Larson, and other Disney greats were still practicing their magic.

"They had an incredible energy and stamina," says Keane. "I remember Ollie was constantly working, always working. I wouldn't see him in the commissary, I wouldn't see him taking breaks, he just worked. He brought his own brown-bag lunch."

The twenty-one-year-old assistant was falling asleep because of the repetition of drawing while Johnston remained enthusiastic at his work.

"I see now that those men were really into their characters. They didn't approach their animation as just drawings they were doing, one after another. They were acting, they were living, performing onstage."

Keane's rare talent was soon recognized, and he worked on scenes in *The Rescuers* and *Pete's Dragon*. As supervising animator on *The Fox and the Hound*, he created the bear fight. He animated Willie the Giant in *Mickey's Christmas Carol*, then the criminal genius Ratigan in *The Great Mouse Detective* which gave him the chance to create a character of strength and dimension.

Lest he be typed as an animator of giants and villains, Keane next undertook Ariel in *The Little Mermaid*—"that was something that really tapped into emotions and feelings more than I ever had before." Next he created a magnificent sixty-foot-wingspan eagle for *The Rescuers Down Under*.

Beauty and the Beast affords Keane the challenge of "what I want to have happen in terms of animating heart and emotion, at the same time doing a character that's bigger than life. Beast combines all sorts of wild animals together in the character and emotions of a twenty-one-year-old guy who's insecure, wants to love, to be loved, but has this ugly exterior and has to overcome this.

Evolution of Beast from an early Chris Sanders sketch to Glen Keane's gorilla/mandrill and the final design.

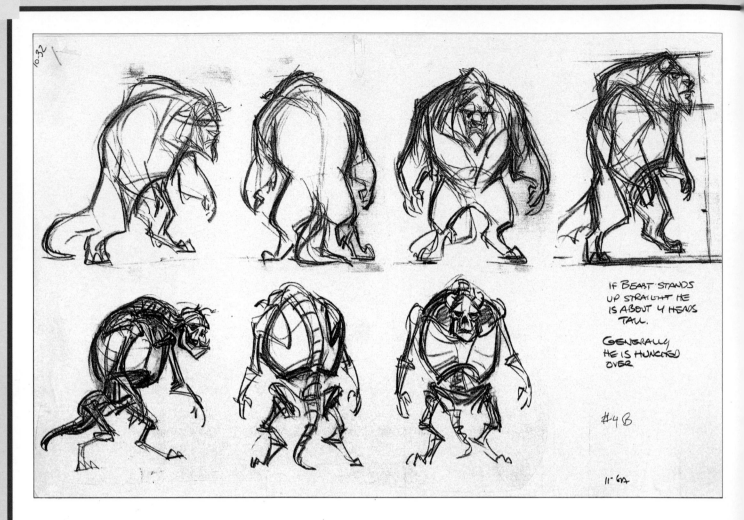

IF BEAST STANDS UP STRAIGHT HE IS ABOUT 4 HEADS TALL.

GENERALLY HE IS HUNCHED OVER

#4B

TOP: *Analysis of Beast's structure by Glen Keane.*

ABOVE: *Glen Keane's rough drawing of the first time Belle sees Beast transformed into the prince.*

OPPOSITE: *The animator also depicted the power of Beast.*

"Usually in our pictures, the characters have an outside obstacle to overcome: the witch in *Snow White*, the stepmother in *Cinderella*. In *Beauty and the Beast*, his enemy is really himself. It's that selfishness of the beast inside him that he has to conquer and overcome."

The keys to Beast, Keane reflects, are the eyes, the hands, and how he moves. "The eyes are the window to his soul. It's in the eyes that we're going to get the clue that this guy is developing his potential, that he can actually love this person and prove he is more than a beast. He's got a heart and feelings.

"It's not just the eyes, it's how he holds her. It impressed me watching *Gorillas in the Mist* and seeing how the gorillas would so gently touch the babies. They're big, powerful figures and they look fierce. But they showed with the movement of their hands that what you saw as ferocity really wasn't. That was Beast, but there's gentleness inside.

"Jeffrey Katzenberg said he wanted to see this character as a beast who is trapped between two worlds. He's neither animal nor man. He's not entirely comfortable in either world. I thought that was really good. He can run on all fours, or he can stand up on two. What happens is that his beast nature takes over control when he becomes angry, and he reverts to one-hundred percent beast. When Belle coaxes him around to his human side, he's gentle, kind, and able to cry.

"To me, he's the deepest character we've ever had."

TOP RIGHT: *Counterpoint to Beast: the handsome guy with the heart of a pig.*

ABOVE: *Animator Andreas Deja remembers nothing of his birthplace, Gdansk, in Poland. In 1958, when Andreas was a year old, the family escaped to West Germany. The Dejas spent months in a refugee camp before being relocated. Andreas started drawing pictures in kindergarten, and he never stopped. His future was decided when he finally saw animation.*

OPPOSITE: *Andreas Deja's drawings of Gaston's arms* (TOP) *and Gaston at his macho best in the tavern number* (BOTTOM).

BELOW: *The early swaggering Gaston.*

ANDREAS DEJA: "LOS ANGELES IS FULL OF GASTONS"

"We didn't have television for the longest time, and then it was black-and-white TV," Andreas Deja remembers of his childhood. "They would run *The Wonderful World of Disney*, and Walt would be speaking fluent German, dubbed. They would show clips of *Pinocchio* or *Bambi*, and there was this fascination, a pounding of the heart. Even when I was four or five years old."

When he was ten, *The Jungle Book* came to Düsseldorf. He earned enough money for a ticket, and "I was totally blown away by the whole thing." So much so that he sat down and addressed a letter to "Walt Disney Studios, America." Looking up words in the German-English dictionary, he inquired how to become a Disney animator. A form letter returned with the suggestion not to copy Mickey Mouse or Donald Duck but to develop his own skills in drawing humans and animals.

Andreas continued drawing through high school, the army, and art school. Reading about the training that Eric Larson was giving young animators at the Disney studio, he decided to write Larson. Andreas received a reply.

He sent drawings to Larson, who responded encouragingly. He wrote that he was visiting Germany for a couple of days on a cruise and perhaps they could meet. Andreas drove seven hours to talk to Larson on shipboard in Hamburg. For the German-speaking young man it was a thrilling experience, yet troubling. "My English wasn't very good at the time, and I just got so frustrated that I couldn't understand every word this wise old man was saying."

Deja's art spoke for him. He submitted a portfolio to the studio and was invited for a test period with Larson in 1980. His talent was unmistakable, and after an eight-week trial, Deja was hired full-time.

His first months at Disney weren't easy. He knew enough English to ask questions and understand the answers, but his conversation was sketchy. Jokes and slang flew over his head. Deja learned that the studio was planning a feature called *The Black Cauldron*. He read the Lloyd Alexander books and started to sketch his ideas for the characters and the action. The studio approved of his work.

Deja and another newcomer, Tim Burton, were teamed to design and research characters for *The Black Cauldron*. "Tim's designs were so outlandish and far-out, and mine were solid Disney drawing, so they thought, 'Hey, put these two together and something unique might come out.' It didn't quite work. You couldn't change Tim's drawings, really. They were great the way they were."

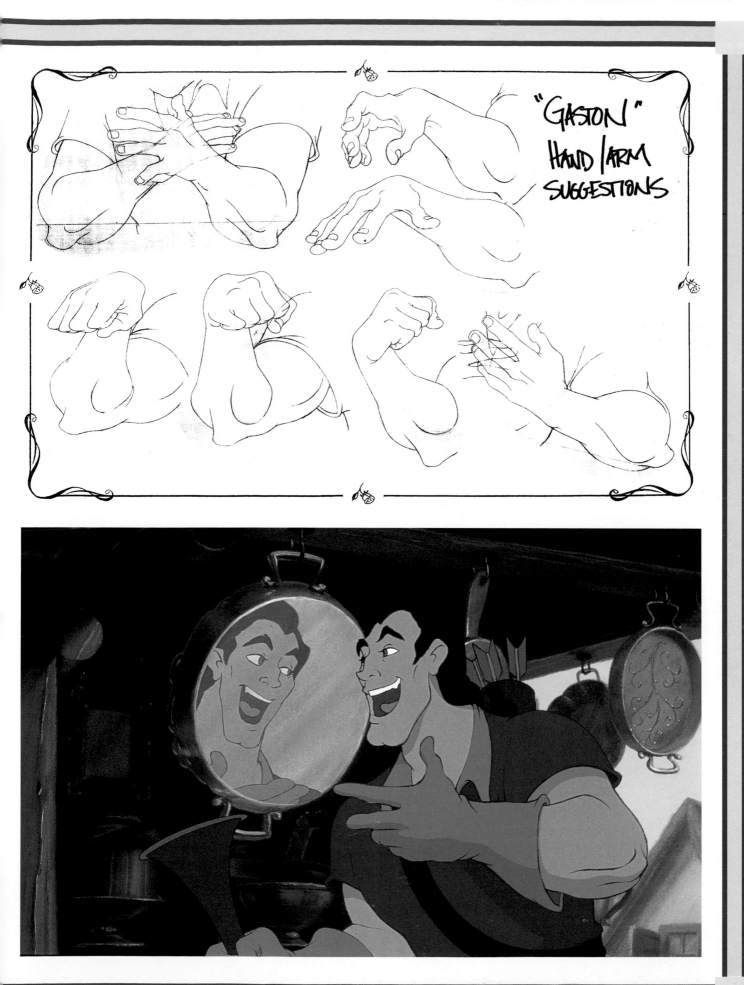

"GASTON"
HAND/ARM
SUGGESTIONS

ABOVE: *Andreas Deja's animation drawings.*

OPPOSITE TOP: *Live-action photography of an actor in the Gaston role provided Deja with a guide for animation overlaid on a color model.*

OPPOSITE BOTTOM: *Finished animation of Gaston with the Bimbettes.*

Burton moved on to make his short films, *Frankenweenie* and *Vincent*, while Deja remained with *The Black Cauldron*. As a newcomer to the studio, he was confused and frustrated by the disarray on the production. Lacking guidance, he produced animation he now considers stiff and ungainly.

After work on *The Great Mouse Detective*, and *Oliver & Company*, Deja was enlisted by Richard Williams for the international crew working on *Who Framed Roger Rabbit* in England. It was a period of artistic flowering for Deja, who animated many of the Toon cameos as well as scenes with Bob Hoskins and Roger Rabbit. He contemplated Williams's offer to stay and work on the long-planned *The Thief and the Cobbler*, but finally decided that his destiny lay with Disney. He was assigned to *The Little Mermaid*, animating King Triton, and later he animated Mickey Mouse in *The Prince and the Pauper*.

Andreas Deja, who is thirty-three with curly brown hair and a neat mustache, was assigned Gaston, the bluff, vain bully of *Beauty and the Beast*. His first efforts were rejected by Jeffrey Katzenberg.

"No, no, no, he's not handsome enough," said the production boss.

"But he's a villain," Deja replied. "Can't we just juice him up?"

Katzenberg explained the concept of the film: "It's not about Beauty and the Beast. It's a matter of 'don't judge a book from its cover.' The Beast is ugly, Gaston's handsome. The Beast has a heart of gold, Gaston's a pig. It's got to be graphically very clear."

Deja reworked Gaston, making him more handsome but striving to give him a wide range of emotions. "He becomes a villain," Deja analyzes. "You don't really think he's a killer when you first meet him. You get an idea of a type. When I saw the first test reels, I thought, 'God, I know such people; Los Angeles is full of them.' You know, the guys who have every hair in place, who just adore themselves. They're everywhere, and there seem to be more and more of them."

Deja makes use of live action of an actor portraying Gaston, but he doesn't study photostats. Instead he makes notes from the video, then animates from his notes. A tilt of the head or a certain expression will inspire the artist, then he pushes it a bit further. He has his own style of drawing.

"Animation is like two different things," he theorizes. "The first approach is out of the stomach, on paper. You just let your emotions go, and you scribble. I can use only one pencil for that, a blue one. It is soft, and I can't do stiff drawing with it.

"I bring it onto paper very, very quickly. I can animate a whole scene, roughly, within half an hour. I test the drawings on video to see the pattern. Then I take my sharp pencil and refine it, make some sense out of it, make sure the form is there and refine the expressions."

On the wall of Deja's room is Milt Kahl's work from *Ichabod*. Andreas comments: "Milt's animation goes through the fingertips. It's not just this thing animated and left to cleanup. Milt drew it all and controlled everything. It's more *your* animation that way. So I go as far as I can with drawing it out."

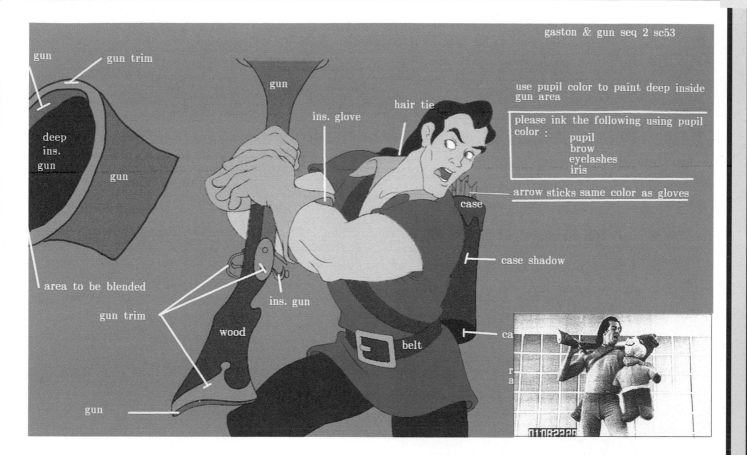

gun

gun trim

deep
ins.
gun

gun

area to be blended

gun trim

wood

ins. gun

gun

gun

ins. glove

hair tie

use pupil color to paint deep inside
gun area

please ink the following using pupil
color :
        pupil
        brow
        eyelashes
        iris

arrow sticks same color as gloves

case

case shadow

belt

TOP: *Early story sketches of the heroine.*

ABOVE: *At twenty-three, animator James Baxter has worked nowhere but in Disney animation, and* Beauty and the Beast *is his fourth film. The neat brown beard does little to hide his youth. But when he draws, his work displays the strength and assurance of a veteran. When he speaks, you hear the gentle tones of Bristol, England, where he was born.*

JAMES BAXTER: PROMOTED ON THE BATTLEFIELD

At sixteen, James Baxter was "messing about" with animation, moving cutouts before a super-8-mm camera. He slogged through a year of animation studies at the West Surrey College of Art and Design, discovered that he didn't like the course or the teachers, and dropped out.

During his summer vacation, he heard that *Who Framed Roger Rabbit* was starting production in London. He submitted a videotape of his work and was hired as an in-betweener.

"I was assisting Andreas for a while, which was very helpful," Baxter recalls. "I started getting hands and feet to do, then short action scenes of the weasels. I moved on to dialogue stuff with the weasels and ended up doing little bits of Jessica and one or two shots of Roger.

"It was my first film. I think it was like a battlefield promotion. They were under such pressure that they needed anyone who could hold a pencil. I think anyone who showed any kind of potential whatsoever would have immediately been given something to do. It would have taken me a lot longer had I been around in a slacker period of production."

Moving to California, Baxter was assigned to *The Little Mermaid*, working with Deja on Triton and with Glen Keane on Ariel. For *The Rescuers Down Under*, he drew "a grab bag of everything, from cockroaches to albatrosses to mice."

Baxter received another "battlefield promotion" on *Beauty and the Beast*. Don Hahn had become acquainted with Baxter's work on *Who Framed Roger Rabbit* and was impressed by his grace of movement with human characters. Baxter became the animator of Belle.

He works surrounded by photos and drawings of female figures, some of them nude. He studies the tape of Shari Stoner, who posed for the live-action scenes of

Belle, "to get a sense of perspective and weird angles that you might not be able to come up with by yourself."

Baxter may examine the live action frame by frame, but he rarely traces anything. Much of the actress's movement is extraneous and must be eliminated or the animation will look strange and unnatural. One of Baxter's guides is a sketch of Belle drawn by Roger Allers, the story man. Baxter recalls: "The directors [Gary Trousdale and Kirk Wise] latched on to that and said, 'Ooh, that's nice, let's use that with the more exotic eyes, slightly turned up at the edges, and fuller lips. Thicker eyebrows, too, to add to a more European look.'"

Baxter usually draws with a red pencil, because it can be easily erased. His first drawings are rough—"just to get the weight, the balance, with hardly any indication of costume." Then he may put another sheet over the drawing and start to refine it. That version goes to the cleanup person, who makes a line drawing with a fine graphite line.

For a complicated scene like Belle spinning, Baxter will draw every frame or every other frame. But if Belle is singing or in a more relaxed scene, he will do every four or six frames. He can average twenty to twenty-five a day.

Baxter's work is supplemented by seven other animators, including Mark Henn in Florida, and he tries to oversee most of their product. The backup is needed. Belle occupies almost a half hour in *Beauty and the Beast*, almost double any other character.

In approaching Belle, Baxter says, "I attempt to go with gut feelings about the story and her part in the story. How I feel she would react in certain situations. I don't go to the extent of writing it all down. I don't try to analyze, 'What's her favorite food?' and stuff like that.

"You start out at the beginning with a certain notion of what you want to do in terms of a graphic style—proportions, personality, different hair, different eyes. But

Finished animation of Belle.

that can be a little tricky, because she has to fit in with the rest of the designs for the film. It has to please everyone, and things fall by the wayside. It has to look 'Disney'"

Asked to define the "Disney" look, Baxter inquires of fellow animator, Rick Farmiloe, who shares the room and draws the clownish Lefou. Both agree that the Disney style in women dates back to the soft, rounded appearance of Freddie Moore's females in the Thirties and Forties, together with Milt Kahl's more angular style of the Sixties, as exemplified by *Sleeping Beauty.*

"You try to do radical things at the beginning of a movie, but invariably they get shot down," comments Baxter, "because they don't live up to what the public now has come to expect from Disney."

But he observes that both Ariel in *The Little Mermaid* and Belle in *Beauty and the Beast* veer from the traditional Disney heroine. Both are real, strong-willed women and not simply "damsels in distress."

"It seems to be very difficult in a lot of the stories to have the female lead be the motivator of the action, instead of just sitting there and having things happen to them. A bit like *Cinderella*, where the Fairy Godmother turns up and does everything for her. There seems to be little Cinderella can do to motivate what happens. The mice make her dress, and all she does is say, 'Thank you.'

"Ariel was a very, very different kind of heroine. The good thing about *Beauty and the Beast* is that we've got a much stronger hero with the Beast, stronger than Prince Eric ever was. He's at least on a par with Belle as far as his character goes, and in certain scenes they try to make him an even deeper character than Belle. So I have my work cut out for me."

LORNA COOK: MAKING A CHARACTER THINK

Animator Lorna Cook grew up in Burbank, not far from the Disney studio, and her parents predicted she would work there one day. "No way," Cook responded, and she pursued an education in fine arts. But a fascination with animation kept nagging at her, and in 1972 she enrolled in the Disney training program. She worked in various capacities, including animation on *Pete's Dragon*, then left with the Bluth group in 1979. Ten years later, she returned to Disney, and now she is one of the animators of Belle for *Beauty and the Beast*. Like James Baxter, Lorna Cook is exhilarated by a different kind of Disney heroine. She sees Belle as a well-read, knowledgeable girl who is mature for her years—about fifteen.

"This seems like her first real romance, yet she's smart enough to know what

she doesn't want," says the artist. "Which is kind of a refreshing female role. Ariel was headstrong, but boom—she sees Prince Eric, and that's it. I like the way Belle thinks a little more.

"Belle is not an easy character," Lorna observes. "Any human character is going to give you fidgets if you don't take heed of how the live action works, and that takes a lot of time. What you try to do is not be overly literal. But there are subtleties here that I just wouldn't be able to see if I didn't have the [photo] stats."

In approaching the character, Lorna started by thinking of actresses who could portray Belle.

"I tried to stay away from what I thought were stereotypes," she says. "Vivien Leigh and Grace Kelly are wonderful to watch, fine examples of feminine beauty. But I tried to think that Belle was someone a little—well, not real quirky, but someone who had beauty of her soul. It's very hard to transcend pencil and paper with such things, but I tried to think of different events in my life. Moments, if you will. Acts of kindness, or things that were good examples for me. Not just a pretty face."

Lorna and others animating Belle coordinate their work with James Baxter, the supervising animator. They are cast for their scenes in accordance to their strong points.

What are Lorna's?

"Personality scenes, medium closeups, I think. I really love doing that. Action scenes are terrific, they keep you limber, and you should be able to do everything as an animator. But to me, the most fun is making a character *think*. Giving the audience a chance to feel the emotion. When you can pull that off, you've really accomplished something."

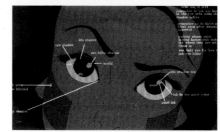

Color model shows Belle's "warpaint" blush, which in final production is blended to create rosy cheeks.

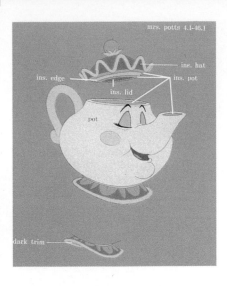

Animator David Pruiksma, who is thirty-three, grew up in a Virginia suburb of Washington, D.C., and became an early addict of animation from the Sunday night Disney television show. Two years at the Pratt Institute in Brooklyn gave him some background in film, but his teachers advised him to go to California if he wanted to learn animation. David took the hint and enrolled at CalArts. He was hired by Disney in his second year, did in-betweens on Mickey's Christmas Carol, became an animating assistant, then animator, on The Great Mouse Detective, and animated the seahorse messenger and Flounder in Mermaid.

TOP: An ink and paint model sketch of Mrs. Potts.

TOP RIGHT: Finished animation of Mrs. Potts and Chip.

ABOVE: Mrs. Potts in an early story sketch, by Brian Pimental, of the "Be Our Guest" number.

DAVID PRUIKSMA: HOW TO MAKE A TEAPOT WALK

"Trust the Process."

That's the sign on David Pruiksma's desk. He explains:

"Sometimes I get into a scene, and I think, 'This isn't going the way I think,' and I get kinda nervous at the beginning. Can I really pull it off? Then I remember that it's all part of the process. If the drawings don't look good now, at some point I'll refine them and hone them down, and they'll be okay in the end. I don't think I've ever downright failed on a scene. I've done scenes that I know I could improve, but I don't think I've ever failed. And I have to remember that, when I'm starting out. It's like, trust that process, you're going to get there. It may take you ten drawings to get one good one, but that's part of the process."

Pruiksma may have found the ultimate test of the process in his assignment for Beauty and the Beast: Mrs. Potts, the cook turned teapot. When Pruiksma first started on the character, a waggish coworker gave him a porcelain teapot with the suggestion: "Oh, we can shoot live action with it; we'll just attach it to wires, and we'll drag it around."

Pruiksma's inspiration comes first and foremost from Angela Lansbury. He has never met the star, but he knows her intimately. He has studied her on Murder, She Wrote and television talk shows and in most of her movies, from Gaslight to The Manchurian Candidate. He has photos of her on his walls, and he listens over and over again to her voice in the Beauty and the Beast dialogue and the title song.

"I want to get a lot of her mannerisms, because she has a really distinctive way of acting," says Pruiksma. "She is very subtle. She's very contained in her movements, I've noticed. She does many little head tilts and short quirky head shakes and things like that when accentuating dialogue. I really like that. As I get into more acting and dialogue scenes on her I want to get those sharp little head nods and things. It's going to be interesting if I can pull it off."

Making a teapot talk is one thing. How about making it walk?

"Mrs. Potts doesn't exactly walk across a background," Pruiksma explains. "She sorta hops. I stretch and squash the pedestal a little bit and use it as sort of feet, other times a skirt, but I still keep the basic structure solid. That's what makes her believable. I pretty much have her hop wherever she goes. Sometimes she might favor one side of the pedestal and then the other, like waddling. That seems to work very well. It helps

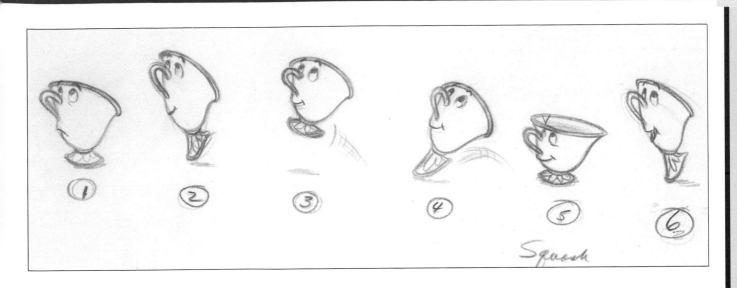

Squash

when she's moving along to have her lid pop on and off. I use that for an accent."

Pruiksma admits: "I had some frustrating years as a young animator. I just wanted to make everything broad and funny and flamboyant, but Mark Henn and I would always be given sentimental scenes. Mark is an expert at subtlety and acting. I'd get so angry because he kept pulling me back and pulling me back. I kept thinking I *had* pulled back, and he'd pull me back some more. Consequently, I sort of developed a flair for doing subtle, expressive characters. I've been on those ever since."

For research on Mrs. Potts, Pruiksma visited the "morgue," where old drawings, paintings, and research materials are stored. He studied everything he could find on animated porcelain. When it was decided to expand the role of Mrs. Potts's son Chip, everyone pointed to David Pruiksma as the man for the job. He has been working on models for Chip, who will move like his mother but on a smaller scale.

"I'm having the same problem with Chip that they had on *Bambi*: the eye-mouth configuration," he says, explaining with a drawing. "The way Chip is designed, his eyes are high on the face, then the handle comes out [as the nose], and the mouth is underneath the handle low on the face. The problem is, the eyes are far from the mouth, so it's harder to get the eye-cheek-mouth relationship that makes a face expressive and appealing. I'm going to have to work out something on that."

The mirror beside Pruiksma's drawing board is a constant point of reference.

"I don't see how you can get the subtlety of acting without it," he observes. "I could sit and struggle all day at my desk trying to draw an expression from memory. But until I actually do it in the mirror a couple of times and sort of draw myself doing it, I don't get the subtlety I want into it.

"I used the mirror a lot when I was doing Bernard on the last picture, *The Rescuers Down Under*. After the picture was out, many people came up to me and said, 'Boy, that Bernard looked just like you!' I think a lot of animators' drawings look like them. It only shows that they're putting a lot of themselves into their work."

This brings up the old saw that all animators are actors. Pruiksma heartily agrees: "I think that's what makes Disney animation what it is. It's the heart of it: the acting. Almost anyone can be taught to make drawings move around. We all drew in our textbooks and flipped the pages to make the figure move. But to make it *live*, to make it *act*—to make it *believable*—that's something we're *all* still working toward."

TOP: *The teacup Chip has the mobility of a small boy.*

MIDDLE: *Conceptual sketch of how Mrs. Potts moves.*

ABOVE: *A story sketch from "Be Our Guest."*

Beauty & the Beast
production 0254

COGSWORTH UPDATE: 1/14/91

WRONG   RIGHT   NO CHANGE ON HOUR HAND

MINUTE-HAND HAS BEEN RE-DESIGNED THINNER, SHARPER THAN ORIGINAL "HEART-SHAPED" VERSION.

PLEASE USE THIS MODEL FOR ALL RUFFS AND CLEANUPS FROM THIS POINT.
— W.F.

COGSWORTH'S BACK!

NO DECORATIONS ON THE BACK OF HIS "WIG."

THE KEY IS HINGED ON A POST IN THE CENTER OF THE BACK OF HIS HEAD.

CARRY SEPARATION LINES TO CLOSE OFF HEAD FROM BODY.

THERE IS ONE LARGE BOLT ON THE BACK OF EACH HAND — NOTHING ON PALMS.

BACK OF BODY IS SOLID WITH NO DECORATION.

BASE/FEET LOOKS EXACTLY THE SAME AS THE FRONT.

Animator Will Finn, who is thirty-two, belongs to the generation who grew up watching Disney, Lantz, and Warner cartoons on TV. Like Andreas Deja in Düsseldorf, Will in upstate New York found his life's work when he saw *The Jungle Book* on the screen. He was studying at the Art Institute of Pittsburgh when the ubiquitous Eric Larson came to town. Will "monopolized a whole day with Eric," who urged the young man to go west if he wanted to be an animator. Larson helped Finn assemble a portfolio that won him a trainee post at Disney in 1979 on *The Fox and the Hound*. After that, Finn spent several years at various other studios, often as a storyman. Returning to Disney, he animated on *Oliver & Company* and was assigned Grimsby, Prince Eric's mentor in *The Little Mermaid*. "I love that kind of British deadpan character," Finn confesses. On *The Rescuers Down Under* he animated the Chairmouse—another "dry Brit."

Will Finn's reasoning in the design of Cogsworth.

"COGSWORTH"

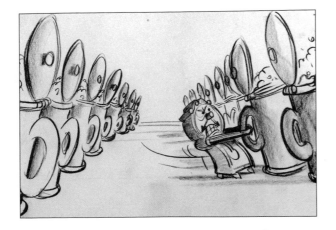

WILL FINN: AN ELEMENT CALLED DISNEYITE

With his bushy hair and wild, bespectacled eyes, Will Finn seems the likely candidate to animate Cogsworth, the castle majordomo turned mantel clock. When Gary Trousdale and Kirk Wise proposed Cogsworth to Finn, he was uncertain at first.

"I saw the storyboards, and I thought: What could you do with a little talking clock?' But I got very excited when I heard David Ogden Stiers's audition—he was so funny and incredibly inventive."

Stiers became a prime inspiration, and Finn studied him on M*A*S*H and at recording sessions. Other sources included John Houseman in *The Paper Chase* and *Fawlty Towers*'s John Cleese. Finn also recalls a breakthrough when he saw John Gielgud in an interview on PBS:

"Gielgud would listen to the questions and look directly at the interviewer," says Finn. "But when he answered, he would always look away or at the ceiling, or even close his eyes. I used this a lot on Grimsby—the head would turn away, even though the eyes may still be looking at the other character."

The next hurdle was the character design itself.

Will Finn admits that in the beginning he was stricken with self-doubt concerning Cogsworth.

"He's wooden, and made up of flat, geometric shapes," Finn explains. "But he turned out to be a lot more flexible than I ever imagined. The subtle part is trying to keep him from looking like just a man in a clock costume. I can twist and stretch him like crazy but I always try to retain the essence of wood. Look at Pinocchio, for example, he has all the flexibility of a human. And Frank Thomas did such a beautiful job on the doorknob character in *Alice in Wonderland*.

"That doorknob was a real inspiration for everyone animating the object characters because it's this fabulously flexible thing, yet you believe he's made entirely of brass. . . . I feel like there's an element called 'Disneyite' that these characters are actually made of. So Cogsworth may be made out of inert materials, but he has all the elasticity of flesh and blood built into him. If you could touch him he would feel like wood, glass, and brass or whatever, but it would have a dimension of a living thing as well."

How does a mantel clock walk?

"It's not easy sometimes," Finn admits. "He's got four little feet and we were going to treat him like a quadruped at first, but Gary [Trousdale] suggested that it would make him look like an octopus or a spider. After trying some walks I realized

Finn is comfortable with offbeat, problematical characters. He analyzes Cogsworth:

"He's a man who has been transformed into this object, and there's a certain amount of discomfort in being wedged into this little wooden frame. But, he has been in there for a while, so he has managed to adapt. I think the hardest part for him is his size—as a human I imagine he was a fairly imposing, portly figure and now he's this little clock only sixteen inches tall. The sheer indignity of not being able to cover the castle grounds with the ease of a full-grown human leaves him fairly stressed out. I'm the same way when I'm on the freeway at rush hour!"

TOP LEFT: *Cogsworth blunders among the beer steins in "Be Our Guest."*

ABOVE: *Animators Will Finn (Cogsworth), Nik Ranieri (Lumiere), and David Pruiksma (Mrs. Potts and Chip) hold symbols of their characters.*

that his personality is so volatile that most of the time he just hops. He's usually bounding or leaping because he has such tiny legs and is so frustrated that he typically covers ground in quick, explosive bursts."

Crucial to the character of Cogsworth is his bristly relationship to Lumiere, the ver-ee French candelabrum. Therein does art imitate life.

Lumiere is animated by Nik Ranieri, another gifted portrayer of offbeat characters, such as *Roger Rabbit*, Ursula the seawitch in *The Little Mermaid*, and Wilbur in *The Rescuers Down Under*.

"On *Rescuers Down Under* Nik and I shared an office together," Will reveals. "Every day was like an episode of *The Odd Couple*—we drove each other nuts! I guess the directors figured we'd be perfect for these two bickering objects. Nik's as flamboyant a showman as Lumiere, and I guess I'm as big a hothead as Cogsworth!"

Maurice Chevalier inspired the suave Lumiere. Blue sketch (TOP); *conceptual drawings* (ABOVE AND RIGHT).

OPPOSITE: *Finished animation from "Be Our Guest"* (TOP) *and Nik Ranieri's model sheet for Lumiere* (BOTTOM).

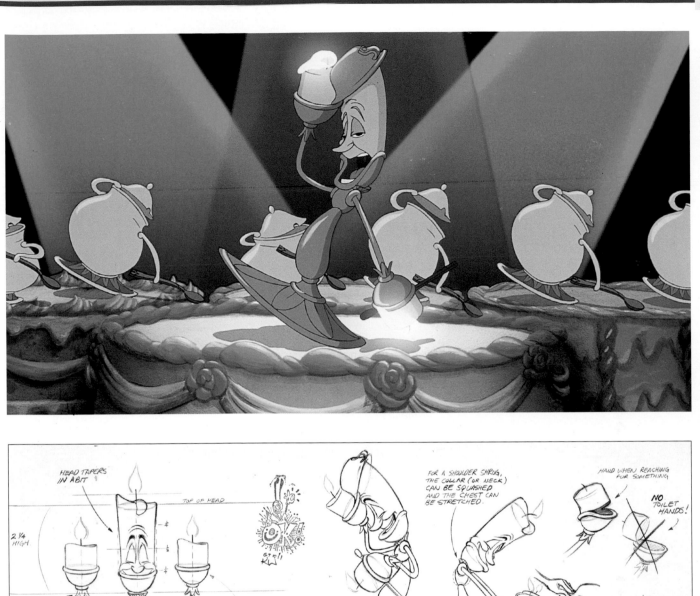

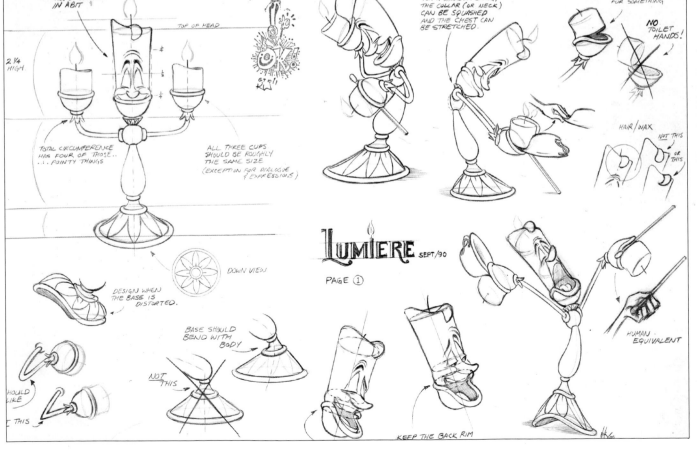

HEAD TAPERS IN A BIT

TOP OF HEAD

2 1/4 HIGH.

TOTAL CIRCUMFERENCE HAS FOUR OF THOSE... ...POINTY THINGS

ALL THREE CUPS SHOULD BE ROUGHLY THE SAME SIZE (EXCEPTION FOR DIALOGUE & EXPRESSIONS)

FOR A SHOULDER SHRUG, THE COLLAR (OR NECK) CAN BE SQUASHED AND THE CHEST CAN BE STRETCHED.

HAND WHEN REACHING FOR SOMETHING

NO TOILET HANDS!

HAIR/WAX

NOT THIS

OR THIS

DOWN VIEW

DESIGN WHEN THE BASE IS DISTORTED.

SHOULD LIKE

THIS

BASE SHOULD BEND WITH BODY

NOT THIS

LUMIERE SEPT/90

PAGE ①

HUMAN EQUIVALENT

KEEP THE BACK RIM

Animator Tom Sito grew up in Brooklyn addicted to the Saturday morning cartoon shows on television. Small wonder he started in animation while still a teenager. After studying at the High School for Art and Design, he worked in commercials, educational television, and Saturday morning cartoons. Bouncing from job to job, he did everything: cel-wiping, inking mattes, assisting on layout, animating, directing.

TOM SITO: HOW TO AVOID ANIMATED PASTA

Tom Sito, a round-faced man with pony-tailed hair, mustache, and goatee, feels a sense of continuity in the animation business. That's because he learned his craft from legendary animators, not at Disney, but at cartoon studios in New York and California with Disney alumni like Art Babbitt and Grim Natwick.

"To meet great animators, then actually to work with them, was just invaluable," he declares. "To me, animation is still a matter of master and apprentice. No matter how good schools become, no matter how the university tries to duplicate the studio experience, to this day the best way to learn animation is to work at the feet of a master animator."

Tom is now thirty-four and astonished to find himself a veteran. At one story conference for *Beauty and the Beast* he gazed around the room and recognized that he was the oldest person there.

Richard Williams hired him to work in England on *Who Framed Roger Rabbit* and that began his "longest gig," for Disney.

"I killed the weasels," Tom says proudly. "Robert Zemeckis, the director, went over the sequence with me and said, 'What I want is "cartoon death." ' So I gave it to him."

Sito was also charged with animating the final scene, the gathering of all the great Toons.

"When I first got this scene, I stared at it for two days," he recalls. "Whenever I would delegate parts to people, *they* would stare at it in horror. We had to calculate we would lose a day every time we added an animator."

Fifteen animators worked furiously, creating as many as twenty-nine levels under the camera. The head count of characters reached one hundred. Even then, Zemeckis sent a FAX instructing Sito: "Put in more Toons." The resulting scene, which took ten weeks to produce, lasted forty seconds on the screen.

Sito's room is crammed with work models of characters in *Beauty and the Beast*. He is creating two major sequences: Gaston's tossing about his cronies in the village and the climactic comic battle between the castle objects and the attacking villagers. He has also been assigned portions of the Beast.

The animator explains his philosophy about crowd scenes:

"You have several characters on one level, and they must all have their personal time in it. There's a group psychology to it, just as in ballet or a successfully visual film.

"There's a graphic sense you have to think about. You have to take note of where the audience's eye is. You have to lead their eye around. You'll notice in earlier films like *Pinocchio* and *101 Dalmatians*, there are huge crowds of characters running around, yet it never looks chaotic; there's a uniformity to it, a graphic uniformity to the frame.

"Some animators try to do crowd scenes, and it just turns into animated pasta. There's all this extraneous movement, and there's somebody inside saying, 'Hey, let's go downtown!' You just can't see what's going on.

"In the scene where Gaston is wrestling his cronies, Gaston clearly has the initiative, and the cronies are subservient, secondary characters. He's leaping on the table and grabbing them and throwing them right and left, tossing them over his shoulder and biting them on the leg.

"So you animate Gaston first, going through his actions with an idea of where the other characters would be. Their actions mustn't overshadow his, or else it would create confusion. There *are* scenes where the catalyst shifts from one to another, so if the character has a line of dialogue, the emphasis would go to him."

Sito approaches each new assignment with a period of brow-furrowing concentration. One of his assistants cracked, "I always dread when Tom looks tired, because it means there's a really hard scene coming up." Sito begins by sketching "some visual shtick, some jokes and things," then seeks the opinions of the story people, layout artists, and directors. Then he starts animating. He seems to thrive on deadlines.

"Once I was joking with George Scribner. I said, 'Animated films are sometimes like battles. You start out with everyone in beautiful lines, flags flying, rifles pointed in the same position. The last two months of production are a melée, with everybody running in all directions and throwing their equipment in the air and screaming. You find out in the end whether you won or not.'"

The decision is made by ticket buyers at the box office. Sito recalls being in New York City when *Who Framed Roger Rabbit* had its premiere. After all the publicity hoopla and the rave reviews, he walked to the Ziegfeld Theater in time for the early evening screening. Police barricades were up, and the six-abreast crowd stretched down the street and around the corner.

Tom says, "That's when I knew we had won the battle."

Tom Sito's animation of Gaston's fight with his cronies. Sito says, "In every scene there's a character who's the catalyst, or the prime mover. There's always one character who is exerting the dynamic that makes the action happen."

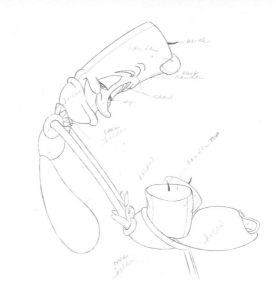

Vera Lanpher, head of Disney's Cleanup Department, seemed predestined to work for Disney. She was born in St. Joseph's Hospital, across Buena Vista Street from the studio. After college she presented her portfolio and started as an in-betweener on Pete's Dragon. *She enjoyed animation, but became intrigued with "actually designing a shape that moved, the final line."*

Cleanup: Achieving the Final Line

For sixty years, Disney animators and cleanup artists maintained a mutually dependent, sometimes uneasy relationship. Vera Lanpher, who heads the ninety-person Cleanup Department for *Beauty and the Beast,* explains:

"Traditionally, department members would literally clean up the animators' drawings. Much of the time, the animators' work would be so clean and beautiful, all we needed to do was clean and touch up the lines. Some would draw rougher; then we would put a new piece of paper over the drawings and copy the lines."

The old system sometimes created friction. Animators were fearful that cleanup people would alter their drawings. The cleanup people sometimes felt they were doing a thankless job.

"That all changed with *The Rescuers Down Under,*" declares Vera. "Management decided to create a better relationship by having the cleanup people work directly with the animators. Now we have carried that a step forward by having one cleanup person overseeing each of the major characters.

"Bill Berg is in charge of Beast. He works closely with the lead animator, Glen Keane, and the others who are animating Beast. Each of them draws the Beast differently, so it's Bill's job to get Beast tied in and drawn so he looks the same throughout the whole film. He redraws every drawing, and, because the animator doesn't always do all the drawings in a scene, he adds in-betweens at the very end.

"Renee Holt does the same for Belle. There are many more animators on Belle than on Beast, so she has an even bigger job of putting Belle together. And it's tougher work because Belle is a female human character.

"It's always a problem, because Disney has created the most beautiful animated females. The human eye is so critical of an animated woman. One little flaw in Belle, and audiences will say, 'Uh-uh, she's not really beautiful,' or, 'She's not a real character.' We've been very, very careful with Belle, to keep her consistent and beautiful."

Vera reviews the work of the nine units of cleanup artists assigned to the nine major characters: Belle, Beast, Gaston, Lumiere, Cogsworth, Mrs. Potts, Lefou, Phillipe, and Maurice. Marty Korth's work on Gaston must be flawlessly handsome,

  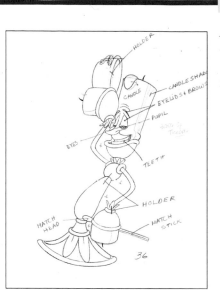

Rick Hoppe's Maurice cleanups warm and appealing, and Emily Jiuliano's Lefou drawings must exude wit and comedy—all male supporting characters, all with a unique approach required by the artist.

As Vera sees it, the cleanup person must have more than the soul of an artist:

"You must also be a team player, and one who has managerial as well as diplomatic skills. The protocol is sometimes quite complex. You have to be a liaison between the directors and the animators. Sometimes the directors have a certain way of seeing a character, and the animators are saying, 'No, we want to do it this way.' Then you're in the middle and must act as liaison between them.

"So you try to say, 'Here, look at this design. Maybe this will work out for both of you.' There has been quite a bit of that on *Beauty and the Beast* because we're dealing with such powerful characters. Belle's personality and Beast's are strong, and so are many of the other characters."

They are also intended to be as real as possible. That was stressed to Vera and the Cleanup Department in early talks with the producer, Don Hahn, and the directors, Kirk Wise and Gary Trousdale, and it continues to be the message from Jeffrey Katzenberg. Cinderella, Sleeping Beauty, and Wendy in *Peter Pan* were stylized heroines who could look the same in every drawing. Not so with Belle. "In every scene she has a different expression on her face," says Vera.

On a film like *Beauty and the Beast*, Cleanup is first in, last out. A couple of months before animating began, the lead cleanup people were collaborating on character design, contributing to the sculptures or sculpting themselves. Alex Topete, who cleaned up Larry White's dynamic wolf animation, visited the Los Angeles Zoo and studied videotapes to observe the wolves and other animals.

For a fall release, the animators completed their work in July. That meant a scramble for Cleanup to complete the film by late August.

"But I think artists do some of their best work when they're given deadlines," Vera observes. "I know if I have only an hour to complete a drawing, I'll just sit and concentrate, and I'll do my best work. I'm most proud of my work when I'm on deadline, and I think the key people are the same. They just reach to the bottom of their souls and put it on paper."

Nik Ranieri's animation of Lumiere.

ABOVE: *In high school, background artist Lisa Keene decided—"I think to my parents' chagrin"—that she wanted to pursue an art career. After art studies at the University of Southern California and the Art Center in Pasadena, she went directly to the training program at Disney and painted backgrounds for all the features from* The Black Cauldron *on. She became supervisor of backgrounds for* The Rescuers Down Under.

OPPOSITE TOP: *From this painting by Doug Ball, computer graphics built and rendered the moving ballroom for the dance sequence.*

OPPOSITE BOTTOM: *Background for the village.*

Background: A Dr. *Zhivago* Kind of Snow

Lisa Keene's workshop is in a far corner of the Feature Animation Building on Flower Street. There are paintings everywhere, some a foot high and six feet long. Lisa is the background supervisor for *Beauty and the Beast*, heading a staff of fourteen artists, three trainees, and an artist of all trades, John Emerson.

She explains how a background artist chooses colors.

"I think emotion is the biggest factor. Emotion is essential because you have to relay the attitude that's happening, the acting, the idea of the moment. . . .

"For a light-hearted scene, I would go for light colors, colors that are high-key, light in nature. If you had a gray scale from one to ten, white to black, I would probably push it up to the higher end of that scale.

"If it was a softer scene, say, Belle's walking through a meadow at a very 'up' moment, you might have very pastel colors, very soft. The 'Be My Guest' number is also an 'up' moment in the picture, but it's a party, and everybody is having a good time. It's confetti, it's loud color, it's high saturation, it's active, it's very punchy."

A violent scene?

"I think I would choose very active dark colors. You could put together colors that might agitate the audience a little bit. The first thing that comes to mind is red, because culturally in our heads, red is a violent, aggressive, angry kind of color. But that's very obvious. If I were to sit here and ponder and try to come up with something different, it could be to play complementary colors against one another in order to make the audience feel uncomfortable or disturbed in some manner or colors that would play off each other in a dramatic way. You would go for something that would create an emotion."

Romance?

"In this film we're having a very soft gold interior when Beauty and Beast are dancing in the ballroom. It's a rich gold with a very vibrant, satisfying blue on the outside. Blue on the screen is a beautiful color. It always translates well, and it makes people feel good for some reason. Everybody loves it. You can't go wrong with a blue sequence.

"At the beginning stages when they're out in the snow, it's going to be a soft, playful atmosphere. For lack of a better description, a Dr. *Zhivago* scene. A crisp winter landscape and maybe some glittering snow scattered about where the light hits it a bit, be a little magical with it."

She adds: "One of the things we try real hard to do is not be predictable with our colors. When you think of a night snow scene, you might figure a blue rather monochromatic night. You may decide to make the snow a very deep violet or maybe throw in some red because it's a fight sequence. If it works well emotionally, the audience will accept it because it's part of the story.

"So you don't have to be as literal with color. Most of the picture takes place at night and in the castle, so you have very dark, gloomy possibilities. You've got to be

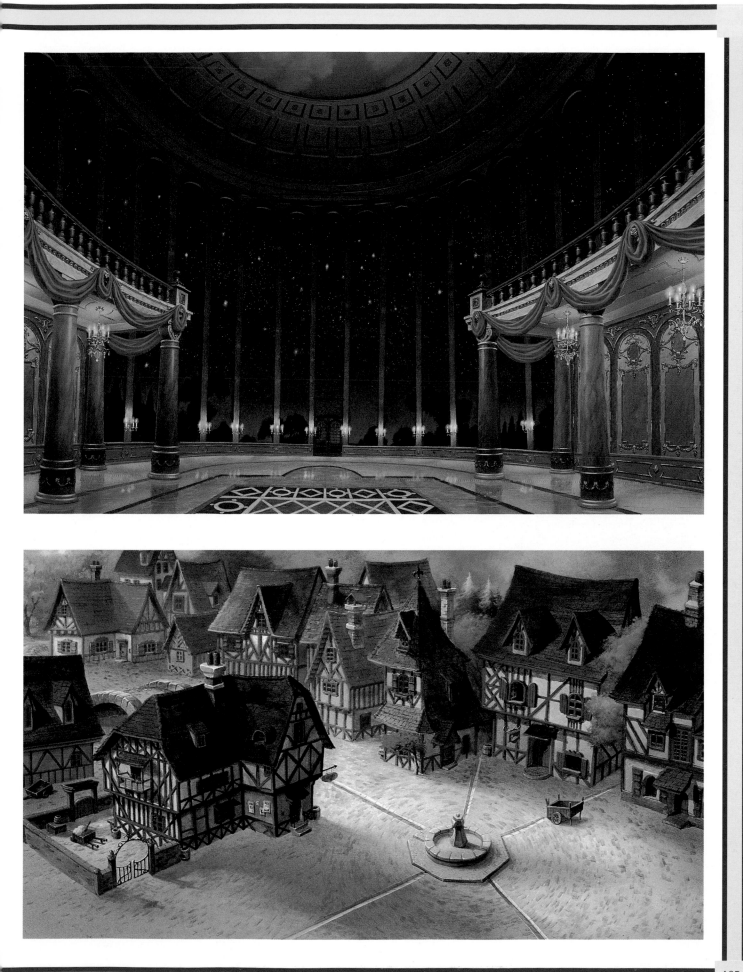

TOP: *A finished background based on the French countryside by Doug Ball.*

ABOVE: The Swing *and other landscapes by Jean-Honoré Fragonard (1732-1806) provided inspiration for Lisa Keene and other background artists.*

OPPOSITE: *A long shot of the castle, painted by Donald Towns.*

able to get creative and come up with something that's going to be fun. Otherwise you're going to have a very dark film."

Before starting to paint, Lisa pores through picture books for ideas. On a wall are photographs of forest scenes, taken especially for *Beauty and the Beast* by Hans Bacher.

"The whole launching point," she says, "was the artist Fragonard, his beautiful landscapes, the way he handles trees. When you start these films, you begin with a certain look, then create a style unique to the film."

Usually in Disney features one person keys the backgrounds. But the department had no lead time on *Beauty and the Beast*, and about 1,100 different backgrounds would be needed. So it had to be a group effort. Lisa and her assistant, Doug Ball, established the color bars (the range of colors) and the style, then others in the department set their own color keys. "Which is good," she observes. "It's generating a lot of enthusiasm. The artists are creative and capable, and it's tough for them to just sit back and copy."

Like Brian McEntee, Lisa Keene found inspiration in *Bambi*: "Some of the things were incredible. Like the stag fight. All of a sudden the meadow dropped off, you have no background, and it turns red. You have just silhouettes of two stags fighting. It ceased to be reality and became the emotion of the situation."

Lisa also admires Eyvind Earle's backgrounds for *Sleeping Beauty*, though she suspects that they may have overwhelmed the animation.

"You've got to remember that a background is a *background*. It is a stage to support the players: that's the goal of a background. It should never be more important than the characters."

ABOVE AND OPPOSITE: *The effects animator can conjure cataclysms at his drawing board. Forks are created by computer animation and combined with hand-drawn splashes and brooms in "Be Our Guest."*

Effects: Everything but Volcanos

"The trick in the way we approach effects," says Randy Fullmer, "is to try to make people not even think about what they're seeing. They should just experience it in a natural way. If you try to dazzle people too much, then you've really lost them."

What are the effects in *Beauty and the Beast*?

"About everything, except volcanos," he explains.

"Take the fireplace scene with Beast. Obviously you've got the fire. The fire emits light, so you've got to cast shadows on everyone who's around the fireplace. You've got the lighted side and the darker sides of each character. You've got glows coming from the fire.

"We're trying to place the characters in exactly the environment they're in. We don't want them to look like flat, drawn characters. If there's a light source in that room, we want them to look as if they are within the room, experiencing what is going on.

"There's a scene where the mob marches to the castle. They all have torches, so there are all kinds of shadows and lighting treatments. We have various elemental treatments. In the beginning a waterwheel is turning next to Belle's house. Belle's father's invention just about blows up their house with lots of smoke and debris. Later, Belle and her horse, while running from wolves in the forest, go over a frozen river and break through the ice, followed by a wild confrontation with the wolves and Beast in the snow.

"Lumiere has a little flame on each hand and one on his head. I've calculated

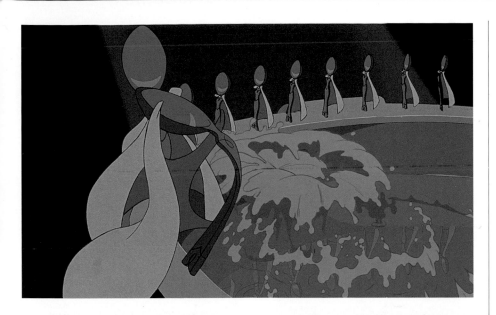

Effects animator Randy Fullmer studied architecture for two years before taking a film class and discovering the incredible freedom of expression possible in animation. So long, structural beams and engineering, and on to CalArts. "I've since learned there are a lot of ex-architects in animation." He made educational and science films with his own company, then joined the Bluth studio in effects. He started at Disney with Who Framed Roger Rabbit.

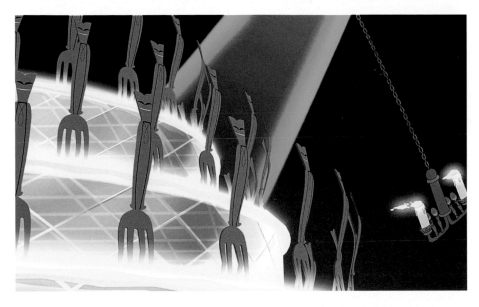

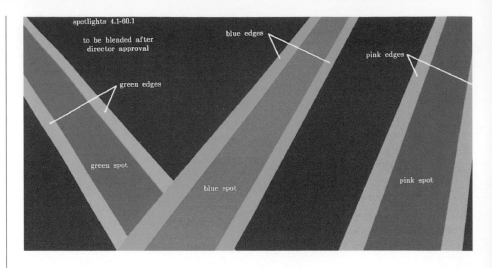

ABOVE: *Lumiere's homage to Esther Williams as drawn by art director Brian McEntee.*

RIGHT AND OPPOSITE: *Hand-drawn candle flames and spotlights join with computer animated dancing forks and a chandelier to create the spectacle of "Be Our Guest."*

that we'll be drawing nineteen thousand flames, all by hand.

"One of the challenging scenes in the picture is when Cogsworth gets his head stuck upside down in Jello and eventually wriggles himself free, while Mrs. Potts waltzes through a kitchen filled with dancing plates and hundreds of floating bubbles.

"When the castle objects are fighting the mob in the castle, they're throwing chairs and buckets of water. Mrs. Potts is pouring tea into cups, and they're poured onto the mob. The stove blows up and fire comes out of it.

"The battle between Beast and Gaston takes place during a rainstorm. They're going to be wet, with lightning flashes illuminating silhouettes and roofs. We want the roofs they're fighting on to have a reflective wet surface."

A large order, and there's more. Fullmer has plenty of help: twenty-five people in the effects department and another four at the Disney-MGM Studio in Florida. For an artist who can conjure storms and earthquakes, he is remarkably low-key. His office in a remote reach of the Flower Street building bears evidence of some of his department's miracles.

"I love effects," he admits. "Some people view it as tedious work, some think there's not the glory because you're not a character acting on the screen. But effects are great if you like abstract painting and freedom of movement. For instance, *The Little Mermaid*. We did all the oceans and millions of bubbles and underseas explosions and the whole storm at sea. There's a lot of design freedom in effects."

The artists of *Beauty and the Beast* are members of a new generation who will carry Disney animation into the twenty-first century. For them, the heritage of the Nine Old Men and others of the past is ever-present. "The ghosts are still here, really," observes James Baxter. "There's still talk about them and how good their stuff was. We've got to live up to that. I think that recently we have been able to live up to that, in cases. So now we can do the stuff ourselves.

"We shouldn't copy what they were doing. We have to push ahead, especially with all the new toys we've got now. There's no real excuse not to. We can really do some amazing things."

The art of animation at Disney has had an amazing history. It is breathtaking to realize that within less than nine years the art progressed from the crude antics of Mickey Mouse and Pegleg Pete in *Steamboat Willie* to the sublime masterpiece of *Snow White and the Seven Dwarfs*. The milestone films, *Pinocchio*, *Fantasia*, and *Bambi*, soon followed, and after the wartime interval, the Nine Old Men and their comrades created a wealth of memorable films and characters. Now it remains to the young artists "to do the stuff ourselves."

Michael Eisner observes:

"Animation gives you the ability to allow your imagination to rule your intellect. In live action, your imagination is limited, though it's getting less so with the technology and the amount of money that's being spent. Spielberg and Lucas have extended the limits.

"You read a script that says, 'Napoleon looks over the Russian troops, and then begins the most fabulous battle ever filmed.' You say, 'That's twenty-five million dollars just for that battle.'

"In animation, there's no limit to what you can do, and no scene is more expensive than any other, because it's all about drawing. Your imagination can go unchecked, except as to your discipline on story.

"It would be very foolish to animate a movie that you could do with live action. But it's hard to train an animal to speak. It's hard to photograph legions of soldiers. It's hard to have your grass be blue. Good times, bad times, there will always be a place for animation."

Glossary of Animation Terms

ANIMATOR: An artist who draws characters in motion.

ASSISTANT ANIMATOR: An artist who works with the animator, "cleaning up" the rough drawings and supervising the work of breakdown artists and in-betweeners.

BACKGROUND: The opaque painting that serves as the scenery behind the animation.

BREAKDOWN ARTIST: An artist who "breaks down" the action of a scene and follows up the assistant animator.

BUSINESS: The action that tells the story.

CEL: A transparent sheet of celluloid on which an animation drawing is inked and painted.

CLEANUP: The process of refining the lines of rough animation and adding minor details.

CLOSEUP: A scene staged with the action or characters close to the viewer.

CUT: The point where the scene ends.

DIRECTOR: Supervisor of the timing, animation, sound, music, and general production processes of a picture.

EFFECTS: The department that creates special illusions, such as clouds, rain, shadows, lightning, trick shots, etc., supporting the main action of the scene.

EXPOSURE SHEET: A form which details the action, dialogue, and music for a scene. Each line represents a frame of film.

EXTREME: The farthest point of an action or expression.

FIELD: The area actually photographed by the camera.

FLIPPING: To hold a group of drawings so that they will fall in an even pattern and give the viewer the illusion of movement.

FRAME: The individual picture on the film; there are sixteen frames to each foot of film, twenty-four frames to each second of running time on the screen.

HOLD: To keep drawings or other art material stationary for a number of frames.

IN-BETWEENER: The artist who finishes the needed number of drawings in between those created by the assistant animator and the breakdown man.

INKER: One who copies drawings onto cels with ink.

IN SYNC: When action is perfectly synchronized with the voices, sound effects, or music.

LAYOUT: The black and white rendering done by a layout man that determines the basic composition of the scene.

LONGSHOT: A scene staged with the action or characters at a distance from the viewer.

MOVIOLA: A small machine for the viewing of motion picture film.

MUSIC ROOM: Director's office and layout room.

OFFSTAGE: Dialogue, narration, or sound effects coming from a source not on the screen.

PAINTER: One who paints colors on cels.

PAN: A sweeping, panoramic camera shot accomplished by moving art material under the camera.

PEGS: The metal pegs upon which drawings, cels, and other material are kept in registry as they move through the studio.

REGISTRATION: To keep drawings, cels, and background in proper relation to each other.

ROUGH: The animator's rather sketchy drawings.

SCENE: A segment of action which completes an idea.

SEQUENCE DIRECTOR: A member of the staff of directors, one who handles an episode or episodes of an animated feature.

SOUND EFFECTS: Miscellaneous sounds added to the soundtrack to enhance the action.

STAGING: The basic visual presentation of a scene or action.

STORYBOARD: A large board on which are pinned sketches telling a story in comicstrip fashion.

STORY SKETCH: A simple storytelling drawing done by a story person.

SWEATBOX: A small projection room in which films are run for criticism; or as a verb to critique a scene.

TAKE: A strong movement denoting surprise or reaction.

TRUCK: A move of the camera, either into or away from the art material on the camera table.

INDEX

Sandra Johnson

Bob Thomas interviewed Walt Disney many times while Hollywood correspondent for Associated Press and in the preparation of two books, *The Art of Animation* and a child's biography, *Walt Disney: Magician of the Movies*. After Disney's death, Thomas wrote the official biography, *Walt Disney: An American Original*.

Thomas is the author of numerous other books, including biographies of Harry Cohn, Irving Thalberg, David O. Selznick, Joan Crawford, William Holden, Walter Winchell, Fred Astaire, and others. His biographies of Howard Hughes and Abbott and Costello became television movies. He continues to report on films for AP and conducts a weekly television interview show, *Hollywood Stars*.

In 1988, Thomas became the first reporter-author to be honored with a star in Hollywood Boulevard's Walk of Fame. He and his wife Patricia live in Encino.